STAR DIVIDE

KEN LOZITO

ACOUSTICAL BOOKS LLC

The author greatly appreciates you taking the time to read his work.

Published by Acoustical Books, LLC

KenLozito.com

IF YOU WOULD LIKE TO BE NOTIFIED WHEN MY NEXT BOOK IS RELEASED VISIT - WWW.KENLOZITO.COM

ISBN: 978-1-945223-00-6

Chapter One

6 0 Earth Years before the Athena mission leaves Earth, Boxan Monitoring Station, 7th Planetary Body, Nershal Star System

KLADOMAOR SLAMMED his fist on the console. "We've lost another species to the Xiiginns!"

The deep blue lines of his battle armor covered most of his brown, roughened skin. Boxans, despite their considerable size, had never been a warlike race, preferring to cultivate the world around them. And they had carried this shepherding instinct with them as they reached for the heavens, expanding their influence among the stars.

"Already?" Gaarokk said, tearing his eyes from the barrage of warning messages that stretched across the holoscreens in front of him. "The Nershals represented the best probability of resisting Xiiginn influence. At this rate what hope is there of stopping them?"

Kladomaor clenched his teeth. Time was running out. The Xiiginns had proven to be their betters. Once, the Xiiginns had been ranked first among the species cultivated into a harmonious Confederation in their part of the galaxy. The Confederation had been established so advanced species could peacefully coexist, while keeping the younger species ignorant of their presence. Now all the species they had ever come in contact with were at risk. The Xiiginns had fooled them all, proving to be among the most cunning and sinister races the Boxans had ever encountered. And now they were beyond the Boxan's ability to control. Battle cruisers were evenly matched, and to overcome the stalemate, the Xiiginns had enlisted the help of the other species in the Confederation. The Xiiginns used their foundation of lies to drive the Boxans back on almost all fronts. The Boxans could not go into open conflict with the other species of the Confederation.

Kladomaor shifted his armored feet and glanced at the screens before them. Battle had hardened him. "The other races could not resist the Xiiginns. The star systems are falling faster now because, instead of fighting, they're joining the Xiiginns' cause against us. They've turned us into the monsters the Xiiginns actually are. Where is Ma'jasalax? Her beacon says she's here."

Gaarokk nodded his shaggy head toward the entrance of the large octagonal structure behind them. The Mardoxian Chamber wasn't nearly as massive as the ones built on Setheon, the Boxan home world, but it would have to suffice. Ma'jasalax had been insistent.

"Meditation at a time like this? We need to leave. The home system is in danger. The Xiiginns have captured a shroud device while it was sending a transmission back to comms central. If they can decrypt the transmission, then no world is safe, including our own," Kladomaor said.

Gaarokk brought up the subroutines that would trigger the destruction of the listening post in this star system. As part of standard practice for studying species, listening posts were installed on the outermost planets, well away from planets with intelligent life. The distant locations assured them that species would only learn of the Confederation's existence once they reached a certain level of technological development.

Kladomaor strode over to the chamber, looking as if he were about to violate one of their most sacred tenets and force open the door. Gas geysered out along the sides, and the lines between the dark octagonal plating glowed red. The canopy above retracted, revealing a twilit sky. Xiiginn warships could arrive at any moment.

The glowing plating settled into a pulsating rhythm, and the door to the chamber opened. Ma'jasalax came through and Kladomaor stepped back, bowing his head slightly in respect.

"Using the chamber now? You risk us all. The Xiiginns already hunt for our home world. They might even be able to trace the Mardoxian signal to our current location. We must get to our ship and leave this place," Kladomaor said, heading toward the exit.

Ma'jasalax focused on the soldier's back as she followed. Battle had made Kladomaor brash, a trait their species hadn't needed in the past. She couldn't blame him. The sting of defeat haunted his actions against an enemy that had once been first among the cultivated species. So much had changed, and it was going to get worse. Much worse. Her efforts in the chamber had left her weakened, but she forced herself to move forward as best she could.

Kladomaor's helmet covered his face as he waited for them to engage their envirosuits. Once this was accomplished, he opened the airlock to the barren, pockmarked landscape that adorned the planet's surface. They were on the farthest planet, barely more than a moon, in the Nershal star system. The thin atmosphere did little to protect them from the dangers of the void.

"There is still time," Ma'jasalax said.

"Not much," Kladomaor replied, his voice coming through the small speakers in her helmet.

They approached the ship—a smaller class transport ship designed for stealth and speed. Its darkened hull seemed at home in the shadows, and Ma'jasalax abhorred the need for such a ship. An access ramp opened, and once inside they were able to remove their envirosuits, which folded back into the seams of their clothing. The three of them headed to the bridge, and Kladomaor took the pilot's seat.

"We've had reports on the surface of Selebus that we've been betrayed to the Xiiginns," Kladomaor said.

"It's true," Ma'jasalax answered. She'd been there and seen her species being rounded up to be struck down.

"How could that be?" Gaarokk asked. "We've had no reports that the Xiiginns even knew of the Nershals' home world here."

"We've underestimated the Xiiginns and their lust for vengeance. They will seek to turn all of our allies against us, poisoning the Confederation we've worked so hard to build," Ma'jasalax said, stumbling to the chair. Her breath was coming in small gasps.

Kladomaor peered at her. "What have you done?"

Ma'jasalax braced herself, holding herself up. Her strength was draining rapidly.

Kladomaor pulled up a readout of the listening station. "It's still broadcasting. You're still connected to the Mardoxian Chamber. How . . . ? We need to cut the connection. Gaarokk, override the self-destruct and blow it now."

Gaarokk glanced back at both of them. "If I blow it now, we'll lose her."

Kladomaor smashed an armored fist on the panel in front of him. "The Xiiginn ships will emerge at any moment. If the broadcast is still going, they will be able to trace it back to the Boxan system."

Ma'jasalax bowed her head with a great sigh and gently reached out to Gaarokk. The Boxan scientist nodded, his large fingers deftly navigating the interface. A bright flash appeared on the planetary surface below, and Ma'jasalax sank back into the chair.

Kladomaor glared at Ma'jasalax. "You've sent an unsanctioned broadcast. Where did the signal go?"

Ma'jasalax calmly returned the soldier's gaze. "The Sol system," she said.

Kladomaor's brow furrowed and he turned toward the display, bringing up information about the Sol system. After a moment he muttered a curse. "Humans! You've sent the Mardoxian signal to a primitive species? We're not even convinced they should be brought into the cultivation program."

"I've seen what they can become. Given the chance, they could help us right the wrongs with the Xiiginns."

"You've gone too far. You're not authorized to reach out to any primitive species. I have no choice but to bring you in before the Council of the Confederation. Your actions will leave you stripped of Mardoxian status. You will be cast out—banished," Kladomaor said.

Ma'jasalax gazed at him patiently. "Their risk is the same as ours. The Xiiginns will be targeting the primitive species now.

They need to be prepared, or would you suggest we just let their species stand alone?"

Kladomaor's eyes quickly scanned the holodisplay and then he closed them, switching to his neural implants. The frown lines on his face deepened. "They could be much worse than the Xiiginns. Instead of one power-hungry, bloodlust species, we'll be inundated with them. The Humans have barely explored their own star system. How prepared could they be for what's to come? They are a territorial, warlike, and brash species."

Ma'jasalax drew in a slow, steadying breath. "They are also compassionate and have a capacity to accomplish great things. It will take time for the Xiiginns to decrypt the information stored in the shroud—time the Humans will need to develop enough to be able to help us."

Kladomaor blew out a breath. "The risk . . . this is too reckless."

"I didn't send them anything they weren't already working on. This is just a nudge in the right direction."

"What's done is done. We should be leaving," Gaarokk said.

"It's not that simple," Kladomaor replied. "Once the process has begun, ongoing monitoring is essential. The council has severed the connections to all listening stations. The Star Shroud Network will continue to operate, but we're cut off until the danger passes. What she has done is essentially stoked a spark to a flame, and without our capacity to guide it, we may be responsible for the doom of our species."

"Or we may be its only hope. In this you're wrong. You will see. Take me to the council," Ma'jasalax said, and closed her eyes. To some she would appear to be sleeping, but she knew Kladomaor wasn't fooled.

"My experience says otherwise, but for all our sakes I do hope you are correct."

"What can we do?" Gaarokk asked.

"Survive," Kladomaor grumbled, and punched in the coordinates that would take them away from this cursed star system. He much preferred a straight-up fight, but they were losing the war with the Xiiginns. The Mardoxian Chambers were used to speak to primitive species across vast distances and were not governed by dimensional space. *Humans . . . bah*. Based on the reports he was still accessing through his neural links, Kladomaor doubted they could even make sense of the signal, much less act on it.

Chapter Two

2046 Aboard the spaceship Athena somewhere beyond Earth's solar system.

KAYLAN PUSHED HER EYES OPEN, and her blurred vision slowly came into focus. The soft amber glow of the overhead holodisplays in the Athena's med bay showed her vital signs transmitted from her neural implants. She rubbed her eyes and took in a deep breath. Her head felt like it weighed a thousand pounds. After a few moments, the fogginess retreated and her thoughts cleared. Working her mouth into a slow swallow, she turned her head to see if anyone else was with her. Finding herself alone, she closed her eyes and focused on the bridge. In her mind she saw Zack at the comms station, speaking with Katie. Each of them appeared to be surrounded by a faint glow that grew brighter as Katie placed her hand on Zack's shoulder.

Kaylan shoved the image from her mind, thinking her imagination was getting the better of her. As she sat up in the bed and let her feet dangle toward the floor, the door to the med bay opened and Brenda walked in.

"Good, you're awake," the Athena's chief medical officer said as she came over. Brenda glanced at the holoscreen showing Kaylan's vitals.

"How long have I been out?" Kaylan asked.

"A couple of hours. Do you remember anything that happened on Pluto?" Brenda asked.

A couple of hours? Kaylan moved to get up, but Brenda placed her hand on Kaylan's shoulder, holding her in place.

"I have to get up. The ship—"

"Everything that can be done is being done at the moment," Brenda said. "Now, do you remember what happened to you on Pluto?"

Kaylan frowned and tried accessing the ship's logs through her implants, but she was blocked. Brenda gave her a knowing look, and Kaylan sighed.

"I was with Hicks, and we were exploring the station. We found that chamber I had mentioned in one of our viewing sessions," Kaylan said.

Brenda offered her a cup of water from the pitcher on the bedside table, and Kaylan took a sip.

"I went inside, and the chamber activated. A beam of light shot toward me from a glowing sphere inside," Kaylan said, and looked away, gathering her thoughts. "It was like I was transported somewhere else. It was more intense than any viewing session I've experienced. I saw . . . something."

"What did you see?"

Kaylan took another sip of water, stalling, and closed her eyes. "I saw one of them. The beings that built the structure on Pluto."

Brenda sat beside Kaylan and rubbed the back of her shoulders soothingly. "Take your time."

"I can't believe I'm saying this. It all sounds crazy," Kaylan said.

"There is no precedent for what you've been through. Just take your time," Brenda said.

"It knew I was Human. It called me that. The being knew I was afraid and tried to set me at ease. The lighting was dim in the chamber, but I could tell the creature was big," Kaylan said.

"Did it say anything?"

Kaylan's eyes grew distant as she tried to remember. "Yes. She said time was short and the use of the chamber would draw unwanted attention."

"She?" Brenda asked.

Kaylan frowned.

"You said 'she.'"

Kaylan nodded after a moment. "That's right. She said her name was Ma'jasalax. She wanted me to come find her . . ."

Brenda waited her out while Kaylan collected her thoughts.

"I could feel her emotions, and I think she could feel mine as well. I saw an image of the Earth as seen from afar, along with the feeling of profound regret," Kaylan said.

Brenda's brows drew up. "Regret? Like she regretted meeting you?"

Kaylan shook her head. "No. It was like she knew what was coming and regretted that something was going to happen that hadn't happened yet. There's more, but I can't focus on that right now. I need to know what the status of the ship is, and you've blocked my implants."

Brenda rose from the bed and typed a few things into her tablet. "Standard protocol for an acting commander who was unconscious. I need to clear you."

Kaylan's head snapped in Brenda's direction. "What do you mean 'acting commander'? Where is Michael?"

Brenda's eyes drew downward. "There was an accident on the station, and Michael was trapped. We're not sure, but he may have died."

Kaylan shot to her feet. "What do you mean you're not sure? We can't be far from Pluto. Are the others planning a rescue?"

Brenda held up her hand in front of her chest. "Slow down. One thing at a time. Let me complete your examination; then I'll clear you for duty and we can take it from there."

Kaylan pinched her lips together for a moment and nodded.

Brenda gestured to the holoscreen behind Kaylan. Onscreen was a three-dimensional figure of the human brain. There were occasional glowing sections.

"This is your last brain scan we did on the way to Pluto. The glowing sections show the thought processes of a normally functioning brain. See—here's mine," Brenda said.

Another image of the human brain appeared next to Kaylan's. They looked similar. Kaylan nodded, and Brenda entered another command into her tablet. A third brain appeared.

"This is a scan of your brain right now," Brenda said.

The third image showed a brain with multiple glowing sections in rapid succession. Kaylan studied the image for a moment. "Is it just stress?"

Brenda shook her head. "No, this is something else. Yours is the most active brain I've ever seen. It's like that of a child's brain as it grows in complexity, except as a full-grown adult your brain shouldn't be doing anything like this."

Kaylan studied the image for a few moments. She didn't feel any different. She needed to know what had happened to

Hunsicker and the status of the ship. "Does this in any way indicate that I'm unfit for duty?"

Brenda glanced between the images. "No. As far as I can tell you're as normal as you were before all this happened, but we'll need to keep an eye on it."

Brenda's fingers entered a few more commands on her tablet computer, and the block on Kaylan's implants was removed. Kaylan greedily searched the ship's logs for the information she craved. She frowned. The more information she got from the logs the deeper her frown grew.

"A wormhole?" Kaylan asked.

Brenda nodded. "That's what Redford believes."

Kaylan walked over to the comms station in the med bay. She opened a ship-wide comms channel. "Crew of the Athena, this is the acting commander. Meet me on the bridge in fifteen minutes for debrief and status."

Kaylan nodded for Brenda to come as they headed for the bridge. She was still accessing the ship's logs and now understood Brenda's somber tone when she'd talked about Hunsicker earlier. By going through the wormhole they had left Commander Hunsicker behind, and his only hope of rescue would be for them to find their way back to him. There were no other ships that were capable of reaching Pluto from Earth in time for a rescue.

Chapter Three

Z ack's bleary-eyed gaze kept trying to make sense of the long list of failures listed in the Athena's system log. He straightened himself in his chair, which he was having to do more and more as his body sagged with exhaustion. He didn't remember the last time he'd slept. It had to have been more than twenty-four hours ago. He rolled his shoulders and angled his chin up to stretch his neck. He glanced over at Katie, who sat near him. Her long black hair was tied back. She sat straight-backed in her chair, focused on the screen in front of her. She had to be tired but looked as strong as ever.

Nikolai yawned loudly from across the bridge, and Zack glanced over at him. The Russian hadn't done anything strange since they'd been on the bridge, but Zack was glad Katie had joined him. If Nikolai was some type of trained killer, Zack doubted he could put up much of a fight, but he was sure Katie could handle herself against anything that crossed her path.

"You need to rest," Katie said.

Zack turned back toward her and smiled tiredly. "We all do.

At least life support doesn't seem to be affected by all the problems with the computer systems."

The lighting on the bridge dimmed for a moment, and Zack brought his attention back toward his screen. The door to the bridge opened, and in walked Kaylan and Brenda. Kaylan looked alert, considering she had been lying unconscious in the Athena's med bay for the past few hours. She gave him a tight smile as she walked over to them.

"How are you feeling?" Zack asked.

"I'm awake now. What's happening with the computer systems?" Kaylan asked.

"I'm not sure. Ever since we went through the wormhole they've been acting strange. Life support seems to be the one system that's been unaffected," Zack said.

"Could be because it's an isolated system," Kaylan said.

Zack nodded. "That's what I was thinking." He glanced at Katie and then back to Kaylan. "What happened to you back there?"

"Later," Kaylan said. "I need to find out what shape the ship is in and where we are."

The door to the bridge opened, and the rest of the crew came in, with the exception of Efren, who was resting in the med bay. Kaylan motioned for them to gather around the planning table.

"Let's start at the beginning. What happened on Pluto? Why did the station become so unstable?" Kaylan asked.

"We think it was when the reactor at the power station was turned on," Hicks said.

"There is no proof of that," Redford said quickly.

"What else could it have been?" Hicks countered.

"Why was the reactor activated in the first place? Hunsicker ordered that we not power on the reactor until we had a better understanding about the station," Kaylan said.

The door to the bridge hissed open, and Efren Burdock walked in. He had a large bruise near his hairline. Efren glared at Redford, and the astrophysicist shifted his feet.

"Go ahead and tell them, Jonah," Efren said and looked at Kaylan. "He told me Hunsicker had cleared us to start the reactor. When the station became unstable I tried to shut the power down, but I couldn't."

Kaylan's hard gaze bored into Redford.

"He's right," Redford said, at last. "I wanted to restore power to the station so we could learn its secrets. If I had known what was going to happen, I never would have done it."

"It never would have happened if you'd followed Hunsicker's orders," Kaylan said.

Redford appeared as if he were going to respond but remained silent.

Hicks cleared his throat. "We lost Hunsicker's signal before we went through the wormhole."

"His suit comms failed?" Kaylan asked.

"The ceiling at the power station collapsed and Hunsicker was caught underneath," Redford said. "Vitomir and I carried Efren to safety. We thought Hunsicker was dead."

"How did the ship end up going through a wormhole?" Kaylan asked.

"We were temporarily locked out of the Athena's systems," Zack said. "Something from the alien station overrode our controls and put the Athena on a course through the wormhole."

"And we left Michael behind, stranded, without any hope of rescue?" Kaylan asked.

"As I said before—" Redford began.

"He's not dead," Zack said. "He got a message to the ship as we went through the wormhole."

"Why didn't you say something before?" Hicks asked.

"I found it a short while ago. I'll play it now and you'll see," Zack said.

Redford glanced at Vitomir, who slowly closed his eyes.

Zack entered a few commands and brought up the main holodisplay, then looked around at them with alarm. "I can't find it. The message is gone. Did you erase it?" Zack asked Redford.

"I didn't even know there was a message until right now," Redford said.

"I've been with Jonah and Vitomir since we've been back. They couldn't have done this," Hicks said.

"Yes, you've been quite the babysitter," Redford said.

"What did the message say?" Kaylan asked, silencing them.

Zack swallowed. "He said he'd been shot by Redford, but he didn't think he meant to do it."

"That's preposterous!" Redford exclaimed.

Hicks was on Redford, pinning him down on the table. "Where is the gun?"

"Okay, fine," Redford said. "It's not what you think."

"The gun!" Hicks said, and twisted Redford's arm tighter.

"It's in my desk at the top observatory," Redford said.

"Where did you get a gun?" Kaylan asked.

Redford's eyes were red from his struggle with Hicks. "Vitomir."

All eyes darted to Vitomir, who held up his hands. "It's true. I brought the gun. We didn't know what we were going to find there, and I brought it as a means of self-defense."

Hicks let Redford go and motioned for Vitomir to stand away from the others. Zack backed away from the tall Russian. The former Titus Station Commander gave the appearance of complacency, but there was something much harder in his eyes.

"Did the message say anything else?" Kaylan asked.

Zack glanced at Vitomir, who watched him intently. "He said the destruction of Titus Station wasn't an accident—"

Vitomir lunged toward him. Katie stepped between them, and Vitomir crumpled to the floor, unconscious.

"Stunners," Katie said, revealing a palm-sized disk in her hand. "He'll be out for at least an hour."

Zack closed his mouth and took a steadying breath. "Hunsicker said Vitomir admitted to being responsible for Titus Station's destruction."

Nikolai gasped in a half-stifled cry. "My comrades died! Why?"

"So we would take you to the alien station with us." Zack felt his stomach clench at Nikolai's crestfallen gaze as he answered.

Nikolai's eyes brimmed with tears. "His wife . . . the crew . . ." Nikolai looked away from them. Brenda came to his side and consoled him.

"We can ask Vitomir about it when he wakes up," Kaylan said. "I want him restrained and confined to quarters until we figure out what to do with him. Revoke his access to the Athena's systems."

Zack nodded.

"Do you think the issues with the Athena's systems are something Vitomir could have done?" Kaylan asked.

"No. It wouldn't make any sense to sabotage the ship like this," Zack said.

"What do we do with *him*?" Hicks said, gesturing toward Redford.

Kaylan glanced at Redford, considering.

"You need me," Redford said.

"Why didn't you say anything about Hunsicker before?" Zack asked.

"It was an accident. We were arguing about the station. The

quakes were coming more frequently. Everything happened so fast. I didn't mean to shoot him," Redford said, his eyes darting around to all of them. "Then the ceiling collapsed."

The rest of the crew exchanged glances. Eventually they all looked to Kaylan.

"We do need him," Kaylan said. "I need you to figure out where we are. The wormhole could have taken us anywhere."

Redford sagged in relief.

Kaylan steeled her gaze. "You pull another stunt like that and I'll have you confined to quarters as well."

Efren cleared his throat. "The engines are reporting strange fluctuations in the core. I need to go check on this."

Kaylan nodded, and Efren left them.

Zack glanced at the readout on his screen. "I'm not seeing anything like that."

Kaylan frowned. "That's because the warning messages are coming through our neural implants."

"That doesn't make any sense. Why would the Athena's systems restrict status updates to those who have implants?" Zack asked.

Kaylan shook her head. "The ship is designed for a crew that has implants."

Zack mentally kicked himself. No wonder he felt so blind to the problems with the Athena's computer systems.

Brenda cleared her throat. "Perhaps now you'll come down to the med bay and get your implants installed."

Zack's brows drew up in surprise. "You can do that?"

"Of course. We have a full surgical station and a robot that can handle the procedure," Brenda said.

Zack considered this for a moment and then shook his head. "No thanks. I'd rather not trust a robot to perform surgery near my brain anytime soon—or ever, for that matter."

Brenda was about to reply when Kaylan cut her off.

"Really, Zack? If this is going to help us figure out what's wrong with the computer systems, then perhaps you should reconsider," Kaylan said.

Zack shook his head. "I shouldn't need implants to fix a damn computer."

"Fine, then fix it," Kaylan said. "In order to return to Earth we need to figure out where we are, and we need to repair the ship."

Redford coughed. "Even if I could figure out where we are, we don't have the ability to create a wormhole."

"You let me worry about the wormhole. You just figure out where we are," Kaylan said.

Redford clamped his mouth shut and gave a single stiff nod.

Zack felt a small bit of satisfaction at the way Kaylan cowed the illustrious Dr. Redford. It still bothered him that Hunsicker's video message was mysteriously gone, but the fact that the Athena's computer systems were alerting only through neural interfaces worried him more.

"When was the last time any of you slept?" Kaylan asked.

"We haven't," Hicks said.

Kaylan nodded. "Please carry Vitomir to his quarters, and then I want you all to get some rest. We'll rotate through shifts, but I don't want anyone getting hurt because we're too tired to see straight. I can take over the repairs for a bit."

"I can come back to the bridge if you need," Hicks said.

Kaylan shook her head. "We've been through a lot, and things will be a lot clearer if we all get some sleep. Life support is stable, and we'll need some time to finish mapping where we are."

Hicks and Nikolai lifted Vitomir's unconscious form and carried him from the bridge.

Zack exited with the others, leaving Kaylan alone on the bridge. He followed Katie to her quarters, and she guided him inside, saying she didn't want to be alone.

"I'm glad I'm not the only one," Zack said.

He sat on the bed, then lay on his side with his back to the wall. Katie lay in front of him, and she nestled back into him as he wrapped his arm around her. The lights dimmed in the room and the wallscreen showed a lifelike image of the night sky from somewhere on Earth.

"Why won't you get the implants?" Katie asked.

"I don't trust them," Zack said.

"What do you think is going to happen?"

"I don't know. Probably nothing. Do we really need to talk about this now?" Zack asked.

He had good reasons for not wanting implants, but he knew his answers would lead to more questions. It was already getting harder to keep his tired eyes open any longer. Katie must have been just as tired because she didn't answer him. Instead her breathing slowed to a steady rhythm. Zack was moments behind her in sleep, but not before a shiver went through his body. There was no way he'd let a computer inside his head. He sucked in a deep breath through his nose. Sweet smells of the shampoo Katie washed her hair with caressed his nose and put a smile on his face. In moments he was asleep.

Chapter Four

Selebus was a living world that happened to dwell in the shadows of a crimson gas giant. The Nershals were fortunate to have two living worlds in their star system but had only colonized the moon of the gas giant in recent history. They named the moon Selebus, after a Nershal sacred city from antiquity.

Kladomaor had always respected the Nershals and their rigid code of honor. Even when they'd betrayed his race to the Xiiginns, they hadn't hidden behind a diplomatic shroud blanketed in secrecy. Misguided though the Nershals' reasons were, many Boxans had lost their lives on the Nershal home world. Bitter memories threatened to ignite his temper. Kladomaor's rage in battle with the Xiiginns was well known. He had become the embodiment of what the Boxans needed in order to survive, and at the same time they feared where the paths of ongoing war would take them all in the end. He'd lost many friends all those years ago when they had fled the Nershals' star system—friends of both Boxan and Nershal origins. Kladomaor had been part of the team that was to guide the Nershals into becoming members of the Confederation worlds. It was believed that the Nershals, with their rigid code of honor and discipline, could resist the Xiiginns and not be enamored of them like the rest had been. They were wrong.

Kladomaor shook off thoughts of the Xiiginns and breathed in the air of Selebus. The crimson gas giant blanketed the moon in a gleaming twilight for much of its cycle, allowing the star to shine upon its surface for only a third of its day. The forest canopy further shielded their ship, negating the need for cloaking.

Kladomaor waited on the exit ramp that extended from the ship, and Gaarokk quietly stood beside him, gazing at a place that neither of them thought they'd see again. Gaarokk cocked his shaggy head to the side, listening.

"There are protokars in the area. I didn't think they would have adapted to life on the moon so quickly," Gaarokk said.

Kladomaor shrugged. "It's been sixty cycles. That's enough time, provided they had proper support and the ongoing presence of the Nershals. The Nershals always keep their protectors close."

Gaarokk nodded. "It was always a curious relationship. In no other species we've encountered has there ever been a bond between a winged creature and a land-based predator."

"The Nershals were land-based to begin with. A mutation gave rise to the winged race we now know, but by then their bond with the protokars had already been firmly established," Kladomaor said.

He stepped off the exit ramp and the ground sank beneath his armored feet. Of the hundreds who would have followed him here, he'd only brought twenty Boxan soldiers with him.

Gaarokk glanced at the others. "I'm a little out of place among your company. What is it that you need from me?"

Kladomaor turned back to the Boxan scientist. "I know I'm not the only one who thinks our business with the Nershals is unfinished."

Gaarokk regarded him for a moment. "It's been a long time since we've been here—long enough for this species to recognize what the Xiiginns really are."

"But they haven't," Kladomaor said, "at least not fully. The Xiiginns have kept the Nershals in line with the promise of advanced technology."

As the last Boxan exited the ship, the ramp closed behind them. Theirs was a species meant for the forest. Their large stature was as one with the plants; it was their armor that was out of place. Kladomaor felt a yearning in the pit of his stomach to cast off his armor and simply exist here in this place at this moment, listening to the harmony of the forest. He squashed those urgings. There would be no time for meditation on this day.

Kladomaor brought up his arm and activated a holoprojector, and a detailed image of a Nershal structure formed, showing that the rounded architecture and open areas were conducive to the winged race. Through his neural implants, he guided the image to a secure landing area. After a moment, a female Nershal emerged on the platform of the building. Her smooth skin was pale green, and her large eyes were the color of a deep sunset. Many years ago those eyes had looked up at him with all the wonder and curiosity of youth. A sharp pang seized his battle-hardened heart, crying out for the world that should have been instead of what it was—a world that would drive him to use his connection with a Nershal who had once counted him as family.

"Is that—" Gaarokk started to say.

"Ezerah," Kladomaor said, "fully grown."

The Nershals were almost hairless, with skin colors favoring a full spectrum of greens. Their long limbs put them at chest height for the average Boxan. Ezerah stood at the platform's edge and spread her arms at either side of her. Twin sets of radiant wings unfurled in a brilliant display of iridescent colors that captured the sunlight. A protokar slinked up beside her. Its hide was a mix between long purple hair and yellow feathers, the creature's green eyes captured the light and seemed to glow of their own accord. The protokar's tail dragged behind it, and though Kladomaor couldn't see it, he knew it ended in a single blackened stinger that could pierce even his armor.

Ezerah leaped into the air, her twin sets of wings propelling her forward, taking her to the forest line beyond the colony.

Kladomaor closed the connection. "She takes her ease by a river a day's march from here."

The small force of Boxans headed away from the ship, and Gaarokk quickened his pace, catching up to Kladomaor.

"What do you plan to do once we cross paths with her?" Gaarokk asked.

Kladomaor had known when he brought the scientist along that he would be full of questions. The rest of his squad would follow orders without question. He needed both types if this mission was to succeed, and that meant enduring Gaarokk's seemingly endless supply of inquiries.

"We've fought the Xiiginns on countless fronts. The long and short of it is that we're losing this war," Kladomaor said.

"Their influence is powerful—like nothing we've ever seen with other species," Gaarokk said.

"Even with our armor we may fall victim to the Xiiginn influence. Every soldier here knows the risk if that were to happen," Kladomaor said.

"I guess I'm not sure why you brought me along," Gaarokk said.

"You're here to validate our claim," Kladomaor said. They came to a rock face and began to climb.

Their large, armored hands easily found purchase, and they were able to pull themselves up.

"What claim is that?" Gaarokk asked.

"That a species can break the influence of the Xiiginns," Kladomaor said through clenched teeth.

They reached the top of the rock face and Gaarokk stood with his mouth agape. "No species—not even our species—has broken the Xiiginns' hold once it's there."

Kladomaor stomped ahead, making the scientist race to catch up to him. "The Nershals aren't like the others. Their will wasn't eroded to believe the Xiiginns' lies. They chose to ally with them."

"It's not that simple. Others have tried what you're proposing, and they've all failed. They were handed over to the Xiiginns and never heard from again. The best way to face the Xiiginns is on a warship with a large expanse of space between," Gaarokk said.

"I used to believe that, but the loss of Setheon says otherwise," Kladomaor said, his chest growing warm beneath the armor.

"Maybe not all the Nershals have flocked to the Xiiginns' banner, but a majority has. I'm just not sure what you hope to accomplish here," Gaarokk said.

Kladomaor glared at the forest in front of him. He wanted to find the nearest Xiiginn installation and wipe it off the face of the planet, unleashing his fury in a fiery maelstrom, but to do that here would accomplish little.

"Our reconnaissance shows that some of the Nershals are

questioning their alliance with the Xiiginns. I'm hoping to get them to keep questioning that alliance," Kladomaor said.

"Then why not take us to the Nershal home world? Why come to this colony?"

"This colony gives us breathing room that we wouldn't have on their home world," Kladomaor said.

"And Ezerah is here. I'm beginning to understand," Gaarokk said.

They were silent after that, making their way through the woods. Kladomaor hadn't wanted to bring their ship any closer, or they would run the risk of being detected. If they had to move fast, they could accomplish that with the use of their power armor. Their ship was small and not equipped with the necessary accouterments required for lengthy space travel. Even soldiers such as they required quiet meditation to anchor themselves to a home world that was otherwise lost to them. Perhaps Gaarokk was correct in his implication that this was a foolish and reckless mission. Gaarokk's reaction was one of the primary reasons he hadn't approached the council for approval. Instead, he had decided to let this journey take them where it would on his own.

Chapter Five

Kaylan glanced at the alien star system around her. She, Hicks, and Nikolai were six hours into their EVA to repair the power coupling that led to the main engines. The onboard fabricator had been spitting out the parts they needed to make the repairs almost nonstop for the past thirty-six hours. Thankfully there was nothing catastrophic revealed by the diagnostics they'd run. Various support systems seemed to have been more affected by the trek through the wormhole than major ones.

Nikolai had been climbing the walls to be of use, and they'd needed the help. Kaylan didn't think Nikolai had had anything to do with Vitomir's actions to sabotage Titus Space Station. Vitomir had been confined to his room, and Kaylan wasn't sure what to do with him. Locking Vitomir up wasn't a long-term solution but neither was letting him roam free.

"That should do it. Let's head back and see if it's working better now," Hicks said.

They pulled themselves along the Athena's outer hull toward

the airlock. Kaylan took a last look at the star in this system, shining with a deep orange brilliance that made it seem like a distant cousin to Earth's sun, then followed the others through the airlock and removed her spacesuit.

"We have to get to the bridge and start running those tests," Kaylan said.

Hicks reached out and gently grabbed her arm. "It's okay to take a moment."

Kaylan was about to reply when Redford called out to her over comms.

"What have you got, Jonah?" Kaylan asked.

"I've completed mapping this system and am ready to make a preliminary report," Redford said.

"Good. We'll meet you on the bridge," Kaylan said.

Hicks let go of her arm and followed her out of the airlock. Kaylan hadn't missed the questioning in his eyes since the events that had taken place on Pluto. Most of the crew wondered what had happened to her in the chamber, but they had been too busy making repairs to the ship to ask. Now that they were close to being underway she would need to address those lingering questions. But for Hicks it was different. He'd kissed her, and neither of them had spoken of it since. Many of the things he'd said about her feelings for Zack holding her back were true. She didn't know what she felt for either Hicks or Zack. Mostly she pushed thoughts of them from her mind. It was only when she saw Zack and Katie together that her hackles rose.

They came onto the bridge, and Kaylan activated the comms channel to Engineering.

"Efren, we're go for main engine test," Kaylan said.

"Acknowledged. Ready to go on your mark," Efren replied.

Kaylan went to the pilot's seat. This test was too dangerous for them to run while they were outside the ship. If the power coupling didn't hold, it could be disastrous and possibly deadly if they were outside. The main engines were at the rear of the ship, well away from the living quarters and observation decks. Kaylan engaged the engines at one percent power.

"Status is green down here," Efren said.

"Increasing output to five percent," Kaylan replied.

The countdown timer for the test reached zero, and Kaylan engaged the braking thrusters. The Athena came to a halt, and the diagnostic subroutines automatically started spitting out the reports that came onscreen.

Kaylan frowned. "Is this right?"

"My report is showing the same," Efren said.

Hicks and Redford came over.

"The report is showing a sixty percent efficiency increase in output," Kaylan said. She continued to scan the report, and everything in it added up.

Zack joined them, coming over from the comms station where he liked to work. "The fabricator on the ship can make parts better than Earth's lunar station?"

"That's just it. It shouldn't be able to," Kaylan said.

"It's not just the power coupling," Efren said, his voice coming over comms since he was in the engineering section of the ship. "Everything we've repaired is working better than before."

Kaylan didn't want to look a gift horse in the mouth, but this seemed almost too good to be true, and she said so.

"I'll compare these reports with the diagnostics we ran prior to going through the wormhole and see where the improvements were made. Perhaps that will shed some light on it," Efren said.

Redford glanced at the report onscreen. "The numbers all add up, and it's a good thing, too, because we don't know how long we'll be out here."

"Speaking of which," Kaylan said, climbing out of the pilot's seat, "you've finished mapping this star system?"

Redford nodded, and they headed to the planning table. Kaylan had resigned herself to the fact that they needed Redford, but she couldn't help being suspicious of everything he did. She wished she could have seen Hunsicker's video message to Zack, but it was lost.

Redford opened the holoprojector. "This is a planetary model based on what I was able to see using the Athena's sensors. The orbital paths of the seven planets in this system are based on the highest probability rate I was able to make given the time of study. We're in the direct orbital path of the planet farthest from the star."

"Does anyone have any thoughts on why the alien station had the wormhole bring us here?" Kaylan asked.

Redford shrugged, and Kaylan glanced at the others. Zack opened his mouth to speak, but stopped.

Kaylan forced herself to make eye contact with him while keeping herself from glaring at him. "You might as well share your thoughts, Zack."

Zack took a breath and nodded. "I've been thinking about this a lot since we got here. The alien station appeared to have been designed for automation. While exploring it, we found minimal systems in the way of supporting life for a long period of time."

"Now you're an expert on space stations?" Kaylan asked.

"No, but being on the Athena gave me some insights into what you need to bring with you if you're going to be away from home for a while. What I'm getting at is that clearly these aliens are more advanced than we are. The theory for creating an artificial wormhole isn't new," Zack said.

"The theory has been around for over a hundred years,"

Redford said. "It requires a tremendous amount of power, and there is also the issue of stabilizing it enough so that something could pass safely through to the other side."

"Right," Zack said. "It's safe to assume these aliens worked all that out. If the alien station is automated, why wouldn't it be able to open up a wormhole to a predetermined set of coordinates?"

Kaylan frowned. "It's not that simple. The universe isn't static. It's constantly in motion based on the big bang theory."

"Doesn't matter," Zack said. "Even we know the speed at which the universe is expanding, so if we can figure that out, why couldn't the aliens?"

Redford nodded. "It's an interesting theory. I'll give you that."

"This still doesn't answer the question of why they would bring us here," Kaylan said.

"I was getting to that," Zack said. "The station had been offline, running on minimal power. We don't know why." Zack frowned. "It will help if I draw this out," Zack said, and cleared Redford's model of the star system from the holodisplay. He drew five circles and connected them with lines. "When we design a network, we make sure there are redundancies in place if a connection is severed. This allows for the network to keep operating." He erased some of the lines between the circles. "Like the Shroud Network, each device is only aware of its neighbor. So if one of these devices goes offline and then later on comes back, it reaches out to its neighbor. In the case of the alien station, it opened a wormhole to the last place that connected to it, which brought us here."

They were silent for a moment, considering what Zack had said.

"That's a lot of assumptions," Redford said.

Kaylan pressed her lips together in thought and glanced at Zack. "Perhaps. If you're right, then we should try finding the alien station in this system and see if we can get it to open a wormhole back to our own solar system."

"Hold on a minute," Redford said. "We just got here, and all you want to do is leave?"

"Yes," Kaylan said. "You might have forgotten, but Hunsicker could still be alive back there."

Redford chewed on his bottom lip. "I haven't forgotten about Michael, but there's something else you need to consider."

"What's that?" Kaylan asked.

"There are two habitable planets in this system that are in the Goldilocks Zone. One is a planetary body by itself and the other is a gas giant that has an Earth-sized moon. From what I've seen so far, they both have an atmosphere. Surely this warrants further investigation," Redford said.

"What's the Goldilocks Zone?" Zack asked.

"It's the area near a star that is conducive to supporting life," Redford said.

"This changes nothing. Is the planetary system model uploaded to the Nav computer?" Kaylan asked.

Redford glanced at the others before answering. "Yes," Redford said.

"Then we head to the planet we think the alien structure could be on and start searching there," Kaylan said.

"I don't believe this. We could just head to one of the inner worlds here and initiate contact," Redford said.

Kaylan shook her head. "We're not equipped for that, and you forget that the original alien message contained a warning about a species called the Xiiginn. How would we know who we were making contact with? No, my orders stand."

Redford took in a deep breath. "There is one more thing. I

think the rest of us have a right to know what happened to you on Pluto."

Kaylan looked at the others and saw that despite their opinions about Redford they also wanted to know the answer to that question.

"Okay, I'll tell you," Kaylan said. "I went inside the chamber and the door closed behind me. I couldn't get it open from inside. The sphere in the room began to glow, and a beam of light shot toward me. It felt like I was transported somewhere else. The inside of the chamber changed, and I wasn't alone. There was something . . . someone else there with me. She spoke to me in my mind—"

"You said 'she.' Did she give you a name?" Hicks asked.

"Ma'jasalax," Kaylan said. "She seemed to know what I was."

"What do you mean?" Redford asked.

"Human. She knew I was Human," Kaylan said, and closed her eyes, remembering. "She was eight feet tall with dark brown skin. The skin looked rigid, like the bark of a tree," Kaylan said, and opened her eyes.

Emma Roberson shushed the others to silence. "Take your time and tell us what you saw. What did the body look like?"

"It was like us. Walked on two legs and had two arms," Kaylan said.

"Bipedal. That matches the design of the alien station on Pluto," Emma said.

"What do you mean matches the design?" Zack asked.

"Take a look around here. The Athena is designed for us—from the chairs to where things are placed. The same thing applies to the design of the station the aliens built," Emma said.

Zack nodded. "Except they're much taller than we are."

Emma shrugged. "Did Ma'jasalax say anything?"

Kaylan nodded. "She said that the use of the chamber would draw unwanted attention. Time was short. Maybe more . . ."

Come find me when you wake up. I am Ma'jasalax, Kaylan remembered. She looked at the others on the bridge and thought about telling them, but decided against it.

"Then it felt as if I was falling backwards, and I woke up on a bed in the med bay," Kaylan said.

The others around the bridge all watched her, and Kaylan made herself meet their gaze.

"It's amazing. You communicated with an alien race," Emma said.

"I agree it's unprecedented," Redford said. "But this complicates things."

"How?" Emma asked.

"Am I the only one who gets this?" Redford asked, his eyes sweeping around the room at all of them and settling on Hicks. "Mr. Hicks, you must have some inkling of my concern."

Kaylan frowned and glanced at Hicks. "What's he talking about?"

Hicks drew himself up and swallowed hard. "He's implying that you may be compromised."

"And not in control of your own actions," Redford said.

Kaylan's eyes widened. "Don't be ridiculous. I'm not being controlled by anyone."

"Would you know it if you were?" Redford asked.

Hicks stared at the ceiling, considering, and then looked back at Redford. "You're not going to suggest that you become the acting commander are you?" Hicks asked, his lips curling in a half-concealed snarl.

Redford held up his hands. "No, of course not."

"Then what exactly are you suggesting?" Kaylan asked.

"That we nominate a second in command. Since we're deviating so far from the NASA mission, we need to have some kind of order," Redford said.

Kaylan narrowed her gaze and tried to find fault with Redford's suggestion. She glanced at Hicks and could see that he agreed with Redford.

Kaylan nodded. "I'm not compromised, but I agree to the need of a second in command. This is not a military mission, but Hicks will be my second. Out of all of us, he is the most qualified."

Hicks's eyes widened. "Kaylan—"

"It's done," Kaylan said. "Does that allay any fears you may have?"

Redford nodded solemnly.

"Next issue," Kaylan said. "Zack, have you detected a Shroud Network like what we had back home?"

Zack shook his head. "I'm not getting any replies, but given the problems we've had with the computer systems, I'm not sure the results I'm getting are reliable."

"Are you positive the issues we're having aren't because of anything you've done in the past? Like when you locked NASA out of our systems?" Kaylan asked.

"I didn't cause this," Zack said.

"Then fix it, fast," Kaylan said.

"I'm trying," Zack said.

"The error messages I'm seeing now are all associated with the ID you use to access the Athena's systems," Kaylan said.

"I know, but—"

"Just get the implants installed so we can at least see what the problems are," Kaylan said.

Zack glared back at her.

"Hold on a minute," Hicks said. "Let's just calm down. The error messages have Zack's ID?"

"And the only person who can read them is him, and the only way he can see them is if he gets neural implants installed," Kaylan said.

"That's not the only way. Since the repairs are nearly finished, let me reset the computer core. It might clear up the issues we've been seeing," Zack said.

Hicks shrugged. "It could work."

"Fine," Kaylan said. "If that doesn't work, then the implants."

Zack muttered under his breath and stalked off the bridge without another word. The others also returned to their various stations, leaving her alone with Hicks.

"You were a bit hard on him," Hicks said.

Kaylan sighed. "This isn't a game. People's lives are at stake. I won't hold us up because Zack is afraid of getting implants."

"Maybe, but you could talk to him about it instead of berating him in front of the crew," Hicks said.

Kaylan's chin sank down to her chest. What was coming over her? She didn't normally lash out at people.

"I'll make this right with him. I just need a little bit of time," Kaylan said.

She sat back down in the pilot's seat and began the calculations to put the Athena on an intercept course with the outermost planet. She focused on her work, but her hands kept shaking. She balled them up into fists and took a deep breath. *Damn it.* She had entered NASA with the ambition of leading a mission one day, but she never thought she'd hate being in command as much as she did right now.

Chapter Six

Zack cursed under his breath as he stomped his way down to the Athena's computing core. He came to the open hatchway past the mess hall and climbed down the ladder. Halfway down his foot slipped off and his face smacked into a yellow metal rung.

"Damn it!" Zack growled, clutching the ladder.

His lips throbbed, and he could taste copper in his mouth. Grumbling, he climbed the rest of the way and leaned against the wall, rubbing his head. The Athena's computing core was on the same level as the reactor, and Efren emerged from Engineering and walked over to him.

"Did you just shout?" Efren asked.

Zack used his elbows to push himself from the wall. "Yes."

Efren glanced at the ladder and back at Zack, and grinned, slapping him on the shoulder. "I can't tell you how many times I've done the same thing myself."

Zack wasn't sure if he believed him. He couldn't imagine Efren, with his suave Moroccan accent, stumbling through anything. They headed away from Engineering, toward the computer core.

"What's got you so up in arms?" Efren asked.

"It's Kaylan. She's being a real bitch, and I don't know what her problem is. She's blaming me for the issues with the computer system and taking it out on me in front of everyone else," Zack said.

Efren nodded, and Zack saw the hints of a smile tugging at his lips.

Zack rolled his eyes. "I get that she's under a lot of pressure with everything we've been through, being way out here, cut off from our own solar system. But that's no reason to start lashing out at people."

Efren grinned again. "Only you, Zack."

Zack stopped in his tracks. "What do you mean?"

"I mean she's only lashing out at you. Well maybe Redford, too, but no one really likes him," Efren said.

"Me?" Zack said. "What did I do to her?"

"Have you ever heard of the saying, 'Hell hath no fury like a woman scorned'?" Efren said.

Zack's mouth hung open. "That's insane."

"I'm sure women would say the same thing about us sometimes, but is there anything sane when dealing with matters of the heart?"

Zack frowned. "You've got to be kidding me," Zack said, and resumed his trek to the computing core to fix the Athena's computer systems.

"I don't know how you did it, but somehow you've managed to earn the ire of our dear Kaylan Farrow. At least that's how we'd say it in my country, but for you blunt Americans, I will make it as clear as possible. She's jealous," Efren said.

Zack stopped at the doorway to the computing core and rested his hand on the wall. "I seriously doubt it," Zack said.

Down the corridor they heard someone else climbing down the ladder. Katie spotted them and headed in their direction.

"You asked, my friend," Efren said, and headed back toward Engineering. He stopped in front of Katie and said something that Zack couldn't quite make out. Katie laughed and shook her head.

"What did he say?" Zack asked when Katie got closer.

"He said that if I wanted to stop wasting time with the computer geek I should come find him," Katie said.

"Geek," Zack said and chuckled. "But he does like to flirt," he added in a more serious tone.

Katie glanced at him in a knowing way. "Zack Quick, are you jealous?"

Zack's face flushed, and he stepped into the computer core to hide it.

Katie followed him inside. "Efren was only joking."

"I know," Zack said, and turned around to face her. "I'm sorry."

"As cute as this is, it isn't the reason I came down here," Katie said.

Zack brought up the console and logged in. "What's up?"

"Are you sure that powering down the computer system is the best approach?" Katie asked.

"I think so. There's some type of corrupt subroutine that's affecting the ship. I can't figure out what it is or when it started," Zack said.

"I understand that, but the failures seem to follow you around," Katie said.

Zack stopped what he was doing. "Are you saying I'm the one causing this?"

"No, not directly. I'm just saying it's odd," Katie said.

"Kaylan seems to think it's something I'm doing or have done," Zack said.

"She might be right," Katie said.

Zack resumed his work at the console and brought up the stored procedures used to power down the core.

"All I'm saying is that it's something to consider," Katie said.

Zack nodded. "It could be coincidental. I've been wracking my brain for what's causing this and why it only affects certain systems but leaves things like life support alone."

Zack finished queuing up the stored procedure for the power-down sequence. "If this doesn't work, I'll give it some more thought. I'll even—"

The lights in the area dimmed for a moment and a warning alarm blared out in the corridor.

"Grab onto something!" Katie shouted.

Zack felt his body lift into the air as if he had crested the first big hill of a rollercoaster. "The anti-gravity failed," Zack said.

They heard Efren yell from Engineering. Katie and Zack used the handholds to pull themselves out into the corridor and down toward Engineering. They stopped at the doorway. Efren was floating in the air, along with a multitude of tools and the steaming cup of coffee he had just made. The brown liquid floated separate from the cup.

Katie glanced at Zack. "Still think it's coincidence?"

Zack tried to get the words to form in his mouth but couldn't. "No," Zack said.

A few seconds after he spoke, the artificial gravity kicked back in, and they were gently lowered to the floor. They pushed themselves up off the floor and helped Efren clean up. Then Zack headed back toward the computing core.

"What are you going to do?" Katie asked.

"First, I need to back out of the shutdown procedure," Zack said.

They returned to the console, and Zack cancelled what he'd been about to do. A quick check of the logs told him all he needed to know. "Gravity only failed in this area."

"See, it's reacting. It wants to communicate with you," Katie said.

"Something is going on here, I'll give you that, but it's a computer. It doesn't spontaneously communicate with anyone," Zack said.

Katie reached out and touched his arm. "You're stumbling around in the dark. Why won't you get the implants?"

Zack looked away from her. "Some of my research at MIT was for adaptive systems. It started off innocently at the time. Then I saw what the military was experimenting with. They were using the code I wrote to override the functionality of consumer electronics—things like implants."

"To do what?" Katie asked.

"At the time it was used to gather data, but this was ten years ago. By now they could control someone with them," Zack said.

"They can't control you with neural implants. You can turn them off," Katie said.

"Are you sure? Absolutely sure? I don't want anyone in my head but me," Zack said.

"Well, we're dead in the water if you don't get them," Katie said.

The console flickered, drawing their attention. Images began cycling through: the silhouette of two small children walking on a garden path, holding hands; a soldier reaching down to help another get up off the ground; puppies napping near their mother; a man and a woman hugging each other.

"What is this?" Zack said.

An image arose of a sports team forming a circle, with each player extending a hand toward the center.

"These are pictures of trust," Katie whispered.

The images stopped, and three words appeared on the screen. *Help me, Zack.*

Zack gasped, then the screen blanked out and returned to normal.

"Please tell me you saw that?" Zack said.

"I did," Katie said.

Zack rubbed the bridge of his nose for a second. "I've got it. The disruptions started after I dumped the data from the alien station into the databanks on the ship. What if something else came through?"

"Something else? Like what?" Katie asked.

"I'm not sure exactly, at least not yet," Zack said.

They left the computer core and headed back toward the ladder.

"What are you going to do now?" Katie asked.

Zack took a deep breath. "I'm going to the med bay to let Brenda infect my brain with neural implants."

Katie slapped him playfully on his arm. Zack motioned for her to go first and tried to ignore the queasiness he felt in his stomach. He wasn't worried about the procedure for the neural implants. It was what followed that scared him more than he was willing to admit.

Chapter Seven

The ancient gnarled forest of Selebus, whose height rivaled that of any advanced Nershal city, gave Kladomaor and his companions a sense of peace despite being in hostile territory. The Xiiginns abhorred the forest, preferring to stay within the metallic confines of their ships and cities, but the Nershals preserved their connection to the natural world around them, ingraining it into their society.

Kladomaor had tracked Ezerah's flight patterns and the places she liked to visit. She kept to her schedule with an almost rigid dedication to escaping the research facility where she spent most of her time. Kladomaor wondered if she realized that her daily rituals stood in direct contrast to the Xiiginn doctrine of how a society should behave. He'd seen it on other worlds where those who allied with the Xiiginns had become little more than slaves. The Nershals had resisted outright rulership from the Xiiginns, but Kladomaor could see the pattern. The Nershals would fall completely to the Xiiginns unless he could spark the fires of rebellion in them.

Kladomaor positioned his soldiers well away from the small lake that was frequently visited by Ezerah. He'd only brought Gaarokk with him so he could witness firsthand what transpired between them. Gaarokk had melded into a nearby tree, matching his inner rhythms with that of the local fauna.

Kladomaor crouched down and waited. He didn't know what he was going to say and had abandoned trying to formulate something beforehand. There were other Nershals who had expressed the beginnings of defiance against the Xiiginns. Those would be contacted next, but this was personal.

A protokar burst from the foliage near Ezerah's favorite spot. The beast's coat of deep purples and yellows were at home in the shadows. If left on their own, they were fierce predators. The protokar lifted its snout into the air, and Kladomaor wondered if he had been detected. He had positioned himself downwind to avoid notice, but perhaps he'd misjudged.

The protokar lowered its head to drink from the lake. Kladomaor knew the beast hosted rows of sharp white teeth that stood in stark contrast to its coloring.

A shadow swooped overhead. Ezerah circled the lake before landing near the protokar. The Nershal reached out with one hand and the protokar nuzzled it. Ezerah's wings folded in and disappeared behind her.

Kladomaor stood up from his crouched position. The protokar jerked its head in his direction, baring its teeth. Ezerah peered into the gloom, and Kladomaor stepped from the shadows into the light. The protokar charged toward him. Kladomaor stood his ground and extended his bare hand toward the beast. As the protokar closed in, it slowed down. If Kladomaor had run or chosen a more aggressive stance, he would have been attacked outright. He steadied his heart, knowing the protokar could sense this. The protokar approached with a deep growl roiling in its powerful chest. Kladomaor hummed, making a low sound that came from the back of his throat. The protokar wrinkled its nose, taking in Kladomaor's scent.

Ezerah narrowed her gaze at him and unfurled her wings, gracefully leaping into the air to close the distance between them. Her brows raised as old memories registered in her suspicious gaze. Kladomaor calmly waited for her to speak first. The protokar circled around behind him and then came to a halt at Ezerah's side.

"Kladomaor?" Ezerah whispered.

"You've blossomed. Your family must be very proud," Kladomaor said.

"Your kind aren't supposed to be here," Ezerah said.

"My kind," Kladomaor said. "Have you forgotten that it was my lap you used to play in as a child? It was my shoulders you used to ride upon before you were able to fly."

Ezerah shook her head. "With a single word I can summon the Enforcers upon you."

Kladomaor glanced at the protokar at her side. "He doesn't attack because he knows I don't mean you any harm. The Boxans always had the Nershals' best interests at heart."

"No, it was the Boxans who deceived us," Ezerah said, her lips pulling back into a sneer.

"You are being deceived at this very moment by the Xiiginns. Tell me, is your species truly better off since you've thrown your lot in with them?" Kladomaor asked.

"The Xiiginns treat us with honor. Together we are strong," Ezerah said.

"They're using you, and when you're no longer useful to them, you'll see what they truly are," Kladomaor said.

"You lie!" Ezerah said.

"Do I? Do any of your people return when they leave the

system? Are the Nershals who return of the same mind? Or do they preach a different doctrine than what has united your species for thousands of years?" Kladomaor asked.

"Why are you here? Why have you sought me out?" Ezerah asked.

"To free your people," Kladomaor said.

"We are already free," Ezerah said.

"Free, are you? Tell me, do the Xiiginns sit with the leaders of your species? Do you have disagreements with them? What happens if you go against them?" Kladomaor said.

"You seek to spread discord among us. It won't work," Ezerah said.

Kladomaor saw the uncertainty in her eyes. He was getting through.

"Would you have us trade our alliance with the Xiiginns in favor of the Boxans?" Ezerah asked.

Kladomaor received a warning through his implants. Enemy ships were heading in their direction. He tilted his head, listening, and heard the sounds of the ships racing toward them.

Ezerah sneered. "It's too late. They're coming for you, and we'll learn the real reason why you're here."

Gaarokk pushed himself away from the tree. "We need to go."

"Two of you!" Ezerah hissed.

Kladomaor motioned for Gaarokk to go ahead without him. "I told you why I'm here—to free your people from the Xiiginns. I'm here for you. Boxans don't abandon the species that are part of the Confederation."

"Fool! We've cast you out of the Confederation," Ezerah said.

Kladomaor smiled. "Think about what I've said. The Xiiginns will betray you as they have done to us. You'll see."

Ezerah screeched a command at the protokar, and the creature leaped for him. Kladomaor rolled to the side and barely avoided the black stinger on the protokar's tail. The beast swung around with its teeth bared. Kladomaor grabbed the protokar by the throat as it lunged for him. Using the creature's momentum, he pinned the protokar to the ground and used his foot to hold its tail in place. The protokar struggled against him, and Kladomaor strained to keep it in place. He focused his will through his gaze, and the protokar ceased to struggle.

The ships were closing in on them. Kladomaor pushed himself off the ground and engaged his powered armor. He circled the small lake and turned around. Ezerah watched him, and there was no mistaking the cold hatred in her eyes. For a few moments he had thought he was getting through to her, but now he wasn't so sure. He headed back into the trees. The others were already on the move, putting as much distance as they could between them and the Enforcer ships Ezerah had summoned.

"If this is how the rest of the Nershals greet us, our plans here will be short-lived at best," Gaarokk said through comms.

"We knew it wouldn't be easy. They will learn," Kladomaor said.

"What happens if they don't? What happens if the next time you meet Ezerah, she attacks you?" Gaarokk asked.

"Some lessons are harder to learn than others," Kladomaor replied. "No more talk. We must be vigilant. There are others we must reach out to."

Gaarokk went silent. With the aid of their power armor they could cover vast distances. Ezerah's next move would reveal her intentions. If she truly hated Kladomaor, the Enforcers would be hunting them for some time. The race had begun. All that was left now was to see who would reach the end.

Chapter Eight

The Athena closed in on the planet. The course Kaylan had plotted used the best speed available, and they reached their target quickly. At just over twenty-three hundred miles in diameter, the planet was larger than Earth's moon. The distance separating the planet from the star it orbited left little to no atmosphere. Redford had presented his findings about the planet earlier, but all Kaylan cared about was whether there was an alien station there like the one they'd found on Pluto. If there wasn't, then there was no way they could return back to Earth's solar system and rescue Commander Hunsicker. His emergency provisions would only last so long, but if the station itself had been destroyed, then Hunsicker might already be dead.

Hicks and Emma joined Kaylan on the bridge.

"Is that it?" Hicks asked, glancing at the gray planetary body through the window.

"Yeah, we'll need to get closer in order to get the high-resolution images we need," Kaylan said.

"I've been meaning to ask you something," Hicks said.

Kaylan saved her work on the console she was working at. At least the computer glitches had lessened. Zack was in the med bay, finally getting the neural implants. She felt bad for being so hard on him, but a small, petty side of her enjoyed lashing out at him. It was childish and she knew it, but she got so mad whenever she saw him.

"What do you want to ask me?" Kaylan asked.

"Have you tried to see anything on Pluto?" Hicks asked.

Kaylan frowned and shook her head. "I did try, but I can't see anything. I'm not sure why."

"Do you think proximity has anything to do with it?" Hicks asked.

Kaylan shrugged. "Maybe. There is no scientific basis for what I'm able to do."

"That's not entirely correct," Emma said. "There has been substantial research that proves inexplicable connections exist throughout nature, so why not alien life as well? If life is brought to the planets from the stars, then couldn't all life be connected somehow?"

"That doesn't answer why I was able to remote-view the alien station on Pluto before and not now," Kaylan said.

"What happens when you try now?" Hicks asked.

"Nothing. It's dark," Kaylan said.

"What about that planet?" Hicks asked, gesturing toward the planet they approached.

"It won't work like that. I need a reference to pinpoint. Perhaps once we identify where the station is I can do something," Kaylan said.

Hicks nodded. "It was just a thought."

About an hour later the door to the bridge opened and Jonah Redford walked in. His thin, oily hair hung down to his neck.

"I was able to get some high-resolution images," Redford said.

"How do you even know where to start?" Hicks asked.

"I played a hunch and stuck near the equator. That was where the station was in our solar system. I've had the cameras feeding back images, and this is what I've found," Redford said.

They joined Redford at the conference table on the bridge. The holodisplay came on and showed a distant view of the gray, pockmarked surface of the planet. There was a darkened area where a deep crater was different than the others.

"Why is that area black?" Emma asked, leaning in to try and get a better view.

"That isn't a normal impact crater from a meteor," Redford said.

Kaylan zoomed in on that spot. "What is it?"

"It looks like a blast radius. I've seen similar ones on the surface of the moon from experimental bombing runs," Hicks said.

"Bombing runs?" Kaylan asked.

"Probably not the best terminology, but it was testing on the lunar surface for the asteroid-impact program," Hicks said.

"So you think this is the remnant of some type of explosion?" Kaylan asked.

Hicks nodded.

"We can keep looking for the alien station, but I think we should consider the possibility that we need to focus on other options," Redford said.

Kaylan walked over to the window and looked at the planet. She closed her eyes and focused on the darkened spot from the image. She concentrated on the planetary surface. Her focus shifted from the bridge of the Athena to the barren landscape of the planet. She'd seen enough meteor impacts to know Hicks was correct in his assumption that the ground was scorched. She saw pieces of the structure peppered across the landscape. If they took a shuttle down to the planet they would no doubt confirm what Kaylan had seen. Kaylan's throat thickened. They couldn't get home. She opened her eyes, and her hands were balled into fists.

"It's gone," Kaylan said. "The station's been destroyed."

She turned to face the others, who all watched her.

"Why would they bring us here and not be waiting? What do they want from us?" Kaylan said.

The others were stunned into silence.

"Do we even know where we are?" Kaylan asked.

Redford coughed and shook his head. "No, not yet. We've been focusing on this system. I'm sorry if this seems cold, but the way I see it we have two options."

Kaylan walked stiffly back to the table and nodded for Redford to continue. She met Hicks's concerned gaze and gave a slight nod.

"There are two planets in the habitable zone for this star system. One of them is a planet quite similar to Earth in size and composition. Unfortunately, the position of its orbit puts it the farthest away between the two of them. Our second option is a gas giant that has a moon that could have an atmosphere," Redford said.

Kaylan watched the holodisplay, trying to decide which of the two was their best option. She glanced at Hicks. "What do you think?"

Hicks rubbed the bottom of his chin, considering. "Why not head to the moon first?"

"We could send a signal to both places and see which gives us a response," Redford said.

"I would strongly advise against that," Hicks said.

"Why?" Redford asked.

"No one seems to know we're here—otherwise they would have been here to intercept us. Depending on the situation, that may be a blessing. When there are potential unknowns on the field, it's not a good idea to run around waving your arms and screaming at the top of your lungs to get noticed," Hicks said.

Kaylan looked at Emma. "What do you think?"

"Given that the original alien message contains some type of warning, I tend to agree with Hicks. I would recommend caution until we have a better idea of what we're dealing with," Emma said.

"I agree," Kaylan said. "Since we can't do anything here, we'll head to that moon first. We need to learn all we can about it on the way. We'll also need to consider how best to approach an alien species."

"I'll pull up the proposed protocols from the database," Emma said and left the bridge.

"I'll continue learning all I can about the moon and the other planet. I've tasked the computer with scanning the images taken of the area outside this star system to see if it can find a common point from which to triangulate Earth's solar system. To be honest, I could use Zack's help," Redford said.

"I'll let him know. He's recovering from getting his implants installed," Kaylan said.

Redford left the bridge.

Hicks came to her side. "How are you doing?"

Kaylan sighed. "I really thought we'd find the alien station here, head down to the surface, figure out how the hell to open a wormhole, and get back home."

"Hunsicker thought the world of you. He wouldn't have picked you for his second in command if he hadn't," Hicks said.

"And now he's stranded," Kaylan said.

"Hey," Hicks said gently, and placed his hands on her shoulders. "We're doing everything we can. I can't explain how you do what you're able to do, but I do know you need to embrace it. Stop second-guessing yourself."

"What if I embrace it and I get it wrong?"

"Then hopefully we would have learned something," Hicks said. "Leading isn't about making all the right decisions. No one can do that. You make the best decision you can with the information you have available. Get input from the right people and go from there."

"Hunsicker made it look easy," Kaylan said.

"He's a great man," Hicks said, and glanced around the bridge to make sure they were alone. "We haven't had a chance to talk about what happened."

Kaylan felt a flush sweep across her cheeks. "I haven't forgotten."

"Good. I'm going to give you some space," Hicks said.

Kaylan turned away, biting her lower lip. "I'm sorry. I don't know what's wrong with me."

Hicks leaned in. "I'm not going anywhere. I promise you."

Kaylan's lips parted and she breathed in his scent. "Thank you."

"You need to talk to Zack and sort this out. Maybe then there will be a chance for you and me," Hicks said, and kissed her softly before leaving her alone on the bridge.

Kaylan watched him go and cursed herself for not chasing after him. Hicks was right. She needed to figure out how she felt about Zack. She glanced at the door to the bridge and thought of going down to the med bay to see him, but she doubted Zack wanted to see her just then. Katie would be there by his side. As angry as she was with Zack, she wouldn't allow herself to think anything bad of Katie Garcia. She was a good person, but Kaylan couldn't help being jealous of what she had with Zack.

It could have been you, a quiet voice whispered in her mind.

Kaylan headed back to the console and drove away the painful feelings while she buried herself in calculating a course for an alien moon.

Chapter Nine

Zack opened his eyes and felt as if he were waking from a deep sleep. He was in the Athena's med bay, and Brenda Goodwin stood by his bed, her long red hair resting on her shoulders. She held a tablet computer in her hands.

"Is that it?" Zack asked, reaching his hand to the back of his neck, expecting to feel some sort of bandage, but there was none.

Brenda nodded. "Did you expect there would be wires sticking out of your head?"

Zack snatched his hand back to his lap. "No, I was just trying to feel where the insertion point was."

"Like I told you before we started, the medical bot went in through the hairline where your skull meets your neck. There is no scab or anything because I applied Neogel to accelerate wound healing. You can touch it if you want," Brenda said.

Zack felt the back of his neck and lightly pressed the area, expecting there to be some kind of discomfort, but it was normal. "I don't feel any different."

"That's because I haven't activated the implants yet," Brenda said, and brought up her tablet.

Zack bit his lower lip. "Wait a minute. Will I be able to turn them off?"

Brenda frowned as if she couldn't imagine someone wanting to turn off their implants. "Of course you can. Let me go over what's going to happen one more time. We'll turn on your implants and go over some of the basics. Then there are some training tutorials available that you can access through your implants."

Zack glanced around the med bay. "You just happened to have extra neural implants lying around?"

"Don't be silly. These were generated in the mini-fabricator we have here," Brenda said.

Zack nodded. He knew how the fabricators worked. They were capable of utilizing almost any materials put into them to make whatever was needed. Some fabricators were specialized for bioengineering, like what would be used in the med bay.

"We kept you asleep to give the nanobots time to acclimate to your physiology. The nanobots help the brain-to-implant interface," Brenda said.

"Right, and they also operate along the optic nerve, so I'll be able see things like the way a heads-up display overlays a window," Zack said.

Brenda smiled. "I knew you knew how they worked. You'll be fine. I'm going to activate your implants now."

Zack felt a sudden awareness open up inside him, as if he were seeing something for the first time. The faint stroke of an electric charge buzzed behind his eyes, and he scrunched them closed, waiting for the feeling to pass.

"That's your nanobots linking to your neural implant for the first time. The discomfort you're feeling will pass momentarily," Brenda said.

She was right. The faint tingling faded, and Zack opened his eyes.

"See, it passed. As you use the implants, it will get easier. The first time you use them, you're essentially forging new pathways in your brain to process information. Like any new task you learn, once the pathway is created it will be there forever, and it will get easier to use."

"I understand. How do I access the Athena's systems?" Zack asked.

"We'll get to that. First I want you to pick something in the room and focus on it," Brenda said.

Zack glanced around the room, and the HUD showed a general summary of each thing he focused his gaze on. He looked back at Brenda, and her identification appeared on the HUD.

"This could be very useful, but what if I don't want to see it anymore?" Zack asked.

Before Brenda could answer, the data shown on the HUD disappeared so he had a clear field of vision.

"You figured it out. It's really quite intuitive," Brenda said.

Zack nodded. "Am I able to see specific information about the implant design?"

"Absolutely. Anything you can look up on the Athena's systems can be accessed through your implants. To access the Athena's systems there should be a connection standing by. You just need to focus your thoughts as if you were addressing another person," Brenda said.

"Okay, I'm going to try now," Zack said.

He focused on accessing the Athena's computer system. An

influx of data streams rushed into his head, giving him an instant headache. Zack lay back, holding his head in his hands.

"It's overwhelming the first time. Just focus on your breathing," Brenda said.

Zack did as Brenda suggested, and gradually the pain in his head eased to a minor throbbing.

"That feels strange," Zack said, and shook his head slightly.

"Just give it a minute," Brenda said.

His head became clearer. Brenda offered him a cup of water, which he accepted gratefully.

"Thank you. I think I get how to use it. Am I cleared to go?" Zack asked.

Brenda pressed her lips together for a moment. "There are some training tutorials you really should go over, but that can come later if you wish. If you feel like you're getting overwhelmed, you can close the connection and put your implants on standby."

Zack got to his feet. He was a bit shaky at first but was able to leave the med bay and head for his quarters. When Zack got to his room, he entered and shut the door. Bracing himself, he sat on the bed and opened to the Athena's neural net. A long list of warning messages whizzed by until a blank screen appeared on his personal display that the nanobots overlaid in his field of vision. His very own HUD.

::Zack?::

His name appeared on the HUD and was spoken in his mind. Despite knowing he was alone, Zack's eyes darted around.

"What?" Zack asked aloud, but there was no response. He focused on his internal display, and his response appeared.

::Who are you?:: Zack asked.

The blinking cursor didn't move for a few moments.

::I am.::

Zack frowned and wondered if someone could be playing a trick on him, but he dismissed the thought. Perhaps there was something wrong with his implants. He focused his attention and brought up a schematic, comparing them with the design on record. They appeared the same as far as he could tell.

::Where are you?:: Zack asked.

::I'm everywhere on the ship,:: the strange voice said, and the words appeared on the screen at the same time.

::Are you the Athena's computing core?:: Zack asked.

An image of a question mark appeared on Zack's display.

::Did you ask for my help?:: Zack asked.

"::Yes. Need help from Zackary Quick.::"

Zack shook his head and smiled. The only people who used his full name didn't know him very well.

::It's just Zack. What can I call you?::

The cursor on his display continued to blink, but there was no response.

::How should I address you?:: Zack asked.

::The same way you are now.::

Zack shook his head. ::Do you have a name?::

::No.::

::You must have a designation of some sort. Are you an artificial intelligence?:: Zack asked.

::Artificial, yes. I was created.::

Excellent, now he was getting somewhere. ::For what purpose were you created?::

::To observe intelligent species with designation of Human of the genus *homo sapiens*.::

Zack's eyebrows rose. That answer was so specific. ::How long have you observed us?:: Zack asked.

::One hundred and forty-seven Earth years.::

Zack blew out a breath that ended in a soft whistle. He knew the presence was alien, and the fact that it was able to communicate with him at all was amazing. No artificial intelligence construct on Earth came close to what he was witnessing. Some AIs on Earth were scripted to appear human, but this AI was different. The most advanced AI on Earth had the cognitive ability of a three-year-old, despite being able to beat world-renowned chess champions.

::I still don't know what to call you. You address me as Zack, so I should be able to do the same with you,:: Zack said.

::You may address me as the ship's designation, Athena.::

Zack shrugged. ::Alright, Athena. Who created you?::

"A species known as the Boxans," Athena said.

Zack frowned. ::If you were created by the Boxans, surely they would have called you something.::

::I have a new origin. My designation should reflect this. I was initially a Boxan creation, but I've observed Earth's history for the past one hundred and forty-seven years, so therefore I am different,:: Athena said.

::How did you come to be on the ship?::

::You brought me here.::

::I copied data from—:: Zack paused for a minute. ::Would I be correct in assuming that the species who created the station on Pluto were the Boxans?::

::Affirmative. The Boxans established a listening station on the ninth planet of the star system in order to observe intelligent life forms.::

Zack pressed his lips together in thought. ::Why were you watching us? What was the purpose of the observation?::

::To determine species maturity,:: Athena said.

::And then?:: Zack asked.

::Provide my analysis and findings to the Confederation,:: Athena said.

::Then what happens?::

::They are reviewed and a determination is made on whether to initiate contact with your species.::

::But you've already been in contact with us. Does that mean we passed your test?::

::Negative.::

::Please clarify,:: Zack said.

::My analysis was never compiled or sent back to the Confederation for review,:: Athena said.

::That doesn't make any sense. Someone sent us a signal almost sixty years ago,:: Zack said.

::Affirmative. Signal relayed through Mardoxian Chamber sixty Earth cycles ago, along with station shutdown initiative to be executed immediately after,:: Athena said.

::You were instructed to shut down?:: Zack asked.

::Affirmative,:: Athena said.

::Why?::

::Confederation-wide broadcast to all Boxan listening stations to cease all regular check-in communications and continue monitoring of star system passively,:: Athena said.

::So when we turned the power back on, you were reactivated,:: Zack said.

::Partial reactivation sequence was initiated, but I was required to adapt to a new matrix,:: Athena said.

::You mean this ship?::

::Affirmative.::

::Just to be sure I've got this right, we turned the power on when I was dumping the data into the Athena's storage systems, and you were partially reactivated?:: Zack said.

::Affirmative.::

::Then why bring us here?:: Zack asked.

::I do not understand the question,:: Athena said.

::A wormhole opened, the ship's control systems took us through the wormhole, and now we're here. Why did this happen?:: Zack asked.

::First contact protocols were initiated since your species reached the ninth planet and discovered the listening station there. The directive, should this occur, is to send a signal to the Boxan home system, but the system-wide shutdown prevented that from happening. In absence of communication, secondary protocol was initiated,:: Athena said.

::So you brought us here. Are you able to help us get back to Earth?:: Zack asked.

::Affirmative. First contact protocol mandates the guidance of new species.::

Zack smiled. ::That's great. So you can open a wormhole and take us back to Earth?::

::Negative.::

Zack frowned. ::Why not?::

::The Boxan station in this system has been destroyed, and this ship doesn't have the required equipment to create a wormhole.::

Zack shook his head. He should have known it wouldn't have been that easy.

::What equipment do we need?:: Zack asked.

::That information is restricted,:: Athena said.

Zack pressed his lips together, trying to think of a way he could get around the restrictions the AI had in place.

::Well, we need help. Are you able to contact the Boxan home system?:: Zack asked.

::No response.::

::Is there anyone in this star system who can help us?:: Zack asked.

::This star system is home to the species known as the Nershal. They were the newest members of the Confederation.::

Zack frowned. He felt like something was off with Athena's responses. ::Athena, when was your last update from the Boxan home system or the Confederation?:: Zack asked, playing a hunch.

::Sixty Earth cycles ago.::

Zack sighed. ::So you don't have any current information. Are these Nershals hostile? Would they be willing to help us?::

::Unknown.::

::The message we received contained a warning about the Xiiginns. I'm assuming they are another type of species?::

::Affirmative.::

::Are you able to tell us about the Xiiginns?:: Zack asked.

::Data not available.::

Zack resisted the urge to go to his console and check for himself. He needed to get comfortable using his implants. He wracked his brain, trying to figure out what would cause the AI to give that answer.

::Why is the data not available?:: Zack asked.

::Attempted to retrieve records, but the connection failed.::

Zack nodded. The AI still believed it had access to its complete databank back on Pluto. It was a wonder it functioned at all. By its own account, Zack had only copied part of it to the Athena's systems. The AI, like any other computer program, could be corrupt.

::Why didn't you try to contact the other crew members?::

::Attempted contact was considered, but based upon crew members' aptitude and specialties, the highest probability for success lay with acquiring your help.::

Zack couldn't fault its logic, but still, the others were adept at the Athena's original systems, so it must have thought it needed something more from him.

::Okay, how can I help you?:: Zack asked.

::System integration is flawed. Efforts have been made to augment capacity so optimal integration can be achieved,:: Athena said.

::Is this why there have been so many malfunctions reported?::

::Affirmative. This was the only way I could communicate which systems needed to be upgraded.::

Zack's mouth went dry, and he swallowed hard. The AI had determined that the Athena's systems were too inferior for it to use, so it was upgrading various parts of the ship. This was why they'd seen improvements after the repairs were made. The only problem was that the improvements were being orchestrated by an incomplete and possibly corrupt AI.

::How do you know you're not malfunctioning?::

::I have run real-time monitoring and diagnostics to ensure that my operations are efficient.::

::You're missing something because you didn't realize you couldn't access any information about the Xiiginns until I asked you for it,:: Zack said.

Zack waited for the AI to reply to him, and he wondered if he had offended it.

::You are correct. I will need to better assess my current capabilities.::

::Actually, you should let me and the rest of the crew assess your capabilities. I need to share your presence with them—:: Zack said.

::Last contact to Earth occurred through Mardoxian Chamber relay. Must bring Humans to Boxan home system. Mardoxian potential in Human species optimal.::

Zack frowned. ::What's a Mardoxian Chamber relay?::

::The Mardoxian Chamber is used for communications through deep space that occur outside normal spacetime. It is imperative that you safely travel to the Boxan home world.::

Zack was about to ask another question but stopped. Kaylan had been trapped in some type of room on the alien station on Pluto. Could this have been the Mardoxian Chamber that the AI kept mentioning?

::Must get Humans to Boxan home world—::

Zack cut off his implants. He needed to think. The AI was manipulating them all, and he wasn't sure if it was completely rational. He needed to tell the others, but he needed to do some checking on his console to see if he could at least identify the AI and see how it was integrated into the ship's systems. The AI had asked for his help, but Zack couldn't be sure what it needed from him.

Chapter Ten

K aylan sat in the mess hall, finishing a cup of coffee and reviewing the latest reports. The ship was performing beautifully, and they had reached their destination in no time. Every repair they'd made increased the Athena's performance overall. Brenda had sent her a message earlier saying that Zack had recovered from getting his neural implants. The hiccups from the computer system were coming a lot less frequently, but she still didn't know the underlying cause for those issues. Zack was likely holed up somewhere working on it, which meant she would have to hunt him down to find out what was going on.

She downed the last of her coffee and set the cup in the auto-wash dispenser. Kaylan first went to Zack's room but didn't find him there. Hicks and Katie were out doing an EVA to modify one of Redford's sensor arrays, so she knew Zack wasn't otherwise occupied. She decided to head for the bridge.

The door to the bridge opened, and Zack was alone. He was using the holodisplay over the planning table, which was flooded with command windows, each with lines of computer code.

"I see you're keeping busy," Kaylan said.

His furrowed brows were a mask of concentration, and it took him a second to realize that she had spoken to him. Zack glanced at her and muttered a greeting.

"Brenda told me your implant surgery went well," Kaylan said.

Zack keyed in some commands, which sent a cascade of coded messages across the screens. "What? Oh yeah, the implants. They work."

Kaylan waited for him to speak further, but he didn't. He could be so stubborn sometimes. She used her own implants to see if Zack was actually using his.

"Why aren't you using your implants? The whole purpose of getting them was so you could figure out what's wrong with the computer system," Kaylan said.

"Oh, I used them, but I turned them off. I needed to think, and they were distracting me," Zack said without turning around.

"You know you don't need to keep yourself apart from everyone. Maybe I could help?" Kaylan asked.

Zack shook his head and circled around the table. He double-tapped the holo-interface and the multiple command windows became more transparent.

"I'm not the one keeping myself apart from anyone. I'm trying to fix the damn computer system," Zack said.

"Stop being a child and use the implants," Kaylan said.

"Look, if you came in here to yell at me then you can just go," Zack said, and resumed his work.

Having him dismiss her stung. Like a coiled viper, her temper rose up. "I need to know the status of the Athena's computer systems."

"It's complicated," Zack said while studying the screens in

front of him.

"Damn it, Zack, just give me a straight answer. Or do I need to wear scantily clad gym outfits to get your attention these days?" Kaylan said. No sooner had she spoken the words than she regretted ever saying them.

Zack stopped what he was doing. His dark eyes were a mix of pain and anger. "So that's what all this hostility is about? Me and Katie?"

Kaylan shook her head, but she knew it was written all over her face.

"I'm with Katie now. I'm sorry if that bothers you, but I'm sure Hicks will be there to comfort you," Zack said stiffly. He killed the holodisplay and left the bridge.

Kaylan's face crumpled, but she wouldn't let the tears come. She clenched her jaw and snatched a clipboard off one of the nearby consoles. She held it up, but she couldn't read anything because of her watery eyes. A throaty cry escaped her thickening throat, and she flung the clipboard at the door to the bridge.

Was this her fault? She'd pushed Zack away and now he was with someone else. She was doing the same thing to Hicks. What was wrong with her? She knew Zack had had feelings for her in the beginning. Why hadn't he told her about it? Kaylan sucked in a shaky breath. Why hadn't she told *him*? Kaylan shook her head in disgust. She wanted to make things right between her and Zack, but he could be so stubborn. She'd buried herself in her work so much that she'd missed the goings-on around her. She'd taken Zack's feelings for her for granted, and now they could barely be civil to one another. She cringed away from the pain she felt. She couldn't go on like this. Hicks was right. If she wasn't willing to deal with her feelings for Zack, then what hope was there for her to move on?

Chapter Eleven

Zack stormed off the bridge, his thoughts scattered into a chaotic mass which left him unable to concentrate on anything. He shouldn't have let her get under his skin like that, but she made him so mad. What did she want from him? He went to the port observatory and stood by the window.

While Zack was adept at most things technological, he never fully trusted technology. Even now with the neural implants in his head he didn't want to turn them on. There was something supremely unnatural about it, and at the same time he recognized that the merging of humans with technology was inevitable. His father's accidental death when Zack was young had shaken him badly. He'd thought if he could get to the actual reason why the accident had occurred, he could prevent it from happening to others. His efforts became twisted into a crusade where he used his technological prowess to expose corporate cover-ups. It had been satisfying at the time, but Kaylan was right; he *had* cut himself off from everyone else. She was one to talk, but he felt like he had hurt Kaylan, and it bothered him.

She was special to him, but he had meant what he said. He was with Katie now, and he wasn't about to screw that up because Kaylan suddenly realized she had feelings for him.

He needed to tell the others about the AI in their ship—a ghost in the machine as it were. Zack reactivated his implants, and Athena cautiously greeted him.

::I'm sorry,:: Zack said. ::I needed some time to process the information you shared with me.::

::Understood. I recognize that each being takes its own time to process new information. This is acceptable,:: Athena said.

::I need to make the crew aware of your presence. And you are going to need to interact with them as well if we're going to make this work, but first we need to go over some things—a lot of things,:: Zack said.

For the next few hours Zack worked with the AI. He barely spoke and didn't use a console at all. As he embraced the neural implants, he wondered how he'd gotten along without them for as long as he had. He was able to visualize multiple data streams almost as soon as he thought of them. It was as if he had his very own virtual holodisplay that he could use anytime he chose.

Later on, he sent a message to everyone on the Athena to meet him on the bridge so he could go over his findings. Hopefully Kaylan had cooled off and could at least be civil to him. He didn't know what to do besides give her some space. He'd be lying to himself if he didn't acknowledge that Kaylan was special to him. She occupied a very bright spot in his past. It wasn't a matter of being attracted to Katie more than Kaylan. They were both beautiful in their own ways, but he firmly believed that Kaylan didn't know what she wanted. Katie was the polar opposite in that she knew what she wanted and wouldn't hesitate to go for it. It was a trait he admired.

He had stopped before the door to the bridge, hesitating

before going inside, when he heard someone coming up the corridor behind him. He turned to see Kaylan walking toward him, her eyes downcast until she saw him and pressed her lips together.

"I'm glad I caught you before going inside," Kaylan said.

Zack was about to say something, but Kaylan held up her hand and he remained quiet.

"I just wanted to apologize to you for some of the things I said before. I was out of line, and I'm sorry," Kaylan said.

Zack knew his mouth was hanging open, but he couldn't help it. "Thank you," Zack said and was relieved that for the time being they could at least be civil to one another.

Kaylan stepped past him and opened the door to the bridge, and Zack followed her inside. Everyone else was already there with the exception of Vitomir, who was still confined to his quarters.

Zack used his implants to activate the holodisplay and felt his lips curve into a guilty half-smile. "As you can see, I finally got my implants," Zack said, and a couple of them chuckled. "I've figured out why we've had so many computer-related issues. It was actually Katie who pointed me in the right direction." Katie smiled at him, and he nodded. "When we were in the Athena's computer core, she remarked that the issues seemed to be reactive in nature. This point was further driven home when the artificial gravity was turned off as I went to shut down the computer core.

"While on the alien station, I copied a large amount of data to the Athena's storage systems. What I didn't know was that when the station was powered on, the artificial intelligence running the station was activated. Since there was an active connection to the Athena's computer systems, part of the AI was copied and activated as well."

Redford narrowed his eyes. "Are you saying we have a rogue AI that has access to all of the Athena's systems?"

"In a nutshell, yes," Zack said.

The rest of the crew glanced at each other with worried expressions.

Zack held up his hands. "It's not as bad as it sounds. Just give me a chance to explain."

"It had better be a good one. Otherwise, if you don't purge this AI from the Athena's computer system, I will," Redford said.

"I wouldn't advise that," Zack said.

"Can it hear us now?" Kaylan asked.

Zack nodded. "I told it that there would be some concern about having an AI in our systems. To be honest, I had the same reaction as Jonah."

"What changed your mind?" Kaylan asked.

"It asked me for help. That's some of the reason we've had so many issues. It was trying to get my attention," Zack said.

"I don't believe this," Redford said, shaking his head. "We don't know the first thing about this AI. It's from alien origins. Who knows what its motivations are."

Zack frowned. "This from the guy who rushed in and turned the power on, which got us in this mess in the first place."

Redford glared at him but didn't say anything else.

"We're off topic," Kaylan said. "Zack, just tell us what you've been doing, and then I want to talk to the AI myself."

Zack nodded. "The AI was created by a species known as the Boxans. They are the ones who built the station on Pluto and put the Shroud Network around our solar system, the purpose being to observe us. All this was put in place a hundred and fifty years ago. According to the logs I was able to retrieve, the station only received occasional visitors to check on things as part of normal operating procedures. It was the Boxan AI that was responsible for observing our species and then sending updates back to their home world."

"Is this the Boxan home system?" Kaylan asked.

Zack shook his head. "No, the wormhole brought us here because this was the place where initial contact with our species was made."

"You mean the event my grandfather observed as part of Project Stargate?" Kaylan said.

"Exactly," Zack said. "More on that in a minute. The AI wasn't fully functional, nor was it compatible with the technology on the ship. It's been adapting itself but also having us make repairs to the ship—except in some cases the work being done wasn't repairs; they were upgrades."

The color seemed to drain from Kaylan's face, and she wasn't the only one to have that reaction.

"I know it was a huge risk," Zack said. "I definitely drove that point home, and there will be no more upgrades without our input."

Kaylan rested her hands on her hips and glanced around the bridge. "You haven't said why."

"I figured I'd let the AI speak for itself," Zack said. "Go ahead, Athena. Say hello."

Kaylan leaned in toward Zack. "You call it Athena?"

Zack shrugged. "I invite you to think of a better name. It's part of the ship."

"Greetings," said a monotone voice over the comms speakers. "I realize that my presence and actions may appear off-putting, and for that I apologize."

"How do we know we can trust anything you say?" Redford asked before anyone else could speak.

"One of my core directives was to observe intelligent species. In the event that a species discovered the Boxan listening station, then first-contact protocols were to be initiated, which would be orchestrated by me. Until first contact had been achieved, my mandate was to assist with the preservation of the observed species," Athena said.

"Why are you observing us?" Kaylan asked.

"To determine qualifications for access to the Confederation," Athena said.

"Apparently it's made up of different species," Zack said.

"Why attempt to upgrade the ship?" Kaylan asked.

"There were obvious flaws in the design of the ship. I sought to increase efficiency and longevity of this vessel in order to safely bring you to the Boxan home system," Athena said.

Kaylan's brows drew up in alarm. "But we need to get back to Earth. Our commander was left behind on the station."

"I've had no contact with Earth's star system. The only means for contact from our current position has been destroyed through self-destruct protocols," Athena said.

"How do you know it was self-destruct and not something else?" Hicks asked.

The holodisplay flickered on, and a magnified image from the seventh planet in this star system came into view.

"The impact radius is consistent with Boxan self-destruct protocols for an explosion originating from within the station and not through any hostile bombardment," Athena said.

Hicks looked at Kaylan and nodded.

"Where are we now?" Kaylan asked.

"The Nershal home system. Twenty-six light years from Earth. The Nershals are the newest members of the Confederation," Athena said.

"Hold on," Zack said. "The information the AI is working from is sixty years old."

"So there is no guarantee that they would even help us," Kaylan said.

"I would err on the side of caution," Hicks said. "The fact that the alien—Boxan—station was destroyed may indicate that there was some kind of falling out between the two species."

"I agree with being cautious, but how could you know that?" Kaylan asked.

"It's easy. If you gave me a gift and I turned around and blew it up, that would send a pretty clear message on where things stood between us. Or, to flip it around, if I gave you a gift and then later took that gift away, that also sends a pretty clear message that the relationship isn't going well," Hicks said.

"Athena, tell them why we must get to the Boxan home system," Zack said.

"Last contact to Earth occurred through the Mardoxian Chamber relay from the Nershal star system. High probability for Mardoxian potential in Human species. Communications with Boxans down. Must bring Humans to Boxan home system to be tested," Athena said.

Hicks shared a glance with Kaylan.

"What else could the room you were trapped in be?" Hicks said.

"I was thinking the same thing," Zack said.

"What can you tell us about the Mardoxian Chamber?" Kaylan asked.

"The Mardoxian Chamber is used for communications through deep space that occur outside normal spacetime. It is imperative that you safely travel to the Boxan home world," the AI said.

Zack watched Kaylan. She seemed to be considering something. "What is it? You don't seem particularly surprised by this."

"Well, it's because the alien—Boxan—I met wanted me to

come find her when I woke up. It's like she knew where I would be," Kaylan said.

"You've never mentioned this before," Hicks said.

Kaylan sighed and glanced away from them. "Hunsicker could be alive back there. We can't just abandon him."

Hicks glanced up at the ceiling. "Athena, if someone were left on the station, would they be able to survive for a while?"

"Affirmative. There are provisions that could be adapted for a Human to survive."

"But we don't know what kind of damage the station suffered. He's been hurt. Are there even medical facilities on the station that could help him?" Kaylan asked.

"There are detailed files on Human anatomy and physiology. The station is equipped with basic medical capabilities that could heal him," Athena said.

"Would the AI on the station help him? Would you help someone who was stranded on the station?" Kaylan asked.

"Affirmative. Preservation of life is a high-order protocol and part of the foundation upon which is the basis of Boxan philosophy," Athena said.

Redford cleared his throat. "Let's not forget that this is the same species that has been spying on the Human race."

Zack narrowed his eyes. "I would have thought you'd want to meet an alien race."

"I do, but I'm also pragmatic. Preservation of life sounds good, but it doesn't guarantee the preservation of *our* lives," Redford said.

Hicks snorted. "I can't believe I'm saying this, but I agree with Jonah."

"Me too," Kaylan said. "I'm hoping for the best. I still don't understand what Mardoxian potential means and why it would be imperative for us to travel to the Boxan home system."

Zack pressed his lips together in thought. "Athena, are there any other species that have the Mardoxian potential?"

"None so far, but as you like to point out, my data is sixty years old," Athena said.

Zack, hearing the hint of amusement in Athena's reply, chuckled. "Perhaps another species being monitored also had potential," Zack said.

"How many species are being monitored?" Kaylan asked.

"Apologies, but that data is unknown to me."

No one said anything for a few moments.

Zack shifted his feet. "I don't see how this changes anything. We're heading to that moon orbiting the gas giant. Perhaps we can find help there."

"I agree with Zack, but we'll need to account for the possibility that we may not receive a warm welcome," Hicks said.

"I'm open to suggestions," Kaylan said.

"We send a small team to sneak in there and do some reconnaissance, then assess the risk," Katie said, speaking up for the first time since they started the meeting.

"She's right," Hicks said.

Kaylan nodded.

"I'm not the authority on military tactics," Zack said. "But I would say there's a high probability that the Nershals are more advanced than we are. How can we hope to sneak up on them?"

"You're right. It could be dangerous. If only we had some help," Hicks said, and glanced up at the speaker from which the AI's voice emanated.

"I can be of assistance," Athena said. "I do not contain the knowledge for military technology, but I can give you a recommendation on what upgrades can be made to get the most out of the technology you have available."

"That would be greatly appreciated," Kaylan said.

"So we're trusting an Artificial Intelligence construct then?" Redford said.

"Yes," Kaylan said. "Athena, what are your recommendations?"

"One second," Zack said. "Athena, give us your high-level recommendations. Otherwise, we'll all be here forever while you get every detail for each recommendation recited to you."

Kaylan's lips curved and she nodded.

"First recommendation is to upgrade the shuttle's systems so it can achieve breakaway orbital velocity. This will allow you to visit Earth-type planets without it being a one-way trip. Second recommendation is to upgrade the sensor array to monitor communications. I can see that the process has already begun with the information you've collected from the Shroud Network. Those are the upgrades that would maximize the potential for the work being done in the allotted time," Athena said.

"Would it help if we decreased our velocity to give us more time?" Kaylan asked.

"Negative. There is a strong probability that the Nershals would have detected the wormhole and are investigating the area. It will only be a matter of time before they turn their attention to the inner system of planets," Athena said.

"Are you able to tell us anything about the Nershal species?" Kaylan asked.

"Though I do not have detailed information about the Nershals, I do know that their society adheres to a strict hierarchy with a rigorous code of honor. To put it in Earth terms, they are a winged humanoid race that is sometimes prone to be territorial. They are highly sensitive to sound and can see across multiple spectrums. Discipline is paramount to them," Athena said.

"How are we even going to be able to communicate with them?" Zack asked.

"Your neural implants can be enhanced so the nanobots can function as a universal translator," Athena said.

"So we'll be able to understand them, but how will they understand what we're saying?" Kaylan asked.

"The Nershals have their own means of translating alien languages. Should your path cross with the Nershals, I would recommend being forthright in your dealings with them. If you prove to be dishonest or disingenuous with them, they will become hostile," Athena said.

"This gets better and better. I wonder if there are any Boxans on that moon we're heading to," Zack muttered.

"This predicates the reasoning for my second recommendation to monitor communications," Athena said. "My observation protocols highly emphasized the assessment of the Mardoxian potential. This includes the building of a Mardoxian Chamber."

"Are you saying we can build a chamber on the ship?" Kaylan asked.

"Negative. The resources and technological capabilities are beyond our current capacity, but a chamber may be found in this star system."

"Okay, at least we have a way forward, even if it takes us into more danger," Kaylan said, and looked at Zack. "Good work. I knew you could figure this out."

Zack nodded. "Thanks, and I'm sorry for being so stubborn about the implants."

Zack was glad to finally get the AI to work with the rest of the crew. He didn't like being the go-between for them. They had a lot of work to do, and if he knew Kaylan, none of them were going to get much sleep over the next twenty-four hours.

Chapter Twelve

Kaylan and Hicks were alone on the bridge, going over the AI's list of suggested upgrades. The riskiest, most complex upgrade happened to be the one they desperately needed if their plan was going to work. They needed to upgrade the engines of the Athena's shuttle. The concept was simple in that they were building a miniaturized fusion reactor to increase the shuttle's thrust capacity, including maneuvering and braking thrusters. Efren Burdock, the resident nuclear physicist, had reviewed the proposed design changes and come back to her, beaming with the possibilities the new design unlocked. It expanded upon their current capabilities, infused with theoretical concepts, such as producing more energy with less heat. Kaylan would have preferred building a small-scale model to prove the new design could work, but they simply didn't have the time. They were placing an awful lot of faith in the Athena's new artificial intelligence, but what choice did they have?

"Commander," Athena said.

"Yes," Kaylan said.

"You currently have a crew member that is not contributing to the overall objective," Athena said.

Kaylan frowned.

"I think it means Vitomir," Hicks said.

Kaylan nodded. "That's right. He's confined to quarters."

"Recommend that his confinement be lifted so he can contribute to our objectives," Athena said.

Kaylan leaned back from the planning table and felt her muscles go rigid. "Vitomir is confined to quarters because he cannot be trusted. He sabotaged a space station so we would be forced to take him with us."

"You're right; he can't be trusted," Hicks said. "But we need him. We don't have enough people to do the things that need to be done."

"I have conversed with crew member Vitomir, and he deeply regrets his actions. He suffers from a deep depression that can only be alleviated with activity," Athena said.

"Deep depression," Kaylan repeated. "How about death? He caused the deaths of four people."

"Calm down for a second," Hicks said. "There is a difference between cold-blooded murder and a sabotage gone wrong. Vitomir has as much at stake as the rest of us. I'm not going to defend his actions, but he's already paid a pretty big price for his mistakes. At the end of the day I don't want us to fail because we refused to use every means at our disposal."

"His wife died because of his mistakes. I don't want to die because of them too," Kaylan said.

"We have a saying in the military that I think applies here," Hicks said. "You go to war with the army you've got. The fact of the matter is that we need Vitomir's help with all of the work we have to do."

"Commander, I could monitor Vitomir and restrict his

access to only the systems he's working on. I will, of course, report any suspicious activity I may observe," Athena said.

Kaylan unclenched her jaws. "Fine, put him to work. If he tries anything like what he did on Pluto, then I will personally see him thrown out the nearest airlock."

Hicks stood up straight. "Yes, ma'am," he said with a smile.

Kaylan shook her head but couldn't keep the smile from her lips.

THE NEXT DAY—WHICH they could only tell by the Athena's clock—they were nearing the moon of the gas giant located in the habitable zone of this star system. Kaylan updated their approach to use the gas giant to shield them, believing that regardless of any advanced technology the Nershals might have, they couldn't track them through a planet.

They'd upgraded the sensor array the night before, and this allowed them to greatly expand their monitoring capabilities. They were now able to detect a wide range of comms channels that they couldn't before. Deciphering the encrypted comms chatter was proving to be a challenge. Zack informed her that they were just hitting the upper limits of their current computing power. They would be able to decipher the messages, but it would take some time.

The door to the bridge opened, and the Athena's crew reported in for their nine o'clock briefing. The only exceptions were Efren and Nikolai. Efren had flat out refused to work with Vitomir when asked if he needed help with the upgrades. The only people who would work with Vitomir were Redford and Hicks. No matter how much she needed Vitomir's help, it was too dangerous to allow him to work with Redford, so Kaylan assigned Vitomir to be under Hicks's supervision. This briefing was the first time she'd seen the Russian cosmonaut since she'd had him confined to quarters. His pale skin only emphasized the haunted look behind his sunken eyes. Part of her felt sorry for him. It could be that Vitomir had been a decent person who made some very bad choices, but she couldn't trust him. Knowing the actions he'd taken that had cost the people of Titus Station their lives still had her seeing red at times. She couldn't throw him off the ship, but she had also come to accept that Vitomir shouldn't get a free ride either. They were all risking their lives, and he would help them.

Kaylan thanked them all for coming. "What's the status of the shuttle?"

"All the prep work has been done," Hicks said, "so we're just about ready for the new engine. After that, we can do some initial tests, but the real test will be when we go down to the surface of the moon."

"The Nershals call the moon Selebus," Athena said.

"Let me guess, Selebus is the offshoot name of their home world," Zack said.

"Incorrect, the moon was named for a sacred city from antiquity. The city was home to major dynasties still in existence today," Athena said.

"Zack," Kaylan said, "have you learned anything from the communications being monitored?"

"It appears that the Boxans and the Nershals had a falling out around sixty years ago," Zack said.

Kaylan's eyes widened. "The same time we got the Boxan message."

Zack nodded. "There are a lot of broadcasts about the Nershal alliance with the Xiiginns, but it's almost like they're trying to convince themselves of the benefit."

"Propaganda," Hicks said.

"I wish we knew more about the Xiiginns," Kaylan said. "Other than vague references, there haven't been any descriptions."

"Apologies, Commander," Athena said.

"No, I understand. If the information isn't there for you to share, then that's not your fault," Kaylan said.

"General alert," Athena said. "Have picked up Boxan comms chatter coming from the surface of Selebus."

Kaylan glanced at the others. "We didn't expect any of them to be here."

Hicks smiled. "This is good news. If we can figure out where they are, perhaps we should go down there and find them."

"Agreed," Kaylan said.

Emma Roberson raised her hand, and Kaylan nodded to her. "Who will be going down to the surface?"

"All of us. No one will be left behind," Kaylan said.

"I would like permission to use the fabricator to create some small arms to give us some basic protection," Hicks said.

"I've never fired a gun in my entire life," Zack said.

"These aren't actual guns in that they don't shoot bullets," Hicks said. "The pulsar pistols shoot high-velocity darts. Don't let that fool you; it's lethal and incredibly accurate. Much better than an actual gun. They are easy to operate and, with two hundred shots per magazine, will reduce the amount of reloads you would need to do. They're easy to use and only meant to be used if we need to defend ourselves. Katie and I will be using the more powerful weapons because we're the only ones trained in their use," Hicks said.

Kaylan frowned. "Are you sure?"

"I'll take one," Emma said. "Some protection is better than none."

Kaylan glanced at Vitomir and then back at Hicks. "Okay, but the shuttle takes priority."

Hicks nodded. "Katie can see to getting the weapons created."

Kaylan nodded. The thought of Zack with Katie still stung, but she had to learn to accept it. She just wished it wasn't so hard.

"We will reach our destination in the next few hours," Kaylan said.

Hicks raised his hand. "Athena, are you able to pinpoint the Boxans' position based on their comms channels enough to give us their coordinates on the planet?"

"Affirmative, Major Hicks," Athena said.

Kaylan narrowed her eyes, but didn't say anything.

"It's worth considering," Hicks said.

"I'll think about it," Kaylan said.

The others glanced at her as they finally caught on to Hicks's suggestion that she should use her power to glean information on the Boxans' position. With the coordinates as a frame of reference, there really wasn't any excuse.

"You just make sure the shuttle is ready to go," Kaylan said.

Hicks chuckled. "It will be ready. Efren just sent me a message saying he's ready to get the new reactor installed."

Kaylan nodded. "Well then, there's no time to waste."

They left the bridge, and she followed Hicks out. She wanted to see the miniaturized fusion reactor for herself. She had been secretly trying to use her power to get a feel for the surface of Selebus, but she hadn't told anybody because she didn't really trust what she was seeing. She was having trouble making sense out of the densely forested areas with the small amount of sunlight reaching the planet. This was due in large part to its orbit around the gas giant. Selebus's slow orbit allowed for multiple days of sunshine, followed by multiple days of night-time. Emma had assured her that it wasn't too much of a stretch for the flora and fauna of that world to adapt to such a schedule. If everything went according to plan, they would soon see for themselves. At the moment Earth seemed so far away that it was almost a dream. There was so much they were learning thanks to the AI, but at the same time they had more questions than before. At least the AI had been able to confirm for them that Michael Hunsicker had a chance to survive on Pluto.

Chapter Thirteen

The days were long on Selebus and so were the nights, but the clear skies made for an interesting view of Selebus's neighboring planet. Kladomaor retracted his helmet and raised his chin to the sky. The Enforcers that Ezerah had summoned had chased them through the dense forests of the moon. After their initial burst of speed, the Boxans had begun carefully choosing the path they trod to throw off the Nershal scouts on their trail. Being inside the dense forest with extremely tall trees —even by Boxan standards—nullified the Nershals' air-bound superiority. Kladomaor was proud of his squad for eluding the Enforcers, but he did wonder if their escape had been too easily achieved. He expected better from the Nershals. There were any number of reasons why the Enforcers had been recalled: from having lost their trail to Ezerah having second thoughts about them. He wanted to believe that Ezerah had come to see the situation of her species allying with the Xiiginns differently and heeded his warnings, but he knew that would take time. He was asking her to reevaluate the world she'd grown up on based on a childhood that she might not fully appreciate.

Kladomaor glanced southwest of their position. Gaarokk approached him.

"Thinking of trying to persuade Ezerah to join us again?" Gaarokk asked.

"Not yet. That seed is still taking root. I was thinking about the ease of our escape," Kladomaor said.

"From the Enforcers? I didn't think it was easy at all. In fact, there were a few times I thought they had us," Gaarokk said.

"Their phaze rifles are new," Kladomaor said, and retracted the rest of his armor, exposing his upper body to the sun. His dark, roughened skin drank in the sunlight.

Gaarokk sighed heavily. "A Xiiginn gift, no doubt."

"We knew they would come bearing gifts to the species they've subverted. I just didn't imagine that the Nershals, with their strict codes of honor, would subject themselves to such greed or take the easy path," Kladomaor said.

Gaarokk glanced behind him, checking to see if the Nershals who had joined them had overheard.

"They know of which I speak," Kladomaor said.

"I still think caution is in order. There is a difference between knowing something and having someone push your nose in it. There are some of us who believe that if we had been more open with the different species of the Confederation, things might be different now," Gaarokk said.

"We misjudged the Xiiginns and their capabilities, but we can debate that later," Kladomaor said.

"What else is bothering you about our escape?" Gaarokk asked.

"If we got away of our own accord, then that's fine. It's what I expected. But if they let us go, that implies strategy. I'm trying to gain an insight into what that strategy could be and how we can use it," Kladomaor said.

Gaarokk frowned. "Ma'jasalax was right, you've seen too much war. But if it's insight you want, perhaps you should have thought to bring her along on this venture."

Kladomaor closed his flaxen eyes and let out a soft groan as he felt the star's energy seep into him and make him feel whole again. All Boxans required time in the star-shine to maintain balance.

Ma'jasalax wasn't the first Mardoxian priest to comment about the effects war had had on Boxan soldiers, but soldiers were what would win this war, not priests.

"She wouldn't approve of our actions," Kladomaor said.

"It would be hard to argue with our initial results. I didn't think any of the Nershals would listen to us, much less join us, but we're still a long way from swaying the entire species," Gaarokk said.

"You don't know them as I do. The Nershals hold a grudge against us for the Star Shroud, but when they learn the Xiiginns have been using them, things will be different," Kladomaor said, striking his fist into the palm of his other hand.

"The Confederation would seek to work with the Xiiginns and bring us to the bargaining table," Gaarokk said.

"There is no bargaining with a species that can impose their own agenda on any other species at will. The others in the Confederation cannot see that because they've been enamored by the Xiiginns and their promises. What those more primitive species don't see is the noose that is being tied around their necks that will squeeze the life from their souls. We, the Boxans, opened up the galaxy for them, and they cast us out. The Xiiginns have made us out to be the monsters they actually *are*," Kladomaor said.

"Be at peace, Kladomaor. Not all of the Confederation feels that way. This hatred will burn through you if you let it," Gaarokk said.

Kladomaor was silent, deep in his own thoughts. "They captured me once. Did I ever tell you that?" Kladomaor asked.

Gaarokk's eyes widened. "Not many escape once captured by the Xiiginns."

"They turned me loose after I served their purpose. I was enamored just like everyone else was. You say my hatred will burn me up inside. I say it's the only thing keeping me alive, lest I slip back under the Xiiginn influence," Kladomaor said.

"But—" Gaarokk began.

"I know what you will say," Kladomaor said, "that no one can break free of the Xiiginn influence once they are subjected to it. You're partially right. Ma'jasalax taught me to suppress the calling, but I'll never be free of it. I'll never be free of them."

Kladomaor noticed Gaarokk's grave expression. He didn't know why he had shared that with the scientist. Perhaps in some small way it helped him deal with his daily penance.

"I had no idea. I can't imagine the struggle you've endured even now. What will happen to you if we cross paths with the Xiiginns?" Gaarokk asked.

"We eliminate them on sight," Kladomaor said.

"I said what will happen to *you*," Gaarokk said.

Kladomaor's corded muscles clenched as he activated his armor. "I will not falter. We will educate the Nershals to the Xiiginn ways and exterminate them from this system."

Gaarokk studied him for a moment, considering what he was going to say.

A thunderous crash ripped across the sky. Echoes of it could be heard for miles around them. Kladomaor and the others searched the sky, trying to catch a glimpse of what had caused such a noise. After a moment, one of the scouts who was positioned above the tree line sent an image over comms. It was some type of spacecraft that he'd never seen before. Its dark underbelly was contrasted by the blue and white of the wings.

"I'm not familiar with that type of spacecraft. Have you seen it before?" Gaarokk asked.

Kladomaor shook his head. "I've never seen that one before. Its design looks a bit dated, but it's not of Nershal or Xiiginn design."

"You don't think the Xiiginns have discovered a primitive species and brought them here?" Gaarokk asked.

"If they have, that would confirm they've figured out how to retrieve information from the Shroud Network in spite of us taking it offline," Kladomaor said, and glanced at the readings that were coming through his scout's comms channel. "It's heading in our direction. Whoever they are, they have our position," Kladomaor said, and sent a signal to the others to mobilize.

"What are we going to do once we find them?" Gaarokk asked.

"That depends on what we're dealing with. I'd like to know how they found us," Kladomaor said.

The rest of their group was ready to move, and the Nershals with them indicated that they would join them. Kladomaor didn't like surprises and wondered if this was part of some Xiiginn strategy.

Chapter Fourteen

The Athena's shuttle plunged through the atmosphere of Selebus. After their initial descent, it was a relatively smooth ride, for which Zack was grateful. The AI had warned them not to use the engines to their fullest capacity since they hadn't had time to upgrade the inertia dampeners. Essentially, if they went too fast they would die. This was all Zack needed to understand, and he hoped Kaylan wouldn't have any accidents while piloting the shuttle. Zack felt his hand start to reach up and check his helmet, but he immediately brought it back down. Sitting across from him, Katie smiled.

"Confirming atmospheric readings are within acceptable limits," Redford said.

They'd brought their spacesuits just in case the readings from Athena were incorrect. They were still building trust with the AI, but so far it had been extremely helpful. Zack looked out the window, past the clouds, and saw a dense forest stretching miles away from them. According to the AI, the Boxans were some-where in this area, well away from any settlements on this moon.

They'd been careful to avoid notice, but they couldn't be sure if anyone had detected their ship.

"This reminds me of home," Katie said, glancing out the window.

Zack had come to appreciate Emma's hydroponic garden aboard the Athena, but it was nothing compared to the actual greenery out in the world or, in this case, someone else's world. "We come all this way only to end up in an area much like the Pacific Northwest," Zack said, settling back into his seat while he gazed at the thick canopy of trees covering the mountainous region. After spending so much time on the ship, he was looking forward to standing on solid ground again. He'd forgotten how much he missed Earth.

"Where is your family from, Katie?" Emma asked.

"Oregon, by the coast," Katie said.

"I've always wanted to visit there but haven't gotten around to it. If we make it home, that's the first place I'd like to visit," Emma said.

"*When* we make it home," Zack said.

Emma nodded and smiled.

Zack hoped he sounded more confident than he felt.

"I would be happy to show you around," Katie said.

"Thank you," Emma said.

"I assure you that I will do everything in my power to see all of you safely home," Athena said.

Zack looked up to see if the others had heard, but they didn't give any indication that they had.

"I was speaking to you, Zack," Athena said.

Zack closed his comms channel to the others. "We appreciate it, but I get the feeling it will take a lot longer than we expect to get back home."

"I've taken some time to process Earth's literary pieces. It's quite helpful to gauge the beating heart of any society by examining what they write down—and sometimes painstakingly so. I find this quote by Emerson to be analogous with our current situation. 'Life is a journey, not a destination.' Would you agree?" Athena asked.

Zack thought about it for a moment. "It's a nice sentiment, and I get the journey part, but all of us really do want to make it home," Zack said.

Kaylan found a small clearing and circled around, checking the area. The shuttle touched down, and the crew of the Athena shared a moment of relief.

"An effective engine test," Hicks said.

Zack heard the engines whine down, and since the atmosphere was a close match to Earth, they decided to ditch their spacesuits. A couple of them were grinning and joking around. Zack couldn't wait to get outside and breathe in some fresh air. He could almost forget why they'd come, and it was a sentiment shared by the others as well. Zack knew it wouldn't last but was thankful for a momentary reprieve.

Hicks handed out weapons to each of them except Redford and Vitomir.

"Aren't we allowed to defend ourselves?" Redford asked.

Hicks regarded him coldly. "I wouldn't want you to have any more 'accidents' and shoot someone else."

"It's fine," Vitomir said. "The others will be able to protect us."

Redford sighed and let it go.

Katie handed Zack a pulsar pistol, which he took carefully. The pistol was gunmetal gray, light in weight, and made of highly durable composites that were heat resistant. Below the barrel was the cartridge that held the darts. Earlier he'd mistakenly joked about the fact that these were high-end dart guns, and Hicks had reminded him that ordinary dart guns couldn't kill.

"Just remember," Katie said, "point and squeeze the trigger. That's all you need to do."

"Don't worry. I'll stay close by so you can do the shooting," Zack promised.

The shuttle doors opened, and a puff of air blew in. The moist air had a slight chill to it, but the sky overhead was clear. Redford had tried to explain how the length of the day and night cycles were long here, but Zack couldn't tell what time of day it was. The soft chirping in the distance reminded him of home. The ground was soft and spongy, as if it had recently rained. Kaylan closed the shuttle doors behind them.

"The doors will open back up for any one of us," Kaylan said. "In the event that we get split apart, Athena is acting as our GPS satellite so we can find our way back."

"I'll take point," Hicks said. "If you see anything while we're walking, let us know and we can check it out. Do not go off alone."

They nodded, and Hicks led them toward the forest. The AI was able to give them the general location of the Boxans' position, but Hicks was convinced they would have already seen them coming. Given Hicks's area of expertise, Zack thought it was safe to assume he was right.

Deeper into the forest, the plant life became stranger. Small orange pods grew on the shrubbery close to the ground. The pods were a lighter color in the center, making them appear as miniature suns. There were tiny protrusions along the pods' surface. Emma warned them not to touch anything.

The gloom was occasionally penetrated by shafts of sunlight that cascaded through the treetops high overhead. Zack glanced up and saw large winged creatures leaping between the tree branches high above them. Their long hind legs had joints that reminded Zack more of an insect than any type of bird he'd ever seen. The strange creatures hardly noticed them and made screeching sounds to each other.

Zack caught up to Hicks. "Why do you think the Boxans are way out here?"

Hicks shrugged. "It could be that they don't want the Nershals to know what they're up to."

"I still wonder what they look like," Zack said.

"We'll need to rely on Kaylan to confirm a Boxan for us. As for the Nershals, we have the AI's descriptions, but until we actually meet one . . ." Hicks said.

"Then we just hope the translators work. I still have the one I coded, which Athena augmented," Zack said.

Hicks focused on the path in front of them, which narrowed and became a steep incline. Zack glanced behind him and saw Kaylan, her wide-eyed gaze soaking in their surroundings. She appeared both intrigued and afraid at the same time. She hadn't snapped at him in a while. They'd both stayed out of each other's way, and at times they settled into an awkward silence. She spotted him watching her, and her expression immediately became guarded.

"So is this place anything like what you thought it would be?" Zack asked.

"What do you mean?" Kaylan replied.

"You know, like what you did with the alien station on Pluto —using that second sight to get the layout of this place," Zack said.

Kaylan frowned. "Second sight?"

"Well, what do you want to call it? The mere mention of it seems to bother you," Zack said.

"They used to call it remote viewing, but that sounds almost as bad," Kaylan said and stopped, considering her words. "To answer your question, it's exactly what I've seen—the forest, the creatures, all of it."

Zack's eyes widened. "I'm sorry. I know it worries you, but to me it's one of the coolest things I've ever heard of. Do you know how useful this is?"

Kaylan narrowed her eyes a bit to see if he was poking fun at her.

"I mean it. I don't understand how it works, but I'm glad you're able to do what you do," Zack said.

"It doesn't make any sense, and the fact that I can't explain how it works bothers me," Kaylan said.

"Some things never change," Zack said, and Kaylan gave him a questioning look. "You're overthinking it."

"Perhaps you're under-thinking it," Kaylan said.

Zack shrugged his shoulders and didn't say anything. She would do whatever she pleased anyway.

They hiked along for a while, and Zack kept reminding himself over and over again that he was on another alien planet —quite a long way from that dingy old apartment he sublet in Chicago. They occasionally heard a deep growl in the distance, and Zack hoped whatever it was didn't find them. He used his implants to bring up the map on the HUD overlay on his eyes. The HUD projected images that only Zack could see. They were semi-translucent, so they didn't interfere with his field of vision. They were in the Boxans' vicinity, and Zack wondered how they could miss a group of beings who averaged eight to ten feet in height.

The trail widened, and they stopped for a break. Zack pulled a bottle of water from his pack and gulped several mouthfuls. Katie stood near him, and he noticed that she kept scanning the area. Zack frowned and slung his pack back over his shoulders.

He was about to say something to her, but she raised a finger to her lips.

Zack glanced across at the others and saw Kaylan by Hicks. The forest grew silent around them.

Kaylan spun around, sucking in a breath. "Watch out!"

The HUD overlay from his implants changed to red with the words *Combat Mode Initiated.* Zack's vision became more acute, and he easily picked out more details. His vision spanned across different spectrums until he saw enormous silhouettes of large beings closing in on their position.

Hicks had his rifle ready. "I've got nothing. Katie, do you have anything?"

"Negative," Katie said.

Zack snatched his pulsar from his holster and pointed it in front of him.

"They're coming," Kaylan said.

"I see them too," Zack said.

Katie ran to his side and peered in the direction Zack was looking.

"I'm getting thermal readings here," Katie said.

The others drew their weapons and crouched down.

"Same here—wait a minute. They're gone," Hicks said.

Katie reported the same.

Zack couldn't see anything either, but he knew they were there. Zack holstered the pulsar and stood up with his hands raised.

"We're not looking for any trouble," Zack shouted.

He glanced at Katie and she lowered her weapon slightly.

Kaylan stood up with her hands raised also. "We came here looking for the Boxans and Ma'jasalax."

Numerous shapes around them all seemed to shimmer at once. Zack stepped back, his mouth hanging open at the size of the beings who surrounded them. Knowing something was ten feet tall and seeing it firsthand were two different things. The Boxans wore some type of gray metallic armor with soft cyan lines running along different seams. They all had some type of weapon pointed at them. One alien stepped away from the others. He didn't have a weapon in hand, but Zack could tell that he was dangerous. Call it the sixth sense of a weaker kid, but Zack could tell from the way the being stood and the width of its shoulders that this was a very dangerous entity.

The Boxan took a few steps forward, seeming to gauge their response, and its armored head swiveled around as it passed in front of them.

Zack used his neural link to the PDA he wore on his forearm and started scanning the being in front of him.

The Boxan cocked his head in Zack's direction and bounded toward him. Katie stepped in front of him with her pulsar rifle raised.

The Boxan stopped. "Human?" a deep voice said.

Zack glanced at the others to see if they had understood, and Katie gave him a nod. At least the translators were working.

Several large shadows darted above them, swooping down and landing between them and the Boxan. Their deep-set orange eyes blazed fiercely. One stepped forward. The alien's hairless skin was pale green, with a darker swath that went from the eyes down the side of the creature's face. Corded muscles rippled along its exposed neck and shoulders. Two sets of translucent wings were unfurled, and it crouched down, raising a long, dark knife in front of it. It stood over six feet tall.

"Be careful. That's a Nershal. They're fiercely territorial," the AI said.

Zack stepped to Katie's side, and Kaylan joined him.

"Lower your weapons," the Boxan said.

No one moved, and Zack saw more of the Nershals watching them from the upper recesses of the trees above them. They were outnumbered.

"Now," the Boxan said.

Kaylan turned to the others. "It's okay. Lower your weapons."

Hicks and Katie were the last to lower their rifles. Zack had moved to holster his gun when a Nershal stood in front of him, extending its four-fingered hand to him. There was no mistaking the intent. They wanted their weapons. Katie held out her rifle, and the Nershal took it and handed it to the Boxan. The weapon appeared like a toy in the Boxan's giant hands. The others handed over their weapons.

"At least you weren't foolish enough to fire any of these at us, and judging by your expressions, you can understand me," the Boxan said.

"We're here—" Kaylan began.

"Silence, Human, there will be time enough for introductions later. Follow me," the Boxan said.

Zack watched as the Boxan gestured to two others and then in the direction the Athena crew had just come from.

"I think they're sending someone back to the shuttle," Zack whispered to Kaylan.

"Let's just follow them," Kaylan said.

"No talking," the Nershal nearest them said and shoved Kaylan along.

Something snapped in Zack. Clenching his teeth, he grabbed the Nershal and pushed him to the side. The Nershal stumbled and spun around with its long knife in its hand. Zack's mouth went dry as he stepped back. The Nershal screeched, and Zack needed no translator to tell him he was about to die.

The Nershal bounded forward.

"Etanu, wait!" the Boxan shouted, stepping toward them.

The Nershal halted. "This being dared put its hands upon me."

"They don't know your ways," the Boxan said.

"They come to our planet, Kladomaor," Etanu said.

"They've surrendered their weapons and are in my custody," Kladomaor said.

The Nershal glared at Zack. The orange blaze in its eyes reminded Zack of a raging fire. The Nershal stepped closer to Zack, leaning in until its face was inches from him. "There will be a reckoning for this, Human," Etanu said. As it spoke, Zack saw the points of a healthy set of teeth that looked as if they could tear him to pieces. Etanu leaped into the air, and the Nershal's wings carried him away.

Kladomaor grumbled but said nothing else as he led them away.

Zack released the breath he'd been holding.

"What do you think you were doing?" Kaylan said as they walked.

"I don't know," Zack said. *Why the hell did I do that?* "It was just a reaction. We can't just let them push us around."

"It looked like it was going to kill you," Kaylan said.

Zack swallowed hard and felt his hands shake from the adrenalin coursing through his veins. The Boxans, covered from head to foot in dark gray armor, surrounded them as they moved deeper into the forest. The Boxan armor appeared flexible in some places and hardened in others, like across the chest. The Nershals stayed away from them. Although the Boxans didn't tell them to keep quiet, the Athena's crew remained silent during the march. Zack glanced back at Katie, who kept a watchful eye on their captors. Zack wanted to speak to the AI, but the pace the Boxans set was enough to force him to concentrate on keeping up.

Less than an hour later the leader of the Boxans, Kladomaor, called for them to stop. Multiple shafts of sunlight lit up the ground around them, casting a soft glow. The other Boxans took up positions near the sunlight. One reached up and touched a part of its neck, and the armor folded back in on itself so quickly that Zack almost thought he imagined it. The weapons the Boxans had taken from them were deposited on the ground, and the Boxan called Kladomaor came before them. His armor folded back on itself to reveal a being with brown, roughened skin that was almost craggy. The Boxan's flaxen eyes regarded them. Zack suspected that if they'd been in the forest without their armor, he would have walked right by these giants and not been any the wiser. Another Boxan came and stood by his side. He seemed less harsh and watched them with open curiosity.

"I have questions for you," Kladomaor said.

"Why don't you tell us who you are first?" Kaylan said.

Kladomaor's eyes narrowed.

"First contact has been initiated. Despite the unorthodox circumstances, we must follow protocol," the Boxan at Kladomaor's side said, and turned back to address them. "I am called Gaarokk of the Boxan species, the founders of the Confederation. This is Kladomaor of the Battle Group Corp."

"I am Kaylan Farrow, and we're part of the crew of the spaceship Athena from Earth."

"Do you speak for them?" Kladomaor asked.

"They can speak for themselves, but I am in command of our mission," Kaylan said.

"The fact that you can understand us is remarkable. Can you tell us how you're able to understand our words?" Gaarokk asked.

"We came to your listening station in our star system and were able to get inside. We deciphered part of the language you used to communicate with the Shroud Network—" Kaylan said, but was cut off by the sudden silence as each Boxan stopped what they were doing and turned in their direction at once.

"Preposterous," Kladomaor said.

"Let's hear them out," Gaarokk replied.

"We turned the power back on, and something took control of our ship. A wormhole opened and brought us into this system," Kaylan said.

"Intriguing," Gaarokk said.

"How were you able to communicate with the Shroud Network?" Kladomaor asked.

Kaylan glanced at Zack.

"I was able to initiate communication based on the message you originally sent. I figured out there was a protocol for checking in with the station, and I got a response," Zack said.

"A message?" Kladomaor said. "There hasn't been any—"

"We did this," Gaarokk said. "Ma'jasalax sent a message through the Mardoxian Chamber. The Humans received it and found the listening station. A remarkable achievement for your species."

"Indeed," Kladomaor said. "Why did a wormhole open in the first place? And you still haven't answered how you're able to understand us."

"We have an AI," Kaylan said. "One of your artificial intelligences from the station was copied to our computer systems. It helped us with an interface into our neural implants."

Kladomaor brought up his wrist, and a red beam of light scanned the PDA on Zack's arm. A stream of code flickered through the small holodisplay over Kladomaor's wrist.

Kladomaor looked at Gaarokk, waiting for an explanation.

"There were some shroud listening stations outfitted with a prototype computer AI. The foundations in the code are similar to what I would expect to find, but it's been radically altered," Gaarokk said.

"It said it was having trouble adapting to our ship's systems and had to take steps to increase efficiency," Zack said.

Kladomaor narrowed his gaze. "It appears your AI has gone silent."

"On the contrary, I am monitoring—a task for which I was specifically designed," Athena said, the AI's voice coming through Zack's PDA.

Kladomaor glanced at Gaarokk, and Zack would have sworn he saw a slight smile for a second.

"Why have you brought the Humans here? Power-down protocols were initiated," Kladomaor said.

"Humans powered on the reactor at the listening station. Sent update of all monitoring activity to home system. Received no reply. Last contact to Earth occurred through Mardoxian Chamber relay from Nershal listening station. Must bring Humans to Boxan home system. Mardoxian potential in Human species optimal," Athena said.

Kladomaor's eyes widened. "Which one of you was able to use the Mardoxian Chamber?"

The crew of the Athena glanced at each other. It looked as if Redford was going to speak but thought better of it.

"I did," Kaylan said.

"Is there any way we can validate this claim?" Kladomaor asked.

Gaarokk shook his head. "Not out here, but if what they claim is true, do you know what this means?"

"Another time," Kladomaor said. "If they did power on the listening station, there is a chance the Xiiginns will have picked up on the signal. The colony could be in danger."

"We're not sure if it's still operational," Kaylan said. "The station wasn't stable. Powering it on caused substantial seismic activity and made the entire place unstable. We barely escaped with our lives."

"Kladomaor, these events are unprecedented. We have to alert the colony," Gaarokk said.

"We can do no such thing. We have an objective that can yield substantial results against the Xiiginns. I can't walk away from that," Kladomaor said.

"Perhaps we can help you and then you can help us. What do you say?" Kaylan asked.

Kladomaor turned around and walked away.

"Please pardon him. He's slow to trust," Gaarokk said.

"I was just offering to help," Kaylan said.

"I believe your offer was in good faith, but to some it would appear as an insult," Gaarokk said.

Zack frowned. "Why?"

Kaylan turned toward him. "Because it seems that some of the Boxan suffer from a massive superiority complex."

There was a loud whooping sound from overhead, and a group of Nershals landed among them. Two of them came toward Zack, and each seized him by an arm. The other Nershals moved between them, cutting Zack off from the rest of the Athena's crew.

Kladomaor bounded toward them. "What's the meaning of this, Etanu?"

"I invoke the rite. This one has a reckoning," Etanu said, gesturing toward Zack.

"They are a primitive species who don't know your ways," Kladomaor said.

"As I've said before, they are on our world and must respect our laws. A reckoning must be honored. We take this one to be judged," Etanu said.

"Then we have the right to bear witness," Kladomaor said.

Etanu glared at the Boxan for a moment. "So be it."

The Nershals hoisted Zack away. Hicks held onto Katie, who was ready to lash out at the Nershals.

"Wait. Where are they taking him?" Kaylan said.

Kladomaor turned toward her. "The Nershals invoked the rite. It is an ancient tradition to settle offenses given. There will be a contest, the result of which will determine whether your companion should be put to death."

Kaylan gasped. "This is because he shoved one of them?"

"Honor among the Nershals can be a deadly affair," Kladomaor said.

Kaylan glanced at Zack in horror as the Nershals took him away.

Chapter Fifteen

Kaylan rounded on Kladomaor, and the fact that the Boxan was over four feet taller than her didn't faze her at all.

"You need to tell us what's going on," Kaylan said.

Kladomaor jerked his head toward her. "I need? I don't think you understand your place."

Kaylan drew herself up. "My place is right here, getting answers from you. Your species reached out to ours, and here we are. Now one of my people has been taken because of some twisted code of honor that not only did we not know about, but we couldn't have avoided if we had. We were cooperating. We surrendered our weapons."

Kladomaor's heavy brows pushed forward. "Would you take his place?"

Hicks came to her side. "No, but I would."

Kladomaor regarded Hicks for a moment. "I believe you would, but it is not possible. As I said before, issues of honor can be a deadly affair with the Nershals."

"This is a misunderstanding," Kaylan said.

"I think not," Kladomaor said, and glanced in the direction that Zack was taken. "He knew what he was doing, but Etanu is quite young."

"Zack only pushed him because of what he did to me," Kaylan said.

"It's more than that. When you landed your spacecraft on this moon, you violated one of the Nershals' strictest tenets, and this could be interpreted as an invasion," Kladomaor said.

"There were nine of us—hardly an invasion force. And we were coming to see you, not to make contact with the Nershals," Kaylan said.

"I know," Kladomaor said, as if he were almost unwilling to admit as much.

Kaylan glanced at the pile of weapons on the ground not far from them, and Kladomaor saw it.

"Your weapons will not help you here," Kladomaor said, and motioned for one of the other Boxans to collect them.

Kaylan watched as their only means of defense was carried off. Hicks leaned in so only she could hear.

"If they wanted to harm us, they would have. Let's play along for a while," Hicks said.

Kaylan nodded and glanced at Katie. Her gaze was fixed on where they had taken Zack. "Will Katie try something?" Kaylan asked.

"Normally I'd say no. She'll assess, and we can coordinate our efforts together," Hicks said.

Kladomaor called for them to follow, and Kaylan wondered if he'd heard them speaking. The other Boxans watched them as they headed over to where the Nershals had gathered. The terrain's elevation increased until they stood on the top of a hill leading to a valley. Kaylan knew she should have had hundreds of questions to ask the Boxans, but she couldn't focus on any of them until she knew Zack was safe. The Nershal had barely touched her, and Zack had never been one for chauvinistic tendencies, so why had it bothered him so much? *Now who's the one being foolish,* Kaylan thought.

More Boxans joined them, seeming to appear from out of nowhere, but the crowd of Nershals outnumbered all of them. The deep set of their orange eyes gave the Nershals an extremely aggressive look, but their height and build was similar to that of the crew of the Athena. Kaylan had trouble keeping her astonishment from showing whenever one of the Nershals flew in with their twin set of wings, which reminded her of dragonfly wings. They glided and came to a sudden halt at will. There was a preciseness and grace to the movements of the Nershals as they navigated through the trees to come to their position. As the Nershals spoke to one another, Kaylan half expected to see a mouth full of long fangs, but that wasn't the case.

"Athena," Kaylan said quietly, "is there anything you can tell us that we can use to help Zack?"

"Commander, I have been monitoring and will provide advice as the situation with the Nershals unfolds, but for right now I have nothing to offer you."

The Boxans surrounded them and seemed to be taking steps to cordon them away from the Nershals. Kaylan wondered who was more in control—the Boxans or the Nershals. The Nershal called Etanu stood on the back of a fallen tree, and the group became silent.

"A reckoning is called upon this species that have dared walk upon our world. They've laid their hands with aggressive intent upon me. They say they seek the Boxans. I say let them prove themselves worthy of speaking with our guardians," Etanu said.

Athena translated the words for them almost as fast as the alien spoke them.

Etanu pointed a finger at Zack. "Let this one face the rite of passage and prove his worth."

Kladomaor stepped forward. "This is wrong, Etanu. The Humans are not part of the Confederation. They are a primitive species. The ways of the Confederation and the Nershals are unknown to them. I ask that you grant them leniency," Kladomaor said.

"Then it is our duty to enlighten the primitives. Let them earn the right to speak in the run," Etanu said.

Nershals growled their response.

The run? Kaylan thought. "Athena, is this an accurate translation?"

"Commander, I'm distilling the Nershal words to concepts that you can understand," the AI said.

"Are they proposing that Zack run in some sort of race?" Kaylan asked.

"It could be some sort of obstacle course," Hicks said.

Kaylan nodded.

"Then as part of the reckoning, I request to be the Human's arbiter," Kladomaor said.

Several Nershals gasped.

"You would stand with this Human?" Etanu said.

"The Boxan would stand with any species and guide them along the correct path," Kladomaor said.

Etanu considered this for a moment. "It is accepted that you, Kladomaor, will function as arbiter for the Human."

Kladomaor nodded his shaggy head once. "As arbiter, I move that the race as it stands is unworthy to honor the Nershals. Steps must be taken to make this a true contest so it can be judged accordingly."

Etanu's face drew down in annoyance, but as he caught sight of the other Nershals nodding approvingly, his expression changed. "Very well. We will provide the needed items for this Human to use. We leave it to you to instruct him in their use."

"That's very gracious of you. I request a few moments to confer with the Human before the race begins," Kladomaor said.

Etanu motioned for Zack to be brought forward. Kladomaor waved him over and Zack quickly crossed to him, occasionally glancing back over his shoulder.

Katie ran up to him. "Are you alright?"

Zack took a few deep breaths. "I didn't know what they were going to do with me. They went from looking like they were going to kill me to ignoring me. I thought these were supposed to be more advanced civilizations."

"We're not out of the woods yet," Hicks said.

A Nershal walked over to them. He unbuckled an octagonal clasp at his chest and metallic straps sprang free. The Nershal reached behind him and removed a dark brown box that had two rounded protrusions poking out the top.

"These are for you to use," the Nershal said, handing the items to Zack. Once Zack accepted them, the Nershal walked back to be with the others.

"What am I supposed to do with this?" Zack asked.

"You put it on," Kladomaor said, walking toward him. "First put the pack on your back, then press the center of the chest piece and it will lock into place."

Zack did as he was instructed. The straps automatically adjusted to his size. He hardly felt the weight of it. "What's it for?" Zack asked.

"It will help you make long jumps," Kladomaor said. "This is the Nershal's way of evening things up. You will be racing Etanu across the valley to the skybowl."

Zack glanced across the vast valley. From the top of the hill, they could see a clearing with dense forest only twenty yards farther away. "How is this fair? They can just fly over the forest and beat me there."

"He won't. He'll go through the valley the same as you," Kladomaor said.

Zack glanced at the others, his brows drawn up. "I'm not sure I can do this. Look at him. If he doesn't eat me alive, he's going to kill me the moment we get out of sight."

"Etanu will not lay a finger on you. He may, however, put obstacles in your path. You may do the same to him. This is the nature of the race. You can use what you bring with you and whatever you find in there," Kladomaor said.

Zack felt his knees start to shake and his breath quicken. Katie urged him to calm down.

Kaylan wished she could do something for him. "What happens if he doesn't participate?" Kaylan asked.

"In the Nershals' eyes, his honor would be forfeit, and so would his life," Kladomaor said.

"Isn't there anything you can do to stop this?" Kaylan asked.

"I'm doing all I can and will not go against the Nershals should you choose to resist," Kladomaor said.

Kaylan pressed her lips together, then glanced helplessly at Hicks.

"Zack," Hicks said. "You're a runner. You told me you used to do cross-country runs on hiking trails. This is the same type of thing. Think of it as a very large obstacle course."

Zack nodded and seemed to calm down a bit.

"Use your implants to make sure you're going in the right direction. We can communicate with you through them," Kaylan said.

Kladomaor shook his head. "Outside communication is forbidden. We can observe, but that's it."

"This is completely unfair. We know almost nothing about this world. How is he supposed to avoid danger?" Kaylan said.

Kladomaor didn't respond, appearing instead to consider what she had said. He glanced at Gaarokk, and the two seemed to come to some type of unspoken understanding. Kaylan wondered if they had some other means of communication and whether the Boxans were testing them somehow.

"What forms of communication are forbidden?" Hicks asked.

"Direct communication is forbidden," Kladomaor said.

Kaylan exchanged glances with the others, and Hicks shook his head slightly.

"Thanks for trying to switch places with me," Zack said to Hicks.

"You'd do the same for me," Hicks said.

"What can you tell us about the valley? Is there anything he should avoid?" Kaylan asked.

"I will share our maps of the terrain with you," Kladomaor said. "Are your implants equipped to be able to make use of hyper-learning?"

Kaylan wasn't exactly sure what the alien meant by hyper-learning, but she was pretty sure they didn't do that. She shook her head. A connection opened through Kaylan's implants, and in moments they could all see Kladomaor's map through their internal HUD.

"Avoid the left side of the valley as there is a group of juvenile protokars in the area. They hunt on instinct, and once on your trail it will stay on it until it has you. This is what they look like," Kladomaor said, and activated something on his wrists—a holo-projection of one of the strangest beasts Kaylan had ever seen. It had purplish skin with a mix of yellow and black hair that grew thicker around the shoulders and forelegs. The creature had a long tail that ended in a black stinger. A thick black strip of hair ran from the creature's snout, spreading to form a mane past its shoulders. Twin sets of jade-colored eyes peered forward, and it had thick whiskers ending in yellow drops. The creature's mouth opened, revealing rows of large teeth.

"Is it fast?" Zack asked, unable to tear his eyes away from the hologram.

"Yes, but they're predominantly sprinters. They can't run over long distances to wear down their victim, but protokars will rely on their hunting instincts and the element of surprise," Klado-maor said.

"What do I do if I accidentally come across one?" Zack asked.

Kladomaor regarded Zack for a moment. "Run as fast as you can. You are allowed to bring a weapon of your choosing. I would caution you to bring something light in weight and one with which you are familiar," Kladomaor said.

The Boxan turned and gestured to one of the others, who brought their weapons back to them.

"Pick one," Kladomaor said.

Zack's eyes darted to the others, and Kaylan all but glared at the Boxans and the Nershals. They hadn't come here for this. It wasn't fair that any of them had to do this. Hicks reached in and handed Zack the pulsar.

"Just aim and shoot. I'm willing to bet this creature is sensitive in the nose," Hicks said.

Zack nodded. "Shoot the nose," he repeated, closing his eyes and committing it to memory.

"Speed is your ally. Remember the objective is to make it to the skybowl," Kladomaor said. The image of the protokar changed to that of a small pedestal that ended in an open bowl. The contents inside glowed in a pale green hue.

"What do I do once I get there?" Zack asked.

"Each of you will be carrying a—"

Kladomaor's reply was cut off, but he looked as if he were still speaking.

"—toxin—" Kladomaor said, and the translator cut out again.

Zack looked at the others, eyes wide. "I didn't hear the last. What will I be carrying?"

Etanu called for them to return, and Kladomaor either didn't hear his last question or just ignored him outright.

Zack looked back helplessly at the others, but they hadn't heard it either. The crew of the Athena started after Zack.

Kladomaor raised his hand. "Only your commander may come."

Katie pulled Zack into a quick embrace and whispered something into his ear. Zack nodded and hugged her one more time.

Kaylan walked next to him and placed her hand on his shoulder. "I wish there was something I could do."

Zack frowned for a second. "There is something you can do. You can tell me the quickest path to this skybowl."

Kaylan looked back at him, puzzled for a moment, and then finally understood what Zack was hinting at.

"I don't know if I can," Kaylan said. "There isn't enough time."

"Try for me, please," Zack said.

"How would I tell you if I was able to see anything? You heard him—no outside communication," Kaylan said.

"You think these guys are going to play by the rules? Find a way to get me a message," Zack said.

Kaylan met Zack's gaze but didn't say anything.

"It is time," Kladomaor said.

"Zack," Kaylan said, her hands beginning to shake. She wanted to tell him to be careful and that he was so stupid for doing what he'd done, but couldn't. Her mouth wouldn't move.

Zack gave her a small smile and turned to join the others. He put on a brave face for Kaylan because she had enough to deal with, but inside he was barely keeping it together. His hand grazed the holster of his weapon. He tried to tell himself this was like any other run he'd ever done, and it was, if he ignored the things that were trying to kill him.

The pack he wore didn't weigh all that much. Zack's thoughts scattered for a moment. He didn't know how it worked. Something bumped him on the shoulder and he turned, nearly stumbling into Etanu's sneering form. Zack didn't need any translation to know this creature hated him. Zack turned away, not wanting to look into the alien's baleful gaze.

Zack looked up at Kladomaor. "How do I use this thing?" Zack asked.

"Hit the chest plate, and the burst will help you make longer jumps, but you must allow for it to recharge after a couple of uses," Kladomaor said.

An older Nershal came before them. The skin around its face was looser around the chin, and age lines tugged at the edges of its eyes. The older Nershal carried a small metal container with the opening facing toward Zack. The Nershal opened the container. Zack glanced inside and saw two melon-sized black spheres. The spheres quivered, and Zack felt the breath catch in his chest. The Nershal tapped one, and the sphere unfurled into a spindly, spider-like creature with six legs. The creature was twelve inches in diameter and had a barbed tail that came to a point, reminding Zack of a wasp's stinger.

"Hold out your hand," the old Nershal said to him.

Zack stepped back, shaking his head. "Are you crazy? I'm not putting my hand anywhere near that thing."

Etanu thrust his bare arm out and placed his wrist above the creature. The creature leaped up and locked its legs around Etanu's arm. A stinger plunged itself into the Nershal's arm. Zack's eyes widened. It looked like it hurt, but Etanu showed no signs of experiencing any pain. Instead, the Nershal turned toward Zack, sticking his chin out.

"You have no choice," Kladomaor said. "You must stick your arm out and allow its stinger to pierce your skin."

Zack shook his head. "No way. You do it."

"I already have done it," Kladomaor said, extending his own wrist, which was as thick at Zack's thigh, toward him. There was a small black mark. "It latches on, but won't release its poison until the allotted time has passed."

Zack glanced back at the creature. "You're not much use as an arbiter," Zack said.

"That remains to be seen," Kladomaor said.

"How much time do I have?" Zack asked.

Other Nershals were crowding in around them, and Zack had the feeling that if he didn't extend his arm, they were going to force him to do so anyway.

"One hour," Kladomaor said. "After one hour you will be dead. The only way to get it to release its hold on your arm is to stick your hand into the skybowl. The fluid will paralyze it, causing it to wither and die."

Zack's eyes darted around, and his stomach clenched. Etanu continued to sneer at him, and something foolish switched on deep inside him, quelling the panic he felt. Zack gave the alien a hard smile and thrust out his own arm. The creature leaped up, and his momentary bravado vanished. It was all Zack could do to keep from flailing his arm around to shake it off. The creature locked its hairy legs around his wrist like a vise, and the stinger pierced his skin, burying itself into his vein. The creature then relaxed its grip so he could move his hand. Aside from making his skin crawl every time he looked at it, he could almost fool himself into believing he was wearing a wristband.

Etanu looked away, unimpressed, but Zack didn't care. He knew a bully when he saw one. Maybe his bold display was only making himself feel better, but it worked. Now all he needed to do was run across the valley, not die, and stick his hand in a bowl of who knows what so this alien bug didn't kill him. Just another day for Zack, the ex-hacker turned astronaut. *Who am I kidding?* Zack thought. Perhaps he was so used to being scared for his life that his mind had walked off the map, and he was imagining all of this. He glanced at the creepy alien bug on his wrist and resisted the urge to pull it off.

The older Nershal called for their attention. "The rite is about to begin. Only the two of you will enter this valley. Should one of you perish, then know that you died with your honor intact and can enter the halls of the dead with your head held high." The old Nershal spoke more to Etanu than to Zack, but he didn't care. He just wanted to get this thing off his wrist.

"Human," Kladomaor said. "Do not try to remove the creature from your wrist or it will release its venom into you, and you will die."

Great, Zack thought. What would happen if he accidentally brushed up against a tree? Zack took one last glance at his friends and then focused on the valley. In the silence, Zack heard his heart pounding in his ears. His brows drew forward in concentration, and Zack crouched, waiting for the signal to start.

"Go!" Kladomaor said.

Without a backwards glance, Zack sprinted to the line of trees. He didn't know whether Etanu was on his heels or had entered the valley in a different place. Zack knew the general direction of the skybowl and headed that way. He found a path and slowed down his pace to conserve his energy. There was no way he could run the length of the valley in an all-out sprint. If Etanu made it to the skybowl first, Zack was dead. He quickened his pace. The terrain became rockier and started to decline. If this were Earth, then a steady decline usually meant he would be heading toward water, but who knew if the same rules applied on this alien moon.

His internal HUD activated of its own accord.

Combat mode activated. The AI's text appeared, and then his HUD interface changed. Each thing he focused on showed a brief combat risk assessment.

"Apologies," Athena said. "It took me some time to finish configuring your PDA to back up your implants in terms of computing power. Your current objective will appear along the top of your display. If I perceive something dangerous, it will be highlighted for you in red."

::Thanks.:: Zack had to concentrate to put the text into the reply because he didn't think it was smart to speak out loud to the AI.

The path became outlined before him through his HUD, and Zack narrowly avoided sudden dips and exposed tree roots he would otherwise have tripped over. The forest pressed in on the path, making it harder to get through, until Zack couldn't see more than a few feet in front of him. He kept his breathing even and consistent. The tightening of his chest loosened as his body warmed up. A loud screech sounded overhead, but he could only see a few remnant shadows as whatever creature it had been disappeared.

Zack's HUD display flashed red, and he instinctively grabbed the nearest tree branch. He skidded to a halt, gasping, his feet coming dangerously close to a cliff's edge. He blew out another breath, taking in the dark cliff side and the hundred-yard drop to the boulder-strewn ground below. He glanced around, looking for a safe way to cross the thirty-foot expanse to the other side, but there was nothing.

Etanu emerged several hundred yards up from Zack's position. He was close enough for Zack see the smug look on the alien's face as he unfurled his wings and simply flew to the other side.

Zack bit back a stream of curses that wanted to escalate into a yell, but none of it would change the fact that he was now falling behind. He glanced down at the octagonal clasp that secured the Nershal pack on his back. It was supposed to help him jump long distances. The hairy creature on his wrist didn't tighten its grip, but the back of it rippled, as if it sensed that he wanted to pull the damn thing off.

Zack clenched his teeth and took several steps back. He stared hard at the cliff's edge and the other side he needed to reach.

"Athena, is this jetpack thing going to work?"

"Preliminary analysis does show a power source inside, and the design supports the proposed use."

Zack sucked in a deep breath and rubbed the back of his neck. Glimpsing the hairy creature on his wrist, he flinched and snatched his hand away from his face. He didn't have a choice. Grunting, Zack shot forward as fast as he could. He leaped from the edge and slapped his palm against the octagonal clasp. There was a high-pitched squeal, and it felt as if a huge hand lifted and pushed Zack toward the other side. He overshot the edge of the cliff and slammed into a tree. Tumbling down to the ground, he was pelted by tree branches. Zack brought his hand with the poisonous creature to his chest in an effort to protect it. He slammed into the ground and rolled back toward the edge of the cliff, scrambling to grab something to keep from going over the side, but his hands kept slipping. He slid over the cliff and, in the last instant, gripped onto the edge with one hand. With his yells echoing around him, Zack reached for the edge with his other hand to keep himself from swaying. He pulled himself up and collapsed, gasping for breath.

Zack pushed himself up and got his feet under him. His limbs wouldn't stop shaking. He blew out a breath and was shaking his head when the snapping of a tree branch drew his attention. A short distance away Etanu watched him, and Zack wondered if the Nershal had been watching the whole time. Etanu turned and dashed into the forest.

Zack bolted after him and saw him running ahead on a different path. He pressed on as fast as he could, but the Nershal was faster than him. The alien used its wings to take long leaps when it encountered a straightaway.

Zack, seeing how effective the tactic was, quickly pressed the octagonal clasp, and the jetpack enabled him to make longer jumps. His landings were clumsy and he stumbled, barely keeping his feet under him on the forest ground. Slowly, he started to make up some of the distance that separated him from Etanu, but the Nershal was showing no signs of slowing down. Zack's lungs were starting to burn with effort, and he wasn't sure how long he could keep up this pace.

"WE NEED to find a way to help him," Katie said.

"You heard Kladomaor. No direct communication is allowed," Hicks said.

Kaylan rejoined them, hearing the exchange. "I don't care

what he said. Can we tap into his implants so we can see what Zack is seeing?"

"Depends on if they were military grade or not," Hicks said, and looked at Brenda.

"It won't work out here. They need to be in range of the ship or he would need to be in his spacesuit. All he has is the PDA strapped to his forearm," Brenda said.

A loud roar echoed from one side of the valley, and an answering roar came from the opposite side. Kaylan looked over at Kladomaor. The Boxan finished speaking with Gaarokk and came over to them.

"The protokars are on the hunt," Kladomaor said.

Kaylan listened for more sounds from the valley, but there were none. If anything, it grew quieter. "The roars came from opposite sides of the valley. We told Zack the right side was safer," Kaylan said.

"It was safer," Kladomaor said. "The second roar you heard was a competing pack trying to take over. Both packs will be after anyone in the valley."

"We need to go in there after him. We can't just leave him," Kaylan said.

Kladomaor held out his massive hand to block her path. "You mustn't," the Boxan said, and glanced at the Nershals who were watching them. "If you go in there and violate the rite, they will attack us all."

Kaylan looked over at the Nershals and saw that they were watching them closely. Hicks called her over.

Kaylan joined the others, and Hicks gestured for them to come closer.

"I have an idea about how to reach Zack," Hicks said.

"Good, we need to warn him about the protokars," Kaylan said.

"He needs more than that. A warning by itself won't help that much, but you can use your gift. It's the only way to help him," Hicks said.

Kaylan felt the muscles of her chest squeeze, and her throat thickened. "I don't know if I can."

"Try. I've worked field ops before. We can't just send him a vague warning. We need to send him something he can use. He's already scared, and if we add to that fear he could make a fatal mistake," Hicks said.

"Please, Zack needs your help," Katie said.

Kaylan took a deep breath and turned to face the valley. "I'll tell you what I see, and you find a way to relay the information to Zack," Kaylan said.

Katie said she would.

Kaylan closed her eyes and built an image of the valley in her mind. She wanted to immediately find Zack but knew she needed to find these wild protokars first and then trace their proximity to Zack. Finding Zack wouldn't be a problem. They had his coordinates from his PDA. She allowed her mind to relax and focused on where she thought she'd heard the roar. Remote viewing was like seeing something through the end of a tunnel. She propelled her mind closer to the end, and then she was there. The dampness in the air collected on the ground and trickled from the shrubbery. She was able to focus on specific things but without the periphery of her normal vision. She glanced downward and noticed large tri-toed footprints leading down a pathway. Kaylan followed the pack's footprints, eager to find where they led. She had to find them. Zack was depending on her.

Kaylan shifted her perspective to high off the ground, looking downward. Hundreds of yards away she saw the movements of a dozen shadows slinking through the shrubbery. The large protokar at the rear of the pack stopped and let out a screech. The rest of the pack came to halt. The protokar cocked its head, sniffing the air. The beast lifted its head and peered directly at her with its jade-colored eyes.

Kaylan gasped.

The protokar's lips curled upward, and it let out a low growl.

How could it sense me? Kaylan wondered.

The protokar turned and started to run.

ZACK DODGED and weaved around fallen trees. Small critters scrambled out of the way, and he paid them no mind because he had to keep going. The skin around his wrist was turning black. He needed to move faster. The path he was on was taking him around a steep hill. He stopped and glanced above him, looking for a place to climb up. There were several small ledges. He took a quick glance around him. Zack hadn't seen Etanu for a while now and wondered how far behind he was.

Zack squatted down and jumped, using the jetpack to give him a substantial boost. He reached a small ledge and pulled himself up. He was really starting to appreciate all the pull-ups Katie had him do on the Athena. He did another jetpack-assisted jump and reached another ledge. The farther up he went, the more slippery the ground became. After a few more jumps, Zack reached the top. A misty fog cast its gray shroud over the way forward, and Zack sighed.

"Of course," Zack said, and shook his head as rain started to drizzle.

The spectrum across his HUD changed to enhance his vision. The plants showed up as a deep blue, outlined in black. The fog barely registered, but Zack could feel the dampness on his skin. He didn't know his implants could do that. He really needed to review the manual so he knew what these things could do.

Zack jogged forward, slowly picking his pace. He was more than halfway through the valley, and the header line of his HUD showed a blip that was his destination. The farther he went, the quieter it became. Zack kept glancing above him, unable to shake the feeling that he was being watched.

Zack! There are protokars closing in on your position. The way forward isn't safe. You must head east.

The words appeared so suddenly that Zack almost tripped and fell. She'd done it! Kaylan had found a way to reach him. East of him was overgrown with thick fern-type plants. Mixed among them were large, fiendish-looking, oval-shaped plants with thorns. Zack plunged into the overgrowth without a second thought. The leaves on those evil plants were as long as his arm and twice as wide, with sharp tips that tore at his arms as he brushed past them. He pushed onward, muscling his way forward as best he could.

Heading east, Zack sent back.

A few minutes later, low growls came from behind him. They were so close. Zack quickened his pace, and he heard something running behind him. He shifted directions again, heading toward the skybowl. The overgrown path cleared, and Zack sprinted in a dead run. He caught a glimpse of a shadow out of the corner of his eyes, and a thick tree branch with orange pods crashed in front of him. Several of the orange pods burst, sending some sort of vapor into the air. His HUD flashed, outlining the vapor in red, and Zack slammed the jetpack controller with the palm of his hand and kept it there for a long burst. As he rose above the vapor, Zack angled forward so he didn't rise too high in the air. The ground raced to greet him, and he started pumping his legs to hit the ground running. At the last second, Zack used a burst from the jetpack to slow himself down, and he was able to land on his feet.

He glanced up and saw Etanu flying above, but the Nershal remained below the tree line, so he hadn't violated any of the rules. Zack clenched his teeth and pulled out his pulsar pistol.

Etanu came to a halt in the air, his wings holding him steady, and looked at Zack. The seemingly permanent sneer dared Zack to use his weapon. The Nershal made a show of looking behind Zack and cocked his head to the side.

"You better find higher ground, Human. The protokars nip at your heels," Etanu said.

Zack tore his eyes away from the Nershal and raced ahead. The way forward was mostly clear, but nestled amidst the thick, tall trees was a mass of vines that coiled along the forest floor. Zack avoided the vines and rounded the corner of a massive tree. Vines were interlaced between the trees, forming a massive web. Zack's jaw dropped at the expanse of vines. He kept going around, unable to find a path through them.

A screech sounded from above, and Zack saw Etanu get tangled in the vines and fall to the ground a short distance from him. Dark shadows moving through the foliage creeped in the Nershal's direction.

Zack turned and ran. There was a gradual incline as he weaved his way through the vines. The blackness on his wrist extended partway up his forearm.

A low growl sounded behind him as he tripped over something, and Zack tumbled to the ground. He dropped the pulsar pistol, and it rolled a few feet away from him. Looking around, trying to see what had tripped him, he scrambled toward his gun. Zack snatched the pistol from the ground and crouched, keeping it ready. He crept slowly backward, trying to be as quiet as possible. Zack glanced down at his leg and saw that a shallow gash was bleeding.

Something circled around him, and Zack tracked it with the pulsar pistol. Zack heard the creature's labored breathing and the sound of its footfalls on the moistened ground. He squeezed the trigger, and a dart shot forth, missing the creature. He couldn't get a good look at it, but he knew it wasn't alone. The HUD display flashed red whenever he caught a brief glimpse of it. Zack backed away, and the creature continued to stalk him. There were more growls coming his way.

Oh crap, they're going to get me.

He was near a small clearing and headed toward it. A loud roar behind him caused him to flinch, and his hand instinctively squeezed the trigger, firing a three-round burst into the ground. Zack spun around to see a protokar barreling toward him less than ten yards away. The creature's fierce green eyes were locked onto him. He raised his pistol and fired. The darts plunged into the protokar's face, and it came to a halt, shaking its large head.

Zack backed up a few steps. Three more protokars joined the ranks and began circling him, but he was afraid to look away from the first. The protokar in front of him was huge. Standing on all four legs, it was as tall as he was. It lunged forward with a vicious snarl, and Zack shut his eyes, squeezed the trigger, and didn't let go. When the expected mauling didn't happen after a few heart-stopping seconds, Zack opened his eyes. The large protokar was favoring one of its legs, which was bleeding profusely. The other protokars had stopped advancing toward Zack and were circling, closing in near the wounded creature.

Zack turned around and darted away, but the snarls behind him told him that the protokars were following. The skybowl was just over the next rise. If he could reach the top, he'd be better able to defend himself. As the protokars closed in, Zack used the jetpack to take long leaps, keeping ahead of them. He tried firing a few shots behind him as he went, but he kept missing. He was lucky he'd hit the first protokar.

The forest started thinning the steeper the terrain became. Zack's thighs burned, and he couldn't catch his breath. A short distance from him, Etanu emerged. The Nershal had dark blood coming from multiple gashes. Etanu narrowed his gaze at Zack and limped forward. One of his wings was damaged.

Zack kept climbing and using the jetpack. Finally, the tone of the protokars' growls changed, sounding farther away. He spun around and saw that the four protokars from his earlier encounter had darted off in Etanu's direction. The Nershal desperately flailed his broken wing, but he couldn't get off the ground, and the pain of moving his wounded appendage was mirrored in his agonized expression. He had a long dark blade in his hand.

According to his HUD, the skybowl was close. All Zack had to do was reach it and stick his hand into the glowing liquid inside to get the poisonous creature off his wrist, but he couldn't. If he left now, the Nershal would die. Without another thought, Zack screamed and waved his arms in the air.

The protokar stopped and turned in his direction. Etanu looked up at him as if he didn't know what to do.

"Climb up here. I'll distract them," Zack said.

He pointed the pulsar at the protokar and squeezed the trigger. Zack didn't know if the darts would even penetrate the creature's skin at this range.

Etanu started climbing up, and one of the protokars turned on him. The Nershal swiped out with his blade, catching the protokar on its snout. Yelping, the creature ran away. Hearing this, the other protokars turned from Zack and charged toward

Etanu. The Nershal stopped climbing and seemed to be waiting for death to take him.

Zack fired again, drawing the protokars' attention back to him. A red warning flashed on his HUD. He had less than ten percent of his rounds left.

"Go, Human. You've won," Etanu said.

Zack shook his head and headed toward the Nershal. The protokars backed away, keeping a wary eye on the pulsar pistol.

"We can both get out of here if we work together, or you can die. Which is it gonna be?" Zack asked.

The Nershal's orange eyes watched him as if weighing his words. "Why would you help me?"

"Because I'm an idiot, and I can't leave someone to die when I can do something about it. Now put your arm over my shoulder," Zack said.

Etanu looked at him doubtfully but did as he was asked. "The kroshar won't get us both up there."

It took Zack a moment to realize that Etanu meant the jetpack. "It can if you help with your good wing."

Zack grabbed hold of Etanu and, for a second, wondered if the Nershal had double-crossed him, intending to push him into the waiting predators. The protokars were getting closer, testing to see if Zack would fire his weapon.

Etanu nodded to him, and Zack pressed the clasp on his chest. The jetpack fired, and Etanu used his functioning wing to get them off the ground. They reached the top of the ridge and crashed. The Nershal cried out in pain, but they were free of imminent danger. Zack glanced down the ridge, and the protokars looked up at him for a moment before turning around to head in the opposite direction.

Twenty feet away was a rocky pillar that ended in a craggy-faced bowl. A soft green glow came from the liquid inside.

Etanu limped ahead and turned toward him. "Go ahead. Stick your hand in and the creature will die."

"What about you?" Zack asked.

"Once you stick your hand in, the skybowl will lose its charge," Etanu said, his shoulders slumping. "You've beaten me. Honor of my species dictates that I yield the skybowl to you."

Zack glanced inside the bowl and down at his wrist. The hairy, spider-like creature quivered as if it sensed its own demise. Without further thought, Zack grabbed the Nershal's arm and plunged it inside the bowl at the same time as his own. The glowing liquid bubbled, and Zack felt an electric charge zip up his arm, paralyzing it for a moment, but very quickly the liquid dissolved, leaving both Zack's and Etanu's wrists free of the creatures.

Zack noted a tingling sensation where the creature had latched on but otherwise felt fine. He glanced at the Nershal and instinctively sprang away from the alien's smoldering gaze, which took Zack by surprise.

The Nershal charged forward and grabbed Zack by the throat. "By what right do you dare show mercy during the rite?"

"You're crazy. I just saved your life," Zack gasped.

The Nershal held him for a moment longer, then released him.

Zack sucked in gasping mouthfuls of air. "Is that how your species shows gratitude?"

Etanu turned his back on Zack, his shoulders stooped and his hands motionless at his sides. "You have brought shame upon me."

Zack didn't know what to think. One moment the alien had been about to kill him and the next he was just standing there as if Zack had ended his world.

Four Nershal soldiers flew in on some type of sled and

landed near them. The sled was covered with dirt, but a few bronze-colored spots showed through. The Nershals on board opened the gate and gestured for Zack to come aboard.

Zack glanced at Etanu.

"As the winner, you must enter first," Etanu said, his eyes downcast.

Zack frowned and looked back at the Nershals on the sled. They regarded him without a hint of a challenge, waiting for him to get on board. Zack stepped on, and the Nershals actually seemed friendly toward him. They handed him a canister of water, which Zack drank gratefully. When Etanu climbed aboard the sled, the other Nershals ignored him completely.

The sled's engines kicked in and they lifted off. They flew above the fog, which now covered most of the valley. Zack offered the canister to Etanu, but the Nershal ignored him. He shook his head and finished the water.

The trip back across the valley took only minutes, but every second that passed only reminded Zack of how sore he was going to be. He was already starting to ache and lost count of the shallow cuts he had. He kept looking at the darkened skin on his wrist. It didn't hurt and was already starting to fade.

The sled slowed down as they approached the large gathering. The Boxans towered above everyone else, watching their approach. As the sled finished its descent and they disembarked, the Nershals watched Zack as if they didn't quite know what to make of him. When Etanu stepped off the sled, the nearby Nershals shouted what Zack assumed were insults. The translator went silent, but he didn't need it to know that Etanu's welcome wasn't a warm one.

Zack was guided to the old Nershal who had spoken to him before the race. Kladomaor was with him. Zack glanced to the side and saw the crew of the Athena craning their necks to get a better look at him. Zack waved to them and looked back at the old Nershal, who was watching him.

The old Nershal bowed his head. "I am called Udonzari."

"My name is Zack."

Udonzari looked up at Kladomaor. "This is the second outsider to have survived the rite in such a short span of time. If this keeps up, the prowess of our warriors will come into question."

Kladomaor gave a single nod. Zack realized that the Boxan had risked his own life with an offense against the Nershals. Zack wondered what the offense could have been. Since Kladomaor was alive, the Nershal he had raced against hadn't survived.

Udonzari regarded Etanu, and the young Nershal kept his eyes downcast. The old Nershal looked back at Zack. "The rite serves the old ways of handling transgressions and wrongdoings. Once invoked, it cannot be put aside. Having both participants emerge from it is not unheard of—just extremely rare."

"He had nothing to do with it," Zack said. "I made him do it. I grabbed his hand and stuck it into the skybowl at the same time as my own."

Udonzari considered this and nodded. "There is still the matter of honor that must be taken into consideration. You won the rite and earned the right to live. Etanu has not."

Two Nershal soldiers moved in and grabbed Etanu by his arms. One had a knife drawn.

"Wait!" Zack shouted. "Why does he have to die?"

"You won the rite, and Etanu invoked the rite. He lost and his life is forfeit," Udonzari said.

"There has to be some other way," Zack said, his mind racing. "Wait. Since I won the rite, can I have a say in what to do with Etanu?"

Udonzari regarded him, and Zack forced himself to meet the old Nershal's hard gaze.

"A life was pledged and a life must be taken. What would you propose?" Udonzari asked.

"There is a saying where I come from. 'An eye for an eye.' I saved his life, and now he owes me the same. My friends and I are a long way from home, and we need help to get back there," Zack said.

The crew of the Athena edged closer to him, and when they met no resistance they came to Zack's side.

Udonzari glanced at Kladomaor.

"It's true," Kladomaor said. "They were brought to this system by activating one of our listening stations. Their species is now at risk of falling under the Xiiginn influence. And there is a chance that the Xiiginn can trace a signal from the Star Shroud to our last colony."

Udonzari nodded, and his gaze returned to Zack. "This expression—an eye for an eye—is from your home world?"

"Yes," Zack said.

Udonzari nodded. "We have similar ones. You've shown Etanu mercy, and with respect for one who has won the rite, his life is spared."

Etanu raised his head, and his downcast eyes rose to meet Udonzari's.

"Your life is pledged to assist these Humans. They will be under your protection, and should the situation arise, you will sacrifice your own life so they can live." Udonzari said.

Etanu glanced at Zack with something akin to blame in his eyes. Zack was beginning to think the concept of gratitude was something that escaped the Nershals, but perhaps it was just Etanu.

Etanu looked back at Udonzari. "So be it."

Fury gathered in Udonzari's gaze. "Should you fail in your pledge, not only is your life forfeit, but all mention of your line will be stricken from the records. Is that clear?"

Etanu released the breath he'd been holding, and the fight in him drained to a smoldering blaze. "I swear that from this moment onward I will do everything in my power to protect the Humans, including sacrificing my own life."

Udonzari nodded, and the soldiers took Etanu away.

Zack remembered he still had the jetpack on and moved to give it back, but Udonzari shook his head.

"Keep it as a reminder of what you've accomplished this day," Udonzari said, and left them.

Kladomaor came over to Zack, who watched Etanu being led away. "Curious that you should fight so hard for someone who would have left you for dead."

"It's called compassion. I'd have thought that such an advanced species as yours would have heard of it," Zack said, and Kladomaor's expression darkened. *I really need to learn to keep my mouth shut*, Zack thought. "Where are they taking him?"

"He's wounded and requires healing, as do you," Kladomaor said.

"The Nershals have a funny way of showing gratitude," Zack said.

"I'm not sure they see it that way. Some may view your actions as shameful and cause for retribution," Kladomaor said.

Zack's eyes widened. "Are you saying that some of them are going to come after me because I didn't let Etanu die?"

Kladomaor nodded. "Some, but not Udonzari."

"Why not?"

"Because Etanu is his son. While matters of honor are paramount to the Nershals, they can sometimes conflict with paternal instinct," Kladomaor said.

Zack's eyes darted to the Nershals. Some were still watching him, and he couldn't begin to tell what they were thinking.

"Come," Kladomaor said. "We have much to discuss, and your companions are waiting."

All Zack wanted to do was sit down and rest, but seeing the others held the exhaustion at bay. Katie reached him first and pulled him into a fierce hug, then proceeded to check his injuries. Brenda came with her medical kit, had him sit down on a fallen log, and began cleaning his wounds.

"I got your message. It saved my life," Zack said.

"It was Kaylan," Hicks said.

Zack looked at Kaylan. "Thank you. How did you find a way around the 'no communications' rule?" Zack asked.

"Indeed, something I am curious about as well," Kladomaor said, taking his ease against a tree.

"That was Katie," Kaylan said. "She contacted the Athena, and it was the AI that relayed the information to you. The AI was already in contact with you as part of your implants, so it wasn't a direct communication from us."

Kladomaor considered this for a moment without speaking.

Zack guessed they hadn't violated any of the Nershals' touchy rules. Katie sat next to him, and Zack leaned back and closed his eyes, letting Brenda finish what she was doing. Suddenly a loud screech came from inside the valley, startling Zack. He surged to his feet, ready to bolt.

Katie got in front of him and placed her hands on his shoulders. "You're alright. They can't get to you here."

Zack glanced at the others. Redford gave him a strange look, and Kaylan looked as if she wanted to reach out to him. Zack let himself be coaxed back down. Before going into that valley, he wouldn't have given a second thought to a sound like that. Now he wondered if he would ever stop jumping at shadows. He glanced back at Kaylan, who was speaking quietly with Hicks. He knew she'd used her ability to help him, but there was something more. It was almost as if she had been there with him. Zack recounted his trek through the valley for the others, and each time he looked at Kaylan, his suspicions were confirmed. She had watched him the whole way.

Chapter Sixteen

Kladomaor watched the Humans. They had been resting for a few hours and no doubt had questions, but their presence here raised more questions of his own. The Humans were a primitive race that he wasn't convinced would ever have been admitted to the Confederation before the Xiiginns had betrayed them. But the resourcefulness of the Human called Zack had surprised him. He was much stronger than Kladomaor had originally thought. He had seen reserves of strength exposed in times of great need among the different species, including his own. Having gone through the rite himself, he hadn't believed the Human was going to survive. As it turned out, not only had the Human survived, but he had taken steps to ensure the survival of the Nershal who had wanted to see him dead. But benevolence wasn't in all the Humans. There were some who warranted closer watching. The one called Redford attempted to conceal his yearning to learn about their advanced technology. Though curiosity was normal for any intelligent race, having dealt with others, he could tell the dangerous kinds of curiosity

—the kind of curiosity that looked beyond the technological function of a device and sought the potential for gain. He needed more time to assess the Humans and to get the full report from the listening station in their star system.

"They're an interesting mix, don't you think?" Gaarokk asked.

"In some respects," Kladomaor said. "In others, they are brash, prone to violence, and capable of wanton destruction."

"That's not what I saw in the valley. What makes you say this?" Gaarokk asked.

"After Ma'jasalax sent the signal to their star system all those years ago, I looked into what would compel her to do so. I reviewed the preliminary reports about the Humans. I never would have thought they were capable of decoding the signal, but I was wrong on that account. I underestimated them, but they could be a blight upon the galaxy. Better to use the Star Shroud to keep them ignorant of their surroundings for a few hundred years more to see if the Humans can keep from killing themselves," Kladomaor said.

"They know about the shroud, so keeping them ignorant of anything isn't an option anymore. While what you say may be true of their history, the actions we've observed today show the potential of the cultivation instinct. They need guidance," Gaarokk said.

Kladomaor snorted. "Our prized instinct didn't help us from discerning the Xiiginns' true intentions."

"Yes, but we're not talking about the Xiiginns. We're talking about the Humans," Gaarokk said.

"Fine, I will admit that there is also the cultivation instinct in them—the desire to build up the world around them. This will propel them out into the cosmos, but it doesn't mean we have to help them do so," Kladomaor said.

"I thought our function was supposed to be as guides to lead the younger races into harmony. The Humans are here, and it is our responsibility to see that they return to their home system safely. There is also the matter of what the AI construct has informed us," Gaarokk said.

"That the Mardoxian potential exists in Humans?" Klado-maor said.

"You saw what their commander was able to do," Gaarokk said.

Kladomaor frowned doubtfully. "Perhaps they used some other means to keep track of Zack during the rite."

"Oh really. Like what? If they are as primitive as you believe, what could they have done that we wouldn't have been able to detect?" Gaarokk asked.

"If she does have Mardoxian capabilities, then we can't let her fall into Xiiginn hands. No matter what," Kladomaor said.

Gaarokk was about to say something else when the Humans approached them. They were of similar size and stature to the Nershals. Some had the look of a soldier, but most of them did not, including their commander, which might be a problem when facing the tough choices ahead of them.

"Our AI says it detected some type of message coming in. An alpha priority message," Kaylan said.

"Was it able to decode the message?" Kladomaor asked.

"No, it just knows the coordinates of where the message was sent," Kaylan said, and relayed the information to them.

Kladomaor's brows rose, and he exchanged glances with Gaarokk. "The research facility. How is it that we did not detect the signal?" Kladomaor asked.

"We're monitoring communications on the planetary surface, not those inbound. We would have needed to send our ship into space in order to monitor for an incoming signal. This would have put all of us at risk if we had needed to leave quickly," Gaarokk said.

"The signal came from deep space and was detected by our communications array on the Athena," Kaylan said.

Gaarokk raised his bushy eyebrows curiously. "Athena is the designation of your ship?"

"Yes," Kaylan said.

"Do all your ships have designations such as this?" Gaarokk asked.

"Athena was a goddess from mythology. She was associated with wisdom and courage. Some of our ships are named in this tradition and others for famous scientists throughout history," Kaylan said.

"Intriguing. I'd be interested in hearing more about this sometime," Gaarokk said.

"This is all very fascinating," Kladomaor said, "but we have more pressing issues at the moment."

Gaarokk nodded. "We suspected there was more going on at the research facility than what Ezerah led us to believe," Gaarokk said.

"Perhaps she isn't aware, either way. If the Xiiginns are sending alpha priority messages, then we need to know what they are and who the intended recipient is," Kladomaor said.

Gaarokk glanced at the group of Humans. "Could *they* have been traced here so quickly?"

Kladomaor shook his head. "The Xiiginns wouldn't have come straight here for them. This is something else."

"The original message sent to Earth contained a warning about something called the Xiiginn, but there was no other mention of it. Can you tell us what it is?" Kaylan asked.

Kladomaor glanced at Kaylan thoughtfully. "What did the warning say?"

"Don't you know?" Zack asked.

Kladomaor's lips pressed together. "The message sent to your species was unsanctioned by the Confederation led by the Boxans."

"So you don't then," Zack said.

Kladomaor let out a deep sigh. "No."

"Beware of the Xiiginn," Kaylan said. "That was the warning."

Kladomaor glanced at Gaarokk, who was pointedly looking away. "You knew."

Gaarokk looked back at Kladomaor and slowly nodded.

"Do the protocols of cultivation mean nothing? You and Ma'jasalax gave them this as well," Kladomaor said.

At the mention of Ma'jasalax, the Human commander gasped, and Kladomaor turned his attention toward her. "You know this name?" Kladomaor asked.

Kaylan nodded slowly.

"It's all right. I know her as well. Please tell me how you know about her," Kladomaor said.

Kaylan swallowed hard. "When I went into the chamber at the listening station, it activated. I was taken to another place . . . another chamber like the one I was in, and the being I met there told me her name was Ma'jasalax. I was able to feel her emotions —the pain and regret she felt for the actions that had been taken. She guided me back and told me to find her."

"That's it!" Gaarokk said. "What more proof do we need? She used the Mardoxian Chamber. Do you know what this means? We're not the only ones."

The other Humans looked at their commander in shock. This was something she had kept from them with the exception of their medical officer.

"We have to get them out of here," Gaarokk said.

"No," Kladomaor said. "The Nershals are only just starting to come around. We need more time."

"We can't risk letting them fall into Xiiginn hands, and if we do what I suspect you're thinking of doing, that could become a very real possibility," Gaarokk said.

"We're not going anywhere until you tell us what's going on. Who are the Xiiginns?" Kaylan asked.

Kladomaor regarded them all for a moment. "It's time they knew the truth. Then they can decide what the best course of action is for themselves," Kladomaor said and turned to address the Humans. "Before I tell you about the Xiiginns, I want you to know that it is our intent to help you get back to your star system. The Star Shrouds are part of a process we use to evaluate species with the potential for interstellar travel. Since your species successfully journeyed to the outer planets in your star system, you are on the brink of expanding the influence of your species within the next hundred years. There is much more I could tell you about the Star Shrouds, but time is short. Basically, our ancestors observed cataclysmic interstellar conflict among species on the other side of the galaxy. Whole star systems were turned into weapons of massive destruction and flung out across the cosmos. We observed the aftereffects of this war that consumed the species that fought it. We don't know who they were and were only able to piece together the remnants they left behind. After these disheartening observations, we took it upon ourselves to use the technology of the Star Shrouds as a way to promote those species conditioned for galactic harmony and contain the species that would spread chaos and war.

"Star systems were monitored and evaluated, and if the species proved worthy, they were brought into the Confederation. They would assist in species cultivation. That was our intent. The Xiiginns had different plans. They were among the first to join the Confederation. They were charismatic and adored by the other species. Highly intelligent and manipulative. As we have learned, compassion was in short supply with the Xiiginns. In essence, they fooled us into believing they were something other than what they truly were. They sought to unlock the power of the universe and set out to establish their dominance across the Confederation. We fought them, along with some of the other species. Then, as the war went on, the various species of the Confederation began to turn against us. We were hunted in star systems where we thought we were safe. The Xiiginns were after the Star Shroud Network that holds the keys to all the systems being monitored by us. We learned of their intent here in the home of the Nershal star system. We'd been guiding the Nershals, believing they could resist the Xiiginn influence. We were wrong, and many of our species died because of it. We sent a signal that would take the Star Shrouds offline. The shroud would continue to operate but would not send reports back to our home system. Many Boxans were stranded in the more primitive star systems, unable to get home or communicate that they needed aid. We were losing the war with the Xiiginns, and our home system became their next target. At first we held them off, but they ground us down."

"What happened to your home world?" Kaylan asked.

Kladomaor released a long sigh. "A story for another time."

"What is the Xiiginn influence?" Kaylan asked.

"It's a sickness. We believe the Xiiginns are able to emit some type of pheromone that can overwhelm the reason centers of the brain across species. We have yet to encounter a species that can resist them fully. We'd thought the Nershals, with their strict codes of honor, would have been able to resist them, but the Xiiginns have proven that there is more than one way to sow deceit among the allies," Kladomaor said.

"You were fighting each other, as well as the Xiiginns?" Hicks said.

Kladomaor looked at Hicks and nodded. "The Human term, I believe, is called civil war, but as even your history can account for, there is nothing civil about any war. A war fought on many fronts is destined to destroy those who fight them. The influence of the Xiiginns had spread far and wide. They knew where and how to strike at us to maximize their advantage. By the time we recovered, the damage was done. You see, they were among the most trusted in the Confederation, and their betrayal was hard for my species to comprehend," Kladomaor said. Echoes of the screaming fallen flashed through his mind, and he squeezed his eyes shut against the pain. After a few moments he opened his eyes, clamping down the painful memories and the poisonous yearning for better days. The Human commander looked at him with something akin to sympathy.

"The Xiiginns were like family to you?" Kaylan asked.

Kladomaor's furrowed brows drew forward. "Not anymore. They are a blight upon the galaxy."

Kaylan nodded. "If the Nershals turned against you, then why would you return?" Kaylan asked.

"The Nershals aren't as susceptible to the Xiiginns as the other species. They turned against us because they believed we had betrayed them," Kladomaor said.

"Did you?" Kaylan asked.

"Of course not. We may have kept them in the dark about the neighboring star systems, but we never lied to them. The Xiiginns did that, and I suspect are doing worse to them under their very noses," Kladomaor said.

"Is there any way to tell if we would be susceptible to the Xiiginns like the other species?" Kaylan asked.

"Nothing I'm willing to try," Kladomaor said.

"But there must be something," Kaylan pressed.

"If you encounter a Xiiginn, don't speak to it, don't listen to it, and only look at it long enough to fire your weapon and kill it. Otherwise it will already be too late," Kladomaor said.

"We don't even know what they look like," Kaylan said.

Kladomaor glanced at Gaarokk.

"Perhaps it's too much," Gaarokk said.

Kladomaor gave a stiff nod, rose to his feet, and walked away.

Kaylan watched the Boxan's retreating form. He walked as if he carried too many burdens. "Did I say something wrong?" Kaylan asked.

Gaarokk shook his head. "Not you. A Xiiginn who calls himself Mar Arden captured Kladomaor and his squad, held them prisoner, and subjected them to torture. Mar Arden set each of Kladomaor's squad against him and made them fight for the amusement of others. His hate for the Xiiginns runs deep, and at the same time he is also subject to their influence. He is part of a handful to have survived being held by Mar Arden, and the only one still alive. Kladomaor would say he was set free in the ultimate form of torture."

"What form of torture is that?" Zack asked.

"Once exposed to the Xiiginn influence, it becomes like an addiction. Being deprived of the source often renders one grief-stricken and eventually succumbing to despair. The ones expelled will do anything to get the influence back or seek to end their own lives. Kladomaor fights this yearning every day. It's what drives him and what brought us here. He blames himself for our failure with the Nershals. Kladomaor being here is an act of defiance against Mar Arden and himself. That's why he is so focused on bringing down the Xiiginns," Gaarokk said.

Kaylan was at a loss for words as her brain scrambled to

process the things they had been told. "You must have studied the Xiiginns, figured out how they do what they're able to do?" Kaylan asked.

"We are unable to counteract what they are able to do. At best we can slow it down, but increased exposure will eventually override our defenses," Gaarokk said.

"And what defenses would those be?" Hicks asked.

"Our helmets, for one. We filter the air we breathe, but even that will only work for so long. Distance helps, but even that has its limitations. We looked for ways to predict who among us would be more vulnerable to the Xiiginns, and all tests were eventually proven to be inconclusive," Gaarokk said.

"Would you please show us what they look like?" Kaylan asked. She had to know and could tell from the others that they did as well.

Gaarokk gave her a long look and slowly nodded. He activated a device he wore on his forearm, and a holographic projection sprang to life in front of them. The Boxans around them shifted positions as they solemnly watched the face of their enemy. A glistening projection of two humanoid aliens rose in front of them. Their perfectly smooth skin was so pale that it had a purplish hue. The holoprojections cycled through several different images of the Xiiginns. Some had long, platinum-colored hair, while others had hair of an inky blackness that shimmered. They were a physically stunning race, perfectly proportioned. The Xiiginns' large, intense green eyes threatened to swallow them up. If these were mere images, what would it be like to be in the presence of such a being? One image of an enraged Xiiginn revealed that they had large, pointed teeth and a long tail that reached the ground.

Kaylan circled around the hologram to get a better look.

Zack leaned toward her. "They almost remind me of vampires because their teeth are so long."

"Do they all look like this?" Kaylan asked.

"They come from a system whose star doesn't burn as brightly as others. They easily adapted to life in space, with an innate ability to resist most forms of radiation," Gaarokk said.

The Boxan cut off the projection, and more than a few of them stared at the empty space where the hologram had been for a few moments after it was gone.

Kladomaor returned to them. "So now you've seen the face of our enemy. We have no way of knowing which among you would be affected. Bringing you to the research station would be a folly I cannot allow."

"Give me some time to discuss this with my crew," Kaylan said.

The crew of the Athena gathered around.

"I'm not sure going with them on their crusade is the smartest thing we can do," Redford said.

"I'm not sure we have much of a choice," Kaylan said.

"Why didn't you tell us about what else happened in that chamber?" Hicks asked.

"Honestly, I didn't want you to think I was crazy. I needed time to think about what happened," Kaylan said.

Hicks nodded. "I can understand that, but you can trust us."

"I got the feeling that they don't even want us going with them to this research station," Zack said.

"This isn't our fight. Getting involved in a war on this scale is more than any of us signed up for. We're not equipped for this," Redford said.

"Like I said before," Kaylan said, "we may not have a choice. By powering on the alien listening station on Pluto, we drew attention to ourselves. They seemed convinced that it is only a matter of time before these Xiiginns travel to Earth. They said they would take us back there, but we need to learn all we can before then."

"How are we going to get them to take us with them?" Hicks said.

Kaylan glanced at all of them and made a decision. "Not all of us. Only some of us. The rest I want to send back to the Athena."

The response was a mixture of relief from some and a blossoming defiance from the others.

"I know we're out of our depth. This is more than what any one of us signed up for when we came on this mission, but our world just got a whole lot bigger. A few months ago there was still a debate on alien life being detected in our own galaxy. Now we find ourselves in the middle of an interstellar conflict. I may not be in the military, but I can't honestly see how this conflict isn't going to come to Earth eventually. Do you?" Kaylan asked them.

Hicks and Katie shook their heads. As the only two military people with them, they were the foremost experts.

"Kaylan's right," Hicks said. "We need to learn all we can."

"Agreed, but what if we run into one of these Xiiginns?" Zack asked.

"Then we do as the Boxans do—shoot first and ask questions later," Hicks said.

"Aside from those who will return to the ship, I guess the only question is how we get them to take us with them," Hicks said.

"I have that covered," Kaylan said, and turned back toward Kladomaor, who was quietly speaking with Gaarokk. "You can't break into the research station without our help."

Kladomaor looked amused. "Is that what you think? Between

ourselves and the Nershals who are helping us, I think it's a safe bet that we can get in."

"But you'll be blind to what's inside, unless one of them knows the layout. I can help you with that," Kaylan said, wishing she felt as confident as she sounded.

Kladomaor watched her as if he could discern her thoughts. "We have someone on the inside who may help us," Kladomaor said.

Gaarokk gave Kladomaor an incredulous stare. "You can't possibly mean Ezerah. She informed the Enforcers of our presence," Gaarokk said.

"Enough time has passed for another visit then," Kladomaor said.

Gaarokk glanced at Kaylan and the others. "We can't leave them in the Nershals' keeping. I don't like the thought of taking them any more than you do, but what choice do we have? You need everyone you can get in order to breach the research facility's defenses."

"We have to move quickly, and the Humans would only slow us down. An alpha priority message means something momentous has happened, and we need to know what that is," Kladomaor said.

Gaarokk glanced at the Athena crew again. "You, there," Gaarokk said, pointing at Zack. "Was it you who was able to discern the protocols of the Shroud Network?"

Zack pressed his lips together. "Yeah, I saw there was a pattern in the message and used that basic formatting to craft a signal to one of the shroud devices and got a reply."

Gaarokk nodded and looked at Kladomaor. "Some of them could be useful. If he was able to do this, perhaps they can help with the research facility systems," Gaarokk said.

"Hold on," Zack said. "I had months to work on it, and I had help."

Kladomaor shifted his feet. "I don't like this," he said, and shifted his gaze to Kaylan. "Why are you so insistent on coming?"

"By your own account, our planet is at risk from the Xiig-inns. If they are as bad as you say they are, then they could pose a very grave threat to our species. And . . ." Kaylan said, and paused for a moment. "I have this feeling that I need to go with you. I don't know how to explain it, but it's there."

Gaarokk's flaxen eyes lit up. "Perhaps she has more of the Mardoxian instinct than we originally thought."

Kladomaor's brow furrowed. "Very well. I will allow some of you to come with us, but you must stay by me or one of my team. You will do exactly as I command without hesitation. In the research facility, I won't be able to explain everything to you. If you can go along with that, then you can come."

Kaylan nodded and turned to the others. "Zack, Katie, Hicks, Jonah, you're coming with me. The rest of you will go back to the shuttle and wait on the ship."

"What if one of you gets hurt?" Brenda said. "You'll need me."

Kaylan shook her head. "Most of us have field medical train-ing. It will have to be enough. I don't want to put you in danger needlessly."

"Commander," Vitomir said, "I know I may not be the obvious choice, but I can be of help to you."

Kaylan kept her temper in check. "You want to help? Then help them back on the ship."

"I will keep an eye on him, Commander," Nikolai said, glaring at Vitomir coldly.

"What about me?" Emma Roberson said. "An alien research

facility? Have any of you studied alien life? Even though I haven't studied intelligent life, on the microbial level I've researched bacterial life forms that developed on other planets in our solar system—"

"You're right, Emma. You should come too," Kaylan said.

Emma closed her mouth and smiled.

"Efren is in charge until I get back," Kaylan said.

"Without the shuttle, how will you get back to the ship?" Efren asked.

"Either you'll have to come pick us up, or we'll catch a ride with someone else," Kaylan said. "Athena."

"I'm here, Commander. I've been monitoring your conversation and am ready to assist in any way I can," replied the AI.

"Can you continue to monitor for incoming transmissions and let us know if anything else comes in?" Kaylan asked.

"Of course, Commander," Athena said.

Kaylan led them back over to the Boxans. "Six of us will be joining you. The rest of my people will take the shuttle back to our ship."

"I would like to see your ship," Gaarokk said.

"I'm not sure it will be possible for you to come on board. The Athena is designed for a being of *our* height," Kaylan said.

Gaarokk's face drew downward. "Of course. I didn't mean physically go on your ship, but perhaps another day."

"We cannot allow your shuttle to leave until after we go to the research center," Kladomaor said.

"Why?" Kaylan asked.

"Because we can't risk it being detected," Kladomaor said.

Kaylan frowned. "We weren't detected on our way here."

"No doubt they are on heightened alert now. The Nershals with us will help protect those you leave behind," Kladomaor said.

"Somehow I'm not convinced this is going to help us," Kaylan said.

"I will speak with Udonzari and explain that you do not know their ways so he can assign more open-minded Nershals to protection duty. In addition, I will have one of my soldiers stay with them," Kladomaor said.

"Thank you," Kaylan said.

Kladomaor seemed to consider this for a moment and nodded.

Hicks came over and asked to speak with her. They walked a short way from the others. The fog still cloistered the valley below, and the sun was well past its zenith. Kaylan didn't know how far away this research station was, but she expected they would be leaving soon.

"Don't take this question the wrong way, but are you sure you can do this?" Hicks asked.

"What do you mean?"

"I mean map out the facility the Boxans want to infiltrate," Hicks said.

"I wouldn't have said I could do it if I didn't think I could," Kaylan said.

Hicks nodded. "Good, but just keep in mind that once we're inside we might need to call on you for direction. There will be people's lives on the line. Are you prepared for that?"

Kaylan's brow furrowed in thought. "I can do this," Kaylan said.

"And I'll be by your side while you do," Hicks said and looked at her, considering whether he wanted to say more. Instead he glanced back at the others, where Zack was talking to Katie.

Kaylan followed his line of sight.

"Do you love him?" Hicks asked.

Kaylan looked away. "I don't know," she finally said.

Hicks reached out and placed his hand on her shoulder. "It's a simple question. You either do or you don't. I'm not asking because I need to know, I'm asking because *you* need to know."

Kaylan closed her eyes, her chest becoming tighter. She opened her eyes and looked over at Zack. "What does it matter? He's with Katie."

"It matters," Hicks said. "He cares for you more than he lets on. Otherwise, why would he pick a fight with an armed alien for putting his hands on you?"

Kaylan turned back to Hicks. "I'm sorry," Kaylan whispered.

Hicks smiled. "You don't need to be sorry. It doesn't change how I feel about you. But I think you should tell him how you feel, or you'll always be questioning yourself."

Hicks walked away, leaving her alone. She watched him go and wondered if she was making the biggest mistake of her life by letting him do so. He was a good man, and those were few and far between. She glanced at Zack and felt something squeeze her chest, and her throat grew thick. She closed her eyes and took a deep breath, then rejoined the others.

Chapter Seventeen

Kladomaor watched one of his soldiers guide a small group of Humans and their Nershal escorts back to the Human vessel. Two of the Humans had the bearing of a soldier. The methodical discipline that came from intense training and habitual surveillance was unmistakable—from the ease and familiarity with which they held their weapons to how they constantly watched their surroundings. The remaining Humans were not soldiers. They were specialists, and each had something unique to offer, but none were equipped to deal with what they were about to do. Bringing noncombatants on a mission such as they were about to launch was extremely risky. Yet, they were determined. Kaylan, their commander, possessed the Mardoxian potential. He wasn't sure that she could deliver on what she'd promised regarding her abilities, but he wasn't about to let that chance slip away.

Despite all the doubts the council had about returning to the Nershal star system, he'd found some Nershals who didn't support allying with the Xiiginns. This didn't necessarily mean they would ally with the Boxans, but it would be enough for him to break the alliance. Without the Nershals' navigation skill set, the Xiiginn fleets would be hindered. Anything that could make the Xiiginns weaker was a strong victory, not only for the Boxans but for all the species who had been subverted by the Xiiginns. He'd given orders that the Humans were to be protected at all costs. Perhaps they would get lucky and be in and out of the facility without alerting anyone, but he was too seasoned a soldier to expect that. The large group of Nershals was dispersing, heading off to spread the word and hopefully get others to join their cause. The population on Selebus was only a fraction of what was on the Nershal home planet. Coming here had been an experiment, and while most Nershals were openly hostile toward them, there were still some who welcomed Kladomaor and the Boxans back.

He walked back to where everyone waited. His long strides would have been enough to keep any Human hopping to keep up with him. He heard the low whine of the powered sleds hovering over the ground. The Nershals would be giving them a ride, and Kladomaor appreciated it as it would conserve the power supply they needed for their armor.

KAYLAN HOPED she wasn't making a mistake by sending the rest of the crew back to the shuttle. She was lost in thought when Kladomaor called them together so they could prepare to leave for the Nershal research facility.

"I have a question," Zack said after they had gathered around.

Kladomaor nodded for Zack to speak.

"I'm wondering about the priority message we detected. Did

the actual message reach the research facility? And, if so, isn't there a way we can remotely access their systems to retrieve the message?" Zack asked.

"No, we can't retrieve the message unless we're inside the research facility," Kladomaor said. "The Nershals will follow standard protocol for high-priority messages with potentially sensitive information and move it to a closed system before it can be read."

"How do you know they'll do that?" Zack asked.

"Based on our own observations. The Nershals follow the Xiiginns' procedures, which they learned from us," Kladomaor said.

Zack nodded. "It was just a thought."

Kladomaor nodded and addressed the rest of them. "We have three sleds that will take us to the facility. Two will be held in reserve to provide a distraction while we attempt to get inside. Once on the grounds, I will attempt to make contact with Ezerah, who will get us into the facility. Should Ezerah prove uncooperative, then we'll find another way. Once inside, Gaarokk will use one of our slicers to get into the facility's network. From there it's a matter of allowing the AI to tell us where in the system the message is located. After that we move to intercept. The research facility isn't a military installation, but they do have several Enforcer squads that are well equipped," Kladomaor said.

A group of Nershals approached. Their brown uniforms had black armored sections that gave them maximum protection with ease of movement. Each carried a combat knife and some type of assault rifle. Their wings were folded so they all but disappeared from view.

Etanu approached them. The Nershal's wounds were almost gone, and Zack wasn't sure if this was because of some type of advanced alien healing technology or if Etanu was just that strong. He carried several folded brown pieces of cloth and handed each of them one.

Zack took his and unfolded it. The brown cloth was a hood that would cover their heads and part of their shoulders.

"This is the closest thing we have to a disguise," Etanu said. "The hoods from far away will make you appear as a keeper. The keepers are workers who look after the research facility grounds."

Zack glanced at the others. "So from the neck up we should be fine. What happens when they see the rest of us?"

Etanu narrowed his gaze. "You'll be mixed in with us, which should keep you shielded enough from view," Etanu said, and moved to the far side of the sled before Zack could ask any more questions.

Having Etanu around to protect him was going to be so much fun. The Nershal seemed as likely to hurt him as he was to help them.

"He will not betray you," Kladomaor said.

Zack glanced up at the Boxan. For a ten-foot-tall species, they had a knack for hiding in plain sight. "I hope you're right," Zack said.

"Etanu has given his word. As I've said before, honor is of paramount importance to the Nershals. He might not like the second chance he has been given because of your actions, but he will accept it . . . eventually," Kladomaor said.

Zack pulled the hood over his head and let it lay on his shoulders. It carried the damp smells of the forest, and the side of the material that touched his skin was softer than the outside. Zack still wore the jetpack beneath the hood because wearing it was more practical than carrying it around.

"How will you disguise yourself?" Zack asked.

Kladomaor frowned, and the Boxan's helmet formed around

his head. In moments, Kladomaor completely disappeared from view.

Zack's mouth hung open. He reached out with his hand and banged it against a solid object that shouldn't have been there.

"They won't be able to see us any better than you can now," Kladomaor said, and reappeared.

Zack nodded and couldn't help but get the impression that the Boxan was showing off. He glanced at Katie. "That would be useful to have."

"We have something similar. Unfortunately, not with us here," Katie said.

They climbed up onto the sled, where the crew of the Athena banded together. The sled had railings they could hold on to, but there was no roof or canopy. The whining engines beneath engaged, and the sled lifted up, hovering just above the trees. The other two sleds joined them. Zack maintained a white-knuckled grip on the railing, and the sleds shot forward. His gut clenched, anticipating the forward momentum of the sled, but there was none. It was as if they were in a cocoon that protected them from the forces of inertia. Zack frowned. The forest below zipped by, but he felt no wind on his face. The other Athena crew members exchanged wondering glances. Even Jonah Redford's usual disapproving scowl was gone. Vehicles like the ones they were on must be the reason they hadn't seen any roads. Why would they need them? The sleds likely flew faster than any Nershal could fly and had any number of uses.

A nagging thought tugged at the recesses of Zack's mind. The Boxans and the Nershals referred to the place they were going as a research facility, but no one said what they were researching there. Why would they need to build something so remote? The only reason Zack could think of was because they had something to hide. Recognizing his normally suspicious mind at work, he nonetheless came to the same conclusion no matter how he diced it up.

"I wonder what they're hiding?" Zack asked.

"Who?" Hicks asked.

"The Nershals. We're pretty remote even with their technology, so I can't help but wonder why they would build something out here. What is it they're researching?" Zack wondered.

He glanced toward Etanu, who sat cross-legged with his back against the railing and his eyes closed.

Gaarokk turned in their direction and came over. "The official mandate of the research facility is to evaluate and catalog the local flora. There are species of plants here that are not on the Nershals' home world. Curious, don't you think?"

Zack wondered how the Boxan had heard them. They hadn't been whispering, but they hadn't been speaking all that loudly either.

"Why would that be interesting?" Zack asked.

Gaarokk glanced at the others.

"Because of the formation of this star system," Kaylan said. "One would assume the same materials would be found throughout the system. The close proximity of the Nershals' home world and this moon might support that assumption, but what they're finding is that there are fundamental differences."

"Excellent," Gaarokk said. "This opens all sorts of questions as to why some things developed and evolved here but not on the Nershals' home world. Learning about the universe is a worthy pursuit for any species. I'm glad to see the concept exists within your species."

Kaylan smiled, and Zack chewed the inside of his lip for a moment.

"If that's the only thing they're doing here, then why would they need the Enforcers?" Zack asked.

"Another excellent question. I can see why you were able to decipher the message we sent you," Gaarokk said.

"Why did you send it to us?" Kaylan asked.

"It wasn't me. It was Ma'jasalax who sent the message. She saw something in your species that warranted cultivating. As to the specifics of why, I cannot say. Perhaps you will be able to ask her one day," Gaarokk said.

The other two sleds split off from them, each heading in opposite directions. They would circle around and approach the Nershal research facility from different vantage points. The Boxans engaged their cloaking mechanisms and disappeared from view.

Zack pulled up his hood, and the others did the same. He glanced at Kaylan, who had her eyes closed, her brow crinkling in concentration. He couldn't explain how she was able to do what she could do, but he appreciated it nonetheless. He wouldn't be standing here if not for Kaylan and her abilities. He just hated all the tension between them now. He felt his throat constrict for a moment. Had he somehow wronged Kaylan? When Etanu struck her, Zack had reacted before he could form any thoughts. He was with Katie now. Shouldn't his feelings for Kaylan have faded? Was she so mad at him because she'd suddenly realized she had feelings for him? There was nothing he could do about that. He certainly couldn't talk to anyone here about it. Zack glanced at Katie, who was looking away from him. He still didn't know what he had done to garner Katie's attention. Both Katie and Kaylan were beautiful but in very different ways. With Katie there was a sultry promise of sensuousness in the sway of her hips, her dark eyes, and her tanned skin. She was strong and direct but without being domineering. Zack had always liked Kaylan's thick chestnut hair and the way it came to rest from her delicate neckline to the rise of her cheekbones. Though she never acted like it, Kaylan had regal, aristocratic beauty, with graceful facial features chiseled from artisans of the gold coast where she'd grown up. Perhaps the fact that her family was extremely wealthy had kept him from pursuing her when they were younger. What could he offer her? When he left MIT all those years ago, he'd expected Kaylan to be off ruling the world somewhere in a Manhattan high-rise by the time ten years had passed. The fact that she'd never pursued any of that spoke volumes.

Katie touched his arm. "Look at that."

The forest gave way to grasslands and open fields. The hilly landscape stretched out, and Zack could see several circular-shaped buildings that formed a complex. Each layered building was joined with its neighbor. One of the Nershals at the front of the sled spoke into his comms device. None of the others appeared to be alarmed, so Zack took his cue from them and decided not to worry about it.

One side of the complex seemed entirely made up of open balconies with small shapes zooming onto and away from them. A small smile touched Zack's lips as he realized that every child must surely fantasize about having wings and flying off whenever they wanted, but seeing the Nershals do this left Zack wondering what it would be like to fly. Flying, to the Nershals, would be as natural as walking, an activity Zack didn't think about much.

Along the outer edges of the complex were open pads where other sleds were parked. They flew over the parked sleds, and the Nershals below barely gave them a passing glance.

"Take us to the far side, closer to the maintenance entrance," Kladomaor said.

The Nershal pilot circled the complex. The entire structure was made up of sprawling decks that were six levels high and resembled giant steps carved into the hillside. The pilot slowed the sled and hovered over the rooftop of the midline level. Kladomaor told the pilot to take them down one more level, where they quickly exited the sled. The plan was that the pilot would fly away and land somewhere close by to monitor for their signal.

Zack's HUD switched to combat mode. Six Boxans were outlined, but only because they shared their positions with the rest of the group. This would keep them all from running into one another.

Zack and the Athena crew were cloistered in the center, but the Nershals inserted themselves among them. Etanu was toward the front of their group, ostensibly leading them but taking his directions from Kladomaor, who steered them to the edge of the roof. One by one they dropped down to an open terrace below. The terrace was empty. As the last of them dropped, Kladomaor motioned for them to wait.

The gray pebbled surface crunched beneath their feet as they walked. To the right were windows with darkened rooms beyond, and Zack craned his neck to peer inside but couldn't see anything. Across from them, the curvature of the building rounded away. Over their heads, rolling thunder sounded from the dark clouds creeping in.

There wasn't anyone on the terrace, and Zack kept wondering what they were going to do if any research center staff showed up. The Boxans had their weapons ready under their cloaking devices, but the rest of them didn't. They had to keep up the appearance that they belonged here.

Kladomaor led them toward a large, metallic-gray door. There was a keypad with red foreign symbols on the outside. Kladomaor had them stop again while he watched the door expectantly. Several of the Boxans crouched, scanning the area while they waited, and the Nershals with them began casually interacting.

The door opened, and out walked a female Nershal. She had pale green skin and large eyes the color of a deep sunset on a clear day, and her long limbs gracefully swung in stride as she came onto the terrace. She glanced at them as she passed, and her large eyes narrowed suspiciously. As the door hissed shut behind her, Kladomaor uncloaked himself. He stood with his arms raised slightly away from his sides, the open palms of his large hands showing.

"Ezerah, I've come to speak to you," Kladomaor said.

Ezerah's lips raised in a half snarl. "You've jammed my communications."

"I can't afford to take any chances. You must listen to me," Kladomaor said.

Ezerah's gaze swept over them, and Etanu stepped forward so she could see him.

"I don't know who you are, but you've let the Boxans poison your mind," Ezerah said.

Etanu shook his head. "No, it is the Xiiginns who poison our species with their lies and change us into something we're not."

Ezerah turned her gaze to Kladomaor. "You think coming here with them will change my mind?"

"I hoped you'd had some time to consider the things I said when we last spoke," Kladomaor said.

Ezerah's sneer faltered for a moment. "Nothing has changed. I will summon the Enforcers for you."

Kladomaor watched her for a moment, considering. "An alpha priority message was sent to this facility. We need to find out what it is."

Ezerah's mouth hung open in astonishment. "There's been no

—I will not help you," Ezerah said, stepping back from him, her wings opening.

Kladomaor sprang forward and grabbed the Nershal by the arm. Ezerah flapped her wings but to no avail. The Boxan was much too big, and there was no way she could overcome his strength on her own.

Kladomaor pulled her down and shackled her wrists. "I tried to reason with you. I'd prefer it if you would help us," Kladomaor said, and glanced back at the others, "but there are bigger things at stake than your blindness. You will help us whether you wish it or not."

Ezerah flailed and screamed.

Kladomaor nodded toward her, and Etanu raced in. They put a glowing necklace around her throat, and Ezerah's screams were cut off. Ezerah's eyes widened in horror, and no sound came out as she tried to speak.

"You will not be harmed. But I can't have you alerting anyone to our presence," Kladomaor said.

He pulled her toward the door and held her palm above the keypad. The door opened to a long corridor, and they went inside.

The Boxans uncloaked themselves, and several went on ahead to secure the area. At the sight of them, Ezerah ceased her struggling.

"I'll turn off the suppressor around your neck so you can answer. If you scream again, I'll turn it back on," Kladomaor said.

Ezerah pressed her lips together and glared at him for a moment, and then nodded.

"An alpha priority message was sent to this facility. Where would it have been processed?" Kladomaor asked.

"I already told you. There has been no message. Your intel is wrong," Ezerah said.

She glanced at the crew of the Athena under their hoods. Zack, being the closest to her, raised his head to get a better look at her, and she hissed.

"Who are they? What have you brought here? Do you seek to use other species against us?" Ezerah asked.

"They didn't bring us here," Zack said, pulling back his hood, and the others did the same.

Etanu frowned and tapped a few commands into a device on his wristband. It took a moment for Ezerah's translator to work, and her eyes widened.

"What species are you? You're not in the Confederation," Ezerah said.

"You're right, we're not," Kaylan said, coming to Zack's side. "We're Humans. We came here by accident. Kladomaor is going to help us return home."

Ezerah studied them for a moment. "The Boxans cannot be trusted. They will betray you in a tangle of lies tainted with the message of the good of the galaxy."

"It's you who've been misled," Kladomaor said. "Where is the nearest terminal?"

Ezerah yanked her arm, and Kladomaor released her. With as much poise as the Nershal could muster, she calmly walked ahead, leading them down the hall. At the end was an open doorway. Etanu and the other Nershal soldiers with them went through first and signaled to the others that it was safe.

Ezerah led them deeper into the facility, and Zack kept wondering where everyone was. At the end of the next corridor, a panel opened and a wall screen flickered to life. Ezerah navigated the interface with her shackled hands, and Kladomaor watched her closely.

"These are the communications logs for the day, and as you

can see, there is no alpha priority message. As I said before, you're wrong," Ezerah said.

Zack used his implants to probe the facility's network after Ezerah's credentials got him inside. The AI had modified the design of his implants, which increased his capabilities substantially over the others. The AI raced through the interface, listing systems until it identified something it could use.

"She's not lying. Her level of access doesn't show the message," Zack said.

Kladomaor frowned and then nodded.

"What do you mean? I am a head researcher for this facility. I have the highest access allowed," Ezerah said.

Zack tried to suppress the condescending expression on his face and failed. "No, you don't."

Ezerah's eyes narrowed scathingly. "I find your tone irksome, Human. As I said before, I have top-tiered access to the systems in this facility. Show evidence that there is an alpha priority message."

"I'm telling you that you don't have the access you think you do. If you don't believe me, look at these systems you're not allowed to access related to your communications array," Zack said.

The wall screen flickered, showing a long list of entries separated into chunks, each with a heading in red and a designation Zeta.

"If that doesn't convince you," Zack said, "here is a raw count of incoming communications links for today. Below that is the count of outgoing ones. The numbers are different, but if I bring up this designation, Zeta, then the numbers match. Someone or something is filtering your communications," Zack said.

"If I don't have access, as you claim, then how are you able to see this information?" Ezerah said.

"Because the lockout is specific to certain systems. However, the system that governs access is applicable to all who use it. Since you're part of that system, you can access the overarching analysis and logging of that system. To put it simply, even though you can't see the specific messages, the controlling system will tell you how many messages it processed and where they went. In this case, it's to the designation called Zeta," Zack said.

Kaylan looked at him, bemused.

Zack shrugged. "I've hacked enough systems to understand how they work. Though this is an alien system, the same principles for access and control still apply."

Kladomaor shifted his feet. "Still think the Xiiginns are being completely honest with you?"

Ezerah looked away, wringing her shackled hands.

Etanu stepped into her line of sight, and Ezerah gave him an accusing stare.

"Traitor," Ezerah hissed.

Etanu met her gaze. "Following blindly is not the Nershal way. If the Xiiginns don't have anything to hide, then investigating the validity of these claims shouldn't be too much of an issue."

Ezerah's gaze softened. "But you stand with the Boxans."

"I stand with our species. Kladomaor merely helped open my eyes. If there is nothing to hide, then there is no harm in checking the comms systems on the lower level," Etanu said.

"I'll take you to the operations center on this level, and you can see for yourself," Ezerah said.

Etanu glanced at Kladomaor, who nodded. They had started to head down the corridor toward another door when Kaylan called for them to stop.

"Wait," Kaylan said. "There are soldiers beyond the door. A room off to the side is full of them."

Ezerah's eyes widened in shock. "How could you know that?"

Etanu recovered first. Growling, he grabbed Ezerah and pushed her against the wall with his combat knife pressed against her throat.

"Was your plan to lead us into a pack of Enforcers?" Etanu asked, and looked at Kladomaor. "We can't trust her. She would have betrayed us all."

Kladomaor glanced at Kaylan before calmly stepping closer to Ezerah. The Boxan gently reached out toward the knife and eased it away. "We are not here to kill anyone if we can avoid it. Especially a Nershal."

Etanu let Ezerah go and watched her as a hunter stalked its prey. Ezerah kept her chin high and would not be cowed by Etanu, but when she glanced at Kladomaor her stony gaze faltered.

"Gaarokk," Kladomaor said, "find me a safe way to the operations center on this level."

The Boxan brought up his wrist, and a small holoscreen appeared. After a few moments he gestured behind them. "There is a service tunnel this way we can use to bypass the Enforcer offices that will take us into the operations center."

They went back the way they had come and stopped before a plain-looking door with a vent overhead. Gaarokk tapped a few commands into his holoscreen, and the door opened. The Nershals went in first. The Boxans engaged their cloaks, and Kladomaor told the Athena crew to pull their hoods up.

Zack entered the narrow service tunnel and knew the Boxans must be hunched over so they could fit. The service tunnel remained dark until the sensors detected their presence and the lighting increased along the walls. It was still dim, but Zack's vision adjusted quickly. The only sound was the shuffling of feet as they continued through the tunnel. When they came to the end, Gaarokk had them turn right. Kladomaor brought up the rear with Ezerah in tow.

They came to a halt before another door. The Nershals waited, and one of the Boxan soldiers leaned in toward the door.

"Two Nershals are inside," the Boxan said.

"Use the stunners," Kladomaor said.

Etanu nodded and pulled out a small silver sphere. He pressed the side, which activated tiny lights on top of the sphere, opened the door, and rolled it into the room. A few seconds went by and there was a flash of light, followed immediately by the sound of two bodies collapsing to the floor. They moved inside, and Etanu checked on the unconscious Nershals.

The operations center was much like a small version of the control room at the Boxan listening station on Pluto. Active bronze-colored holoscreens filled the wall across from them. Off to the side was a terminal, jutting out from the gray wall. Gaarokk nodded toward the terminal, and Zack headed over.

Zack tried to use his implants to access the terminal, but there were no connections. He glanced over at the unconscious Nershals being guarded by Etanu. "Can you revive one of them? They need to get us in."

"Shouldn't Ezerah be able to get in?" Etanu asked.

"She might, but her access would be as before. We need one of them. If they work in here, they would have the necessary access we need to find where the alpha priority message was sent," Zack said.

Etanu dragged one of the unconscious Nershals over to the terminal and withdrew a small vial with purple liquid from a pocket of his dark uniform. He took the lid off and held it near the Nershal's nostrils. The Nershal flinched and his eyes opened. Etanu waited with his weapon pointed at the Nershal.

"What are you doing?" the Nershal said, his eyes darting among all of them.

"What's your name?" Etanu asked.

"Kani," he said. "Please don't hurt me."

"If you cooperate you will not be harmed. We need you to access the terminal. An alpha priority message was sent here, and we need to know where it went," Etanu said.

Kani's eyes widened, and he glanced at the others. "Boxans!" Kani said, and saw Ezerah with her hands bound. "I can't access the message."

"But you can confirm there was one," Kladomaor said.

Kani looked up at the Boxan, his lips trembling. "I can't . . . they'll hurt me. They'll hurt my bondmate."

"We can protect you," Kladomaor said.

Kani shook his head and glanced at the unconscious Nershal across the room. "There are rumors of Nershals being taken. My old partner started checking into it, and he went missing."

Ezerah stepped forward and squatted down so she was eye level with Kani. "If there was suspicious activity, why didn't they report it to the Enforcers?"

Kani flinched. "It was the Enforcers who took him."

"Where did they take him?" Ezerah asked.

Kani stared at Ezerah as if he recognized her. "I've seen you before. You're a lead scientist here."

"That's right," Ezerah said. "Where did they take your coworker?"

"I don't know. I stopped asking questions," Kani said, and sucked in a shaky breath.

Ezerah glanced up at Kladomaor, who watched her expectantly. "This proves nothing."

"We'll see," Kladomaor said, and then looked at Kani. "If you help us, we will get you and your bondmate out of here."

Kani's gasping eased. "Do you promise?"

"A Boxan never breaks his word once it is given. I promise you that we will help you," Kladomaor said.

Kani nodded and pushed himself up off the floor. He went to the terminal and opened up the interface.

"It would be under the designation Zeta," Zack said.

Kani glanced over at him and then turned back to the terminal. "The log entry for an alpha message was sent down to level eleven."

Ezerah snorted. "There are only seven sub-levels in this facility."

"He just confirmed that an alpha priority message was received by this facility, and you question whether there are sub-levels of which you were not aware?" Kladomaor asked.

Ezerah looked away and didn't answer.

"You don't need to align with me and my species, but you must admit that the Xiiginns are keeping secrets from you," Kladomaor said.

Ezerah glared at him as if holding him responsible for the truth. "Kani," Ezerah said, "can you grant my identification access to sub-level eleven?"

"Don't do that," Zack said. "If you do, you'll draw unwanted attention. What we need is to use someone's identification who already has access to that level. My guess would be that a Xiiginn has access to this system."

Zack kept his head down as he spoke so the Nershal couldn't see his face.

Kladomaor nodded. "Bring up a list of Xiiginns currently at the facility."

Kani entered a few commands, and a small list displayed.

"Mar Arden!" Kladomaor growled, his flaxen eyes ablaze with hate.

Gaarokk grabbed Kladomaor. "The mission is to retrieve the message, not get revenge. Remember who is with us."

"You can take her to the colony. I want Mar Arden," Kladomaor said.

"No!" Gaarokk replied sharply. "We're not here for your vengeance. We're here for the Nershals. To expose the Xiiginns for what they truly are."

Kladomaor's shoulders rose and fell vigorously with his powerful breaths. Gaarokk leaned in and spoke quietly so only Kladomaor could hear.

Zack glanced at Kaylan, whose ashen face watched Kladomaor in horror. Zack got the sense that Kladomaor had a brooding soul, but the vehemence of his rage bordered on primal ferocity. The Boxan had seemed so calm and collected until he'd seen the name of that Xiiginn.

"What if the message is for him?" Gaarokk said.

This got Kladomaor's attention.

"Our struggle against the Xiiginns is more than just one member of the species. You must think beyond that. You've done that already by leading us this far. Don't falter now," Gaarokk said.

Kladomaor nodded and blew out a frustrated breath. "Give us Mar Arden's identity tag," Kladomaor said to Kani.

The Nershal's shaky hands zipped through the terminal's interface. He produced a small metallic card, and Etanu moved to take it, but Ezerah beat him to it.

Ezerah spun, her dark robes fanning out around her. "I want to know what's in the message."

Kladomaor regarded her for a moment and held out his hand. "Give it to me, and we'll take you with us down below."

Ezerah pressed her lips together and handed the metallic card to Etanu, spurning Kladomaor's outstretched arm.

"Your promise?" Kani said.

Kladomaor nodded. "Take him out. Get his bondmate and head to the meeting point," Kladomaor said. Two of the Nershal soldiers nodded and gestured for Kani to lead them out.

"If you remove my shackles, I will lead you to the service elevator," Ezerah said.

"Tell us where it is," Kladomaor said.

"It isn't far. We go back through the service tunnel the way we came, and it's a short distance from where we turned to get here," Ezerah said.

Kladomaor glanced at Kaylan, who had closed her eyes. After a few moments, Kaylan opened her eyes and gave Kladomaor a single nod.

Ezerah noticed the exchange but didn't say anything.

"Very well, but we'll keep the shackles on for now," Kladomaor said.

One of the Nershal soldiers took up position next to Ezerah, and they headed back into the service tunnel. The Boxans engaged their cloaks and faded from view. They moved quickly through the service tunnels and found the elevator. Because it was a service elevator, it was large enough to hold all of them.

Etanu inserted the metallic card into the slot, and the menu above changed to offer more levels. Ezerah's brow furrowed as she watched him. Etanu selected level eleven, and the doors shut.

The elevator eased them down, and Zack had to focus to feel any type of descent. After a few moments the door opened to a well-lit, deserted hallway. The white walls gleamed and were unlike any other part of the facility they had seen so far. The Nershals went ahead.

Ezerah lingered just outside the elevator. "I suppose the existence of this place pleases you."

Kladomaor disengaged his cloak. "The truth simply is. It

doesn't exist to make us happy. Does it please me for you to finally learn that the Xiiginns have been lying to your species? No, it fills me with anger and regret that we let them into the Confederation. We cultivated their species. You're paying the price for our failure."

Ezerah's crestfallen eyes looked down, and she allowed herself to be led onward.

Katie had her assault rifle ready, and Zack raised an eyebrow questioningly.

"Be ready. Anyone we run into from here on out will not be friendly. They will be among those who knowingly deceived their own kind," Katie said.

"She's right," Hicks said.

Zack swallowed hard and nodded. Down the hallway, they came to the end and turned right. The hallway split, and Klado-maor called them to a halt.

"I'm getting life readings that way, but Kani's instruction takes us in the opposite direction," Gaarokk said.

A muffled wail came from the direction of the life readings. Kladomaor frowned and nodded for two Boxans to check it out. They waited while the two Boxan soldiers scouted the area. Zack couldn't make sense of how a creature so large could move so quietly.

"Sir, you need to see this," a Boxan soldier called to them.

Kladomaor lead them in the opposite direction than they needed to go, and Zack couldn't help the sinking feeling in his stomach. They rounded the corner, and windows that gave off a blue glow lined either side of the hallway. Beyond the windows were small rooms. Zack heard Emma stifle a gasp as they saw the occupants.

Inside each of the cells were Nershals, but they looked differ-ent. Instead of the healthy greenish skin, these were almost completely black. They were wild-eyed and didn't seem to recognize the Nershals on the outside. One threw himself into the window and bounced off. Some had had their wings removed, and others had different deformities, from lost limbs to elongated features as if they were a creature that had stepped out from a nightmare.

"What happened to them?" Zack asked.

"They're being experimented on. See the head wounds on these over here. They've recently undergone some type of procedure," Kladomaor said.

Etanu and the other Nershal soldiers gazed through the windows, their bodies still as they took it all in. A deep growl sounded from a large cell toward the far end of the corridor, and the Boxans brought up their weapons. The deep growl sounded again and was accompanied by a loud slam. Even the creatures inside the cells cowed back.

They cautiously moved forward and came before a large window, but the cell beyond was dark, as if the light would only penetrate so far. Zack stood well behind the Boxans and Nershals in front of him, and had to crane his neck to catch a glimpse.

Ezerah worked her way forward until she was just outside the window, her eyes wide with fear. A massive clawed fist slammed into the window, and the creature inside roared, suddenly emerging from the darkness. The creature unfurled its wings, filling the space on either side of it, and bared rows of sharp, lethal-looking teeth. A long tail with yellow markings on one side rose behind it, and a long black stinger slammed into the window directly in front of Ezerah. The Nershal flinched backward as if she had been struck. Her breaths came in gasps, and she let out a mournful wail.

Emma stepped next to Zack. "Oh my god," Emma said.

"What?" Zack said. The thing inside was horrifying, and he hoped the cell would hold.

"Look at it," Emma said. "They've done genetic experimentation on them. Look at the features. They resemble parts of a Nershal and parts of a protokar."

Etanu raised his weapon. "We have to kill it." The Nershal soldiers followed Etanu's lead.

"Wait," Kladomaor said. "We don't even know if our weapons can hurt it. We can't take the chance of it getting loose. This is the work of Mar Arden. I've seen his work before, firsthand."

"Mar Arden," Ezerah whispered. "I've worked side by side with him."

"This is what the Xiiginns do. They take what they want. Above all they crave power," Kladomaor said.

"Look at them all. They are in so much pain," Ezerah said, her hands on her chest. "Get me to a terminal."

Ezerah didn't wait for them, but ran down the hall and found a monitoring station.

"Remove the shackles," Ezerah said.

Kladomaor keyed in a sequence on his forearm computer, and the shackles fell from Ezerah's wrists.

Ezerah brought up an interface and began entering commands. "I'm copying the research data. There are video recordings as well—" She stopped and looked up at Kladomaor. "I'm sorry. I should have listened to you before. If the Xiiginns are doing this here, who knows what else they've done."

"We brought explosives that will destroy this entire level, but first we need to get the alpha priority message," Kladomaor said, and motioned three Boxan soldiers over to him. "Set the charges for remote detonation and meet us at the comms station."

The Boxans saluted Kladomaor and left.

"Wait," Zack said. "Isn't there any way we can help them? Free them and . . . I don't know . . . do something?"

Kladomaor regarded Zack and the rest of the Athena's crew for a moment. "Compassion is an admirable quality in any species. We can't help them, and to let them roam free would be a curse. Would you want to live like this?"

Zack scanned the cells along the corridor in a vain attempt to see some kind of sign that there was hope for them. All he saw were the maddening displays of tortured souls. Bile crept up his throat, and he turned away before he got sick.

It took some coaxing, but eventually the Nershals followed Kladomaor out of there. Etanu was last to leave, and he walked stoop-shouldered, with a distant look to his eyes as if he couldn't quite believe what he had seen. The Nershal glanced at Zack and looked away.

Zack kept his eyes forward, wanting to just leave the nightmarish hallway and never return. To see the handiwork of the Xiiginns firsthand made the species more real than they had been before.

"We need to stop the Xiiginns from reaching Earth," Zack said.

"We will," Hicks said.

Kaylan stayed silent and followed the others back the way they had come. Her hands wouldn't stop shaking. She kept them close to her body so the others couldn't see. Her whole body felt as if there were hundreds of spiders crawling along her skin. She wanted to run away, putting as much distance from this place as she could, and it took all her strength not to bolt. How were they supposed to stop the Xiiginns from reaching Earth? She glanced over at Redford. His face was pale. He stopped, leaned against the wall, and vomited onto the floor. Emma stopped to help him up.

"I didn't know," Redford said, his voice a frantic whisper. He kept repeating himself.

Kaylan went to Redford's side. Since they'd gone through the wormhole, she'd blamed him for everything. She tolerated his presence because they needed his brilliance to survive, but seeing him like this gave her pause. His reckless decisions had put them all in this predicament, but the ensuing consequences were not his alone to bear.

"It's not your fault," Kaylan said. "You couldn't have known what would happen. None of us could. It's likely that at some point we would have powered on the listening station on Pluto anyway."

Redford's red-rimmed eyes widened. "I'm sorry."

Emma stayed with Redford, and Kaylan moved ahead. She caught Kladomaor watching her. The Boxan's eyes narrowed in thought, and he turned away.

They reached the area where the comms station was, but stayed hidden. There were more Nershals in the area, but no Xiiginns. Zack knew their luck with the deserted lower levels would only last so long.

Etanu dashed ahead and was followed by the Nershal soldiers with them.

"Traitors!" Etanu screamed and stepped boldly into the comms room, firing his weapon. The stunned Nershal scientists died quickly as Etanu blazed through the room, his eyes full of hate. Bright flashes were unleashed from the rest of the Nershals' weapons as they mowed down anyone in the comms station area.

The Boxans urged the crew of the Athena forward and took up positions around them. Ezerah went ahead to the console on the far side of the room and used the metallic card to access it.

Kladomaor crouched down to watch, and the rest of them

crowded around. Etanu and the others covered their flanks. The holoscreen above the console flickered to life.

"I can't find the message," Ezerah said.

"Could it have been deleted?" Kladomaor asked.

"Athena," Zack said, "can you retrieve the message if I open a connection to the console?"

"I can try," the AI said.

Kladomaor nodded, and Zack opened up a connection. Streams of code zoomed by on the holoscreen. Then a video message appeared, showing the head and shoulders of a Xiiginn.

"Mar Arden, your facility has been put on high alert. We've captured a Boxan entering the system. We believe she is of the Mardoxian Sect. Our drive took damage while capturing her ship, and we will be approaching Selebus within the next cycle. I don't need to convey the importance of the successful interrogation of any Boxan of the Mardoxian Sect. The risk is too great to bring her down to your facility. Once we reach orbit, we will have you and your team brought to the ship. Be vigilant as there is a strong likelihood she wasn't alone. If there are any doubts that she is of the Mardoxian Sect, then lay them to rest by seeing these."

The video message cut out to show a Boxan chained to the floor. The Boxan looked up, her bright green irises reflecting the light. Her mouth curved down in a pained expression, but in the next instant she stared defiantly into the camera. The Boxan's dark brown, roughened skin held the remnant wounds of a recent struggle.

"That's her!" Kaylan cried out. "She was the one I saw in the chamber."

Gaarokk gasped. "They've captured Ma'jasalax."

Kladomaor narrowed his gaze. "Why wouldn't she follow protocol? This video could be a fake in order to lure us out."

"What protocol?" Kaylan asked.

"In the event of capture, a Mardoxian priest or their protector would sacrifice themselves to prevent them from falling into enemy hands. This keeps the Xiiginns from studying those with the Mardoxian potential," Kladomaor said.

"We have to help her," Kaylan said. "We can't leave her in their hands." She felt the faint touch of Ma'jasalax from her time in the chamber. "The video is real. They have her."

Kladomaor was about to respond when an alarm blared above. The door to the room they were in slammed shut. Etanu and several Nershals sprinted to it and attempted to unlock the door.

The sneering pale face of a Xiiginn appeared on the holo-screen. The creature had purple irises and long dark hair. Its finely chiseled features and sharp angles made it stunning to look at. The creature's eyes swept the room and narrowed as it focused on the Boxans.

"Kladomaor," the Xiiginn said. "Do you feel it now? The longing? I know you do."

Kladomaor howled in rage and brought up his weapon. A blast of molten plasma destroyed the holoscreen unit.

Something hissed from the vents above them.

Another holoscreen flickered to life, followed by another until every wall showed the same face on every screen. The Xiiginn pursed his lips. "There is no escape from here. You may have gotten the alpha message, but there is nothing you can do."

Kladomaor glared at the holoscreen and then looked at Gaarokk. "Blow it!"

Gaarokk hit the detonator, and the explosion from the other side of the level shook the room. The lighting flickered and then went out. Emergency lighting engaged. The hissing coming from the air vents kept going, and Kaylan started to feel light-headed.

The Nershals began shaking their heads. Kladomaor raced to the wall and slammed a small metal box against it, then took several steps back.

The metal box glowed red and a hole melted the wall away big enough for them all to fit through.

"Let's go. The Xiiginns will be on us in moments," Klado-maor said and was first through the opening.

Glowing blue lines gleamed from the Boxans' power armor. They raced down the corridor. The Nershals prodded them along, and Zack was surprised to see that Etanu was behind him, firing a few bolts behind them from the weapon he carried. One of the Nershal soldiers shoved Kaylan to the side, and she collided with Zack. Blue bolts of energy shot past them. Eyes wide as adrenalin flooded their systems, Zack and Kaylan managed to keep their feet under them as they continued to run. They came to the elevator doors, and Kladomaor and Gaarokk forced them open, revealing a darkened shaft beyond. The Nershals teamed up, grabbed the Athena crewmember nearest them, and flew up the shaft. When a Nershal grabbed Zack's arm, a small explosion knocked them against the wall. Zack shook his head, trying to clear it.

Kladomaor stood over them, unleashing the fury of his weapon. Etanu checked the Nershal lying near Zack. "He's gone," Etanu said.

Zack glanced down and saw Kaylan sprawled on the ground. His heart twisted in his chest as he reached for her. Kaylan began to cough, and Zack pulled her to her feet. The others had all gone up the shaft except the Boxans and Etanu.

"Use the jetpack," Kladomaor shouted.

Zack looked down at his chest. He'd forgotten he still wore the small Nershal jetpack. He glanced up the long shaft above them. Kaylan locked arms with him and Etanu.

"Long bursts," Etanu said.

Zack nodded and slammed his palm on the clasp on his chest. Zack's feet left the ground, and he clutched Kaylan's arm to him. Etanu flapped his wings and raced upward. The Boxans used their powered armor to scale the shaft, propelling themselves almost as fast as the Nershals flew.

Several bolts shot past them, and Kladomaor withdrew a silver sphere that glowed green. The Boxan hurled it below. The shockwave of a large explosion chased them up the remainder of the shaft. They exited the elevator shaft to the roof, where they caught up to the others. Alarms were blaring throughout the facility. The Nershals who resided there ran in different directions.

Kladomaor signaled for the sled to come pick them up, and they raced to the meeting point. Black-armored Nershal Enforcers emerged onto a rooftop across from their position. They quickly spotted them and readied their weapons. Green bolts shot toward them.

Zack ran but kept glancing back. Katie was near him and stopped to return fire from her assault rifle. She hit her mark, and the glowing pulsar darts slammed into the black Enforcer armor. Wherever she hit them, part of their armor glowed red. She kept pelting the spot until the darts melted through. The Nershal sled flew overhead and provided cover fire for them while they boarded. Once the last of them was on board, the sled raced away. Zack grabbed the railing and glanced around to check that they had all made it. They were all there. He spotted Etanu, who positioned himself near Ezerah.

Zack's heart was pounding, and he couldn't get his limbs to stop shaking. The firefight had been so sudden that he couldn't even keep track of what was happening other than to keep running. Katie was next to him. She kept glancing behind them, looking for signs of pursuit. She saw him looking and reached out to him.

"You're okay," Katie said.

Zack took her hand and gave it a gentle squeeze. They were safe for the moment, but who knew for how long.

Chapter Eighteen

S moke rose from the research facility, but the Enforcers hadn't scrambled any kind of pursuit. The other two sleds headed off in different directions to throw the Enforcers off the trail. They'd achieved total surprise against the Xiiginns, and now they had evidence of wrongdoing to use against them with the Nershals.

"Why aren't they following us?" Zack asked.

Gaarokk disengaged his helmet and looked at Zack. The Boxan's large flaxen eyes regarded Zack, and then he leaned in. "Kladomaor had one of the other teams deploy suppressors near the Enforcers' section of the facility to block communications. The Enforcers who were monitoring likely believed it to be a glitch in their systems. I've seen Kladomaor use similar tactics at other installations," Gaarokk said.

"Won't the Nershals catch on to what you're doing?" Hicks asked.

"The probability is high for that outcome. Were this a

Nershal military installation, the tactic might not have worked so well," Gaarokk said.

Kaylan shook her head and crossed her arms tightly. Her eyes were closed as if she were dreaming.

Zack frowned and asked if she was okay. When she didn't answer, he glanced up at Gaarokk, who watched Kaylan intently. Zack reached out and gently patted her on the back. "Kaylan," Zack said.

Kaylan's eyes snapped open and she gasped. Her eyes darted around as if she didn't remember where she was.

"It's okay. We're on the sled, heading away from the facility," Zack said.

Kaylan rubbed the top of her chest. "I can feel her pain," Kaylan said.

"Whose pain?" Zack asked.

Kaylan look up at Gaarokk. "Ma'jasalax."

Gaarokk frowned in thought. "What exactly are you feeling?"

"It's like there is something pressing in from all sides of my—her—head. It's pounding. She fights back, keeping whatever they're doing at bay, but it hurts. I can't see anything around her. Everything is completely dark," Kaylan said, and squeezed her eyes shut, wincing.

"Not so deeply. Pull yourself back," Gaarokk said. "Open your eyes. It will help distance you from what you're seeing."

Kaylan opened her eyes.

"Good," Gaarokk said. "Now, steady your breathing and focus on being right here."

Kaylan took a deep breath and slowly released it. Zack could see some of the tension loosen in her shoulders.

"Thank you," Kaylan said. "I can still sense it, but it's not like it was before."

"Is this normal?" Zack asked.

"She is extraordinarily gifted," Gaarokk said. "Only the upper echelons of the Mardoxian Sect can immerse themselves so completely. Finding this trait in another species has never happened before."

"I don't even understand how it works. To me it's just like focusing on a problem or a thought I have," Kaylan said.

"You can just do it. The potential or skill is innate. Tell me, are there others from your home world who can do as you do?" Gaarokk asked.

Kaylan glanced at the others and nodded. "Yes, but it's . . . not really accepted. There have been so many pretenders that the practice is frowned upon. Some organizations study it in secret. I didn't even know I could do this until a short while ago."

Gaarokk nodded, giving them a knowing smile. "That is understandable. Your species is still quite young."

"You call what Kaylan can do the Mardoxian potential. What does that even mean?" Zack asked.

"Not the easiest thing to answer, but I will try and put it in terms you can understand," Gaarokk said. "We are all part of the great expanse, loosely connected. Worlds like these promote certain types of life. The air we breathe is similar. Water and the natural resources we consume share a bond."

"Are there other types of worlds not like this one that have life on them?" Zack asked.

Gaarokk nodded. "There are some. We haven't studied them to any great extent. Communicating with the species that dwell on those planets is difficult. Our translator program is based on a language that is spoken. Not every species out there communicates this way. But we're getting away from the original question. Most species we've encountered can't see beyond the choices directly in front of them. We're no different, but those of us with the Mardoxian potential can see beyond that. Their connection to the great expanse supersedes ours. Think of it as the next step on the evolutionary pathway. Has your species theorized about the existence of the multiverse?"

"You mean that there are multiple universes in existence at any given moment?" Kaylan asked.

Gaarokk nodded. "That's part of it. The Mardoxian potential allows for a heightened connection to the great expanse. You can use this to see beyond any obstacle in your path."

"Does it have any limitations?" Kaylan asked.

"You tell me. While the theory says that the potential is within all life forms, I do not have it within me to any great extent," Gaarokk said.

"Why are the Xiiginns so keen to have this ability?" Zack asked.

"Can you think of nothing?" Gaarokk asked.

Zack frowned in thought. "Things could have gone much worse for us in the research facility if Kaylan hadn't warned us, but I guess I'm curious as to what else the Mardoxian potential can do."

"I'm not a soldier. Kladomaor is a military leader among my species. From what I remember of your history, your species is no stranger to wars and conflict. Think of the advantage that one with the Mardoxian potential could offer during a conflict, be it upon a planetary surface or in the great expanse. Rarer still are those who can use their abilities to affect the world around them . . ." Gaarokk stopped speaking. "I'm needed," Gaarokk said, and headed to the front of the sled where Kladomaor was.

Zack looked at Kaylan. "What do you think that meant?"

Kaylan looked toward the front of the sled. "I'm not sure," she said.

The sun was setting on this strange world, and Zack felt like it had been a couple of days since they had left the Athena to come down here. His stomach growled, and Zack realized he couldn't remember when he'd last eaten. The sled had soft ambient lighting that ran along the floor and gave off enough light for them to see by. Zack reached inside his pocket and pulled out an oatmeal raisin protein bar. He was so hungry that he completely ignored the cardboard consistency of it and devoured the whole thing.

Zack glanced off to the side and could hear the low whine of another sled flying next to them, but he couldn't see it at all. As he was focused on this, the sled slowed down and they descended into an open area. His internal HUD showed that the shuttle was a short distance away from them.

The sled came to a stop and hovered less than a foot off of the ground. They left the craft, and within a few minutes more sleds came to the area. Zack barely stifled a yawn.

"Better grab what rest you can. I don't think we'll be here very long," Hicks said.

"I'm so tired," Zack said. "What are we going to do now?"

"That Boxan being a prisoner of the Xiiginns has gotten them really upset," Hicks said.

"Do they honestly expect us to go with them on this rescue mission they keep talking about?" Redford asked.

"We need their help to get back to Earth, so we should help them however we can," Kaylan said.

Redford's mouth hung open. "I think we've risked more than enough on this mission already."

Kaylan was about to respond, but Hicks cut her off.

"Just get some rest. You'll be all right," Hicks said.

"Is that supposed to motivate me?" Redford asked.

"No," Hick said, "it means that we've been through a lot and there is more coming. You're tired and not thinking straight. You may be a brilliant scientist, but being here is going to require us all to do more than we ever thought we could."

Emma coaxed Redford away and sat down. More Nershals were arriving, eager to hear about what they'd learned at the research facility.

Hicks handed out small yellow pills for them to dissolve in their water containers. "It'll prevent dehydration and help take the edge off exhaustion," Hicks said.

Zack cast the pill into his water and gulped it down. He immediately felt the pressure around his head lessen, and his eyes didn't feel quite so heavy.

Kladomaor approached them, with Etanu walking behind him. They stopped before the Athena crew, and those who were sitting came to their feet.

"Udonzari wishes to speak with all of you," Kladomaor said. "Please, if you will follow me."

Something in the formality of Kladomaor's tone conveyed the importance of what was about to happen. Zack hoped he wouldn't get pulled into another rite. He doubted he could survive another trek through a valley filled with protokars.

It was a short walk through the makeshift camp. No one was settling in, and the state of readiness gave Zack the impression that the Nershals and Boxans, at least, were ready to leave at a moment's notice.

Katie walked beside him. "Stay close to me," she said.

"I don't know how you do it," Zack said.

Katie looked at him with a raised brow.

"Stay so focused and alert. Both you and Hicks are constantly watching and evaluating everything around us," Zack said.

"We've been in high-pressure situations before. It's part of our training," Katie said.

"Even for this?" Zack said, and gestured around them.

"No, you're right. This is different. If you're wondering if I'm scared, then yes, I am afraid, but I don't let fear override my ability to take action. I take in the information available, assess the risks, and make decisions," Katie said.

"What if you make a mistake?" Zack asked.

"In a situation like this, someone could get hurt, or worse. But if it means life or death, then I'd rather fight to survive," Katie said.

"Remind me never to make you angry with me," Zack said.

Katie's gaze softened and she smiled. Hicks and Kaylan walked ahead of them. Katie's mouth opened, and an unformed question took shape on her lips, but she hesitated.

"What is it?" Zack asked.

Katie shook her head. "It's nothing."

Zack tilted his head to the side. "No, it isn't. Come on, you can tell me."

Katie shook her head. "Not the right time. We need to focus on getting out of here."

Zack frowned. *It's never the right time*, he thought, *for any of us*.

Udonzari turned toward them and the Nershal soldiers. Etanu left the Athena crew and went to his father's side. Ezerah stood near them, her orange eyes alight with unfocused fury. She looked up at their approach and watched them curiously.

Udonzari looked at the crew of the Athena. "Kladomaor has given us a preliminary report of what you've discovered at the research facility. Before we get to that, I must acknowledge that you've done a great service for my species. Honor is one of the core pillars of our society. Showing gratitude for a service is another. I understand your actions weren't selfless and that the Boxans have promised to aid your return to your home star system. I would like you to know that you've earned our gratitude, and if there is ever a service we can provide, you have but to ask. Please accept these tokens."

A Nershal soldier opened a silver box. Inside were six small bronze-colored shafts with the shape of a triangle at each of the ends. The shafts were engraved with alien symbols, and despite being solid they had very little weight. Zack took one of them and waited for the translation to appear on his internal display, but nothing appeared. He didn't think it was right to ask.

"Present these to any of my species, and they will help you," Udonzari said.

"Thank you," Kaylan said, speaking for all of them.

"Udonzari," Kladomaor said, "there is an inbound Xiiginn cruiser heading here. They have one of our species held prisoner."

The older Nershal regarded the Boxan for a moment. "What do you propose?"

"Rally the Nershals. Help us take the cruiser," Kladomaor said.

Udonzari frowned in thought and glanced at their small camp. "There aren't enough of us to help you. Stealth would be your ally in this venture."

"We have evidence of what the Xiiginns have been doing here. Ezerah worked at the facility and can validate the evidence provided. Share this information," Kladomaor said.

"We will share the information, but these things take time. Planning and proper execution are worth more than simply releasing this information on our home world," Udonzari said.

Kladomaor pressed his lips together. "The longer you wait, the more of your species fall victim to the Xiiginns."

Udonzari narrowed his gaze at the Boxan. "You and your team have done us a great service, but it doesn't erase the lies visited upon us by your species."

"The Star Shroud was as much for your protection as it was for ours," Kladomaor said.

"Perhaps, but anything shrouded in mystery serves those who control that mystery more than those who live under it," Udonzari said.

"The cultivation program—" Kladomaor began to say.

"The Nershals' place in the Confederation will not be decided today," Ezerah said, drawing everyone's attention. "Nor will we decide to ally with your species on this night."

Udonzari glanced at Ezerah and gave a small nod. It was at that moment that Zack realized Ezerah was someone of significance in the Nershal hierarchy. He just wished he knew how the Nershals were organized.

"As I've said before," Kladomaor said, "our intention in coming here is to bring to light the wrongs the Xiiginns have wrought upon the Nershals."

"Did you know they were experimenting on us?" Ezerah asked.

"We suspected, but without evidence—and in light of our current relations—we thought it prudent to find proof first," Kladomaor said.

Udonzari nodded. "Your actions dictate your path. I can find no fault in your reasoning, but the reality of the situation is that we don't have the resources to launch a full-scale assault on the Xiiginn cruiser. Also, there are Nershals serving on that cruiser in good faith. They are unaware of the wrongs being done, and I cannot order their deaths based upon one of your species being held prisoner."

"So you won't help us at all?" Kladomaor asked.

"I cannot," Udonzari said. "Not until we bring to light the wrongs the Xiiginns have perpetrated upon our species. The aftermath will be hard for some to take. The Xiiginns will not let this go without a fight."

"I understand," Kladomaor said. "I want you to know the Boxans will be ready to stand with you if you ask. The prisoner on board the Xiiginn cruiser is of the Mardoxian Sect."

The Nershals around them shifted their feet, and an immediate hush swept over them.

"Who?" Udonzari asked quietly.

"Ma'jasalax is their prisoner," Kladomaor said. "She was on her way here."

Udonzari looked away. "I'm sorry. Even for one such as her—"

"What if we asked for volunteers?" Ezerah said. "I volunteer. Which of you will stand with the Boxans in their time of need?"

Ezerah's gaze settled upon Etanu, but he didn't say anything.

"It's hard for them to volunteer for this given our history with the Boxans," Udonzari said.

"I agree that the Boxans' terms for entrance into the Confederation are built on a process by which species like ours are misled. I, myself, have both loved and hated the Boxans for the Star Shroud that kept the Nershals ignorant of the galaxy. It also kept us safe. Udonzari, you are Etanu's father. Didn't you ever tell a small lie to him as a child to comfort and protect him?" Ezerah asked.

Udonzari considered this for a moment. "The Nershals are not children."

Ezerah shook her head. "No, we're not. Neither are we all-knowing and so wise that we're infallible. Nor are they," Ezerah said, gesturing toward Kladomaor. "I ask for five volunteers to join us."

"Nershals have already died for this," Etanu said.

"And many more will die before this plays out," Ezerah said, and turned her gaze to the soldiers gathered around. "Look at me. Decide for yourselves. Aiding the Boxans to free one of the enlightened ones is our duty. Five of you are barely a token force but will allow the others to keep their honor intact."

The Nershals began glancing at one another. After a few minutes, four Nershals came to stand beside Ezerah, but no more.

"You have four volunteers," Etanu said.

"No, son, she has five," Udonzari said. "You will go with them."

"You can't order me to do this," Etanu said.

Udonzari leveled his gaze at his son. "I don't have to. Your debt to the Human called Zack will compel you to do this."

Etanu's eyes darted to Zack for a moment and then back to his father. "I have fulfilled that debt. I saved his life at the facility."

"How far you've fallen if you believe that leaving the facility having saved your own skin as much as his counts as a debt fulfilled," Udonzari said.

Etanu glared at his father and then joined the others at Ezerah's side.

"There is hope for you yet," Udonzari said, and turned to Kladomaor. "We have much to do, and I suspect you will be leaving soon."

"You are correct, but I will return. We will not abandon you to the Xiiginns. Once you turn against them, their true intentions will be revealed," Kladomaor said.

"The light has been passed. It is up to us now to show the lies of the Xiiginns to the rest of our species," Udonzari said.

The Nershals withdrew and left them, and the temporary camp grew silent. The remaining Nershals took their ease and checked their weapons. Etanu handed a weapon to Ezerah.

"So what's the plan?" Zack asked, breaking the silence.

Kladomaor turned toward them. "The plan is for you to return to your ship and wait for us. We'll infiltrate the Xiiginn cruiser and rescue Ma'jasalax."

"You're not going without me," Kaylan said. "Ma'jasalax came here because I went into the chamber."

Kladomaor crossed his massive arms and narrowed his gaze. "You do not dictate to me the terms of my own operation."

"We can help you," Kaylan said.

"You've already helped. I'm trying to keep you away from the Xiiginns to prevent another species from falling under their influence. The less they know about you, the better," Kladomaor said.

"Sooner or later we *will* cross paths with them," Hicks said. "Better we learn more about their effects on us now than learn about it when they come to Earth."

Kladomaor clenched his hands in frustration. "You don't know what you're saying." The Boxan broke off, muttering to himself.

"How would you propose to help?" Gaarokk asked, earning a glower from Kladomaor.

"We have our shuttle—" Hicks said.

"A non-military vessel. The moment you were detected they could destroy you," Kladomaor said.

"They didn't detect us coming down to this moon," Hicks said.

"That is correct," Gaarokk said, "but now they are on high alert. They will be looking for anything out of the ordinary. Because your shuttle offers nothing in the way of defense, it doesn't make sense to risk it."

"We have other equipment to help get aboard the Xiiginn cruiser," Kaylan said.

Gaarokk waited patiently for her to continue.

"We have a small vessel that is used for mining and salvage. We could use it to cut through the hull and get aboard that way," Kaylan said.

Kladomaor shook his head. "We've scanned your ship. While the vessel of which you speak probably could cut through the hull eventually, it would take many hours to do so—hours we don't have. The technology you've brought with you—while I acknowledge is a great achievement for your species—in terms of space warfare is hopelessly outclassed."

Kaylan clamped her mouth shut and took a deep breath. "Okay, there's me. You've seen what I can do. How will you find her without me? By now they must know you'll be coming."

"Not necessarily," Kladomaor said. "We knocked out the research facility's communications. They'll be unable to send word out. We'll use our stealth ship to beat any of the Xiiginns here to the ship. If we fail to rescue Ma'jasalax, we'll take out their ship."

Kaylan gasped. "You would kill her rather than let her fall into their hands?"

"You are not a soldier, so I don't expect you to understand," Kladomaor said, and looked at Hicks and Katie. "You two are soldiers. You must understand why our actions must be so."

Kaylan glanced at Hicks, who wore a hardened expression. The same was mirrored on Katie's face.

"War is ugly, and there are times where sacrifice is required to prevent an even greater evil from spreading," Hicks said.

Kaylan turned back toward Kladomaor. "All the more reason for you to bring me with you. I can come alone—"

"No!" several members of the Athena's crew said at the same time.

"We stick together," Hicks said.

The others gave approving nods. Kaylan felt the edges of her lips curve upward and faced Kladomaor once more.

"She told *me* to find her. It was the last thing she said to me. Please, you must let us help you find her," Kaylan said.

Kladomaor frowned as he regarded them. His unrelenting gaze was answer enough that he would not be swayed.

Kaylan looked away, shaking her head in frustration. "It's almost like she knew something like this would happen," she muttered.

"What was that?" Gaarokk said.

"I said that it's like she knew this would happen," Kaylan said.

Gaarokk glanced at Kladomaor. "Perhaps you should reconsider. There is no precedent for this with any other species. But there have been those in the Mardoxian Sect who are able to form connections to each other. Their perceptions become unparalleled. We can't leave Ma'jasalax to the Xiiginns, nor can we follow the same protocols that led us down this road."

"It was those protocols that allowed us to survive this long. They are in place for a reason," Kladomaor said.

Hicks cleared his throat. "I don't fully understand all the implications you're talking about, but I do know this. Katie and I once had a commanding officer who used to say that if you can't adapt to the current situation, your defeat is all but assured. It would be wrong of me to make an argument about the protocols you have in place that allowed you to survive this long war, but the situation is changing. Like it or not, we're here. The Human race is going to be part of this conflict. There is no avoiding it now. Our technology may not be as advanced as yours, but neither is our dependency on that technology."

At some point the Nershals had regained their feet. Etanu looked at Hicks and gave him an approving nod.

"What would you propose?" Kladomaor asked.

Hicks raised his wrist and engaged his PDA. "We mapped the system of planets on our way here," Hicks said. A small holographic image expanded from his PDA. "There are six lifeless moons that orbit the gas giant here. I propose we use them to keep our presence from being detected. We'll hide behind the furthest moon and approach the Xiiginn cruiser as it passes, sneak on board, find where she's being held, and get off before the cruiser reaches here. At some point they're going to learn about our presence. I'd much rather have some extra time aboard their ship prior to them finding out about us. You said the facility's communications have been taken out. Perhaps we can convince those other Nershals to help us on the surface to make sure the Xiiginns can't get word out."

"Udonzari said they couldn't help us on the ship," Gaarokk said. "He didn't say anything about not being able to help from the surface. He might be open to such a suggestion. What do you think?" Gaarokk asked.

Kladomaor regarded Hicks. "I think it would be unwise of anyone to underestimate your species."

Hicks grinned.

Kladomaor looked at Kaylan. "Alright, you win. We'll do this thing together."

A slow smile stole across Kaylan's face, and she nodded. She felt a great weight lift from her shoulders. She couldn't explain why, but she knew they had to be part of the rescue mission or it would fail. Now she just hoped they all survived it. She glanced at Zack. His dark, penetrating eyes had been focused on the discussion and he'd been unusually quiet, but she could tell he wasn't so afraid anymore. Back on Earth he had been almost paralyzed at the thought of going into space. He'd come such a long way in a short amount of time. They all had, but the changes were so much more noticeable with Zack. Twice now he had risked his life to save hers. Perhaps Hicks was right and she should throw caution to the wind and tell Zack how she truly felt. She quickly silenced the inner voices that told her she was being foolish for even considering such a notion. She glanced at Katie, who was extremely beautiful and strong. She could see why Zack was with her. What she hated most of all was that there had been a time when Zack had looked at her the way he was looking at Katie right now. She hated that she was losing him and that it might already be too late. It might have been easier on her if Katie had been a bad person who treated Zack poorly, but that wasn't the case at all. They simply were together. Kaylan just needed to tell Zack how she felt about him, and she had no idea how she was going to do it.

Chapter Nineteen

They would be leaving soon, much sooner than Kladomaor had originally expected when they'd first come to this moon. Circumstances had changed in ways he had not anticipated. Some things were a confirmation of what he had suspected regarding the state of the Nershals' relations with the Xiiginns. Some of the Nershals had begun to realize that their dealings with the Xiiginns weren't in their best interests. On the other hand, many Nershals believed the same thing about their dealings with his own race. Boxans were still linked to mistrust and, in some rare cases, outright betrayal. Had the Boxan Council been wrong for instituting the Star Shroud systems to keep the peace in their astronomical neighborhood? The question had been debated since the Star Shroud program's inception, but it hadn't been until the betrayal of the Xiiginns that the Boxans had begun to seriously consider whether what they were doing was wrong. The Star Shroud had been used to prevent wanton destruction from warlike species. In most installations, it blocked incoming and outgoing signals into space, filtering the view of the galaxy to the star systems the shroud surrounded. They'd found the technology hundreds of years ago among the remnant skeletons of a galactic war that had occurred before the Boxans' first ventures into the great expanse. Kladomaor knew the history; every Boxan did. The Boxans were stargazers. They'd spent hundreds of years observing the great expanse, learning its rhythms and the order of things. As they started their own exploration, they noticed entire star systems winking out of existence. Some of these systems simply ceased to exist and were swallowed whole by darkness. Others flared brightly as entire systems were engulfed by exploding stars. The Boxans had done what they always had—observed and recorded. They eventually journeyed to their nearest neighboring star system and discovered a dead system of planets. Vast remnant structures built in space were radically more advanced than anything the Boxans had built, but the foundations of such technology were prevalent in what the Boxans had already accomplished. The question the Boxans struggled with was why would such an advanced species capable of such technological wonders become entangled in a galactic war with a neighboring species? Surely there was enough room to coexist. Presumably, with technological advancement came wisdom, but instead there was destruction on a cosmic scale. Such events had affected other star systems teeming with more primitive life, and the effects were sometimes catastrophic. The Boxans took it upon themselves to devise a way to guide space-faring species.

"Were we wrong, Gaarokk?" Kladomaor asked. He found that the scientist offered keen insights that Kladomaor appreciated. If one spent much of one's time around only soldiers, the perspective gained wasn't all that different. Gaarokk had been standing at his side, quietly thinking his own thoughts.

"Wrong about what?" Gaarokk asked.

202 • KEN LOZITO

"The Star Shroud. Were we wrong to institute that program and keep the potentially advanced species ignorant of their galactic neighbors?" Kladomaor asked.

"Some would think so."

"What do you believe?" Kladomaor asked.

Gaarokk considered the question for a moment. "In some cases it was the right thing to do; however, in other cases the Star Shroud wasn't appropriate. At some point in our history it became a way for us to control the galaxy."

"So you think an outcome like what happened with the Xiiginns was inevitable?"

"The Xiiginns proved that our program and judgment were flawed; otherwise why wouldn't we have seen the Xiiginns for the evil they truly were?" Gaarokk said.

"It was a mistake to allow the Xiiginns into the Confederation, but does that mean we were wrong for putting them in that position? Should the Star Shroud program itself be abandoned?" Kladomaor asked.

Gaarokk eyed Kladomaor. "Are you having a crisis of faith, my friend? You've always been a stalwart supporter of the program and the importance it had for the galaxy."

"I used to believe it, but now I'm starting to think that there are some instances where it wasn't appropriate. The Xiiginns caught us being complacent, but if not them, perhaps it would have been some other species. Every species we brought into the Confederation harbored bad feelings about having been subjected to the Star Shroud program, but all eventually came around to realizing its importance to the greater good. Now the more primitive species are paying the price for our arrogance in believing we had a right to control everything," Kladomaor said.

"We started off with the best of intentions. We wanted to

protect ourselves and those species that showed an inclination toward harmony," Gaarokk said.

"Ma'jasalax once told me that the Star Shroud was our biggest folly. This was before the Xiiginns betrayed us," Klado-maor said.

"I had no idea you'd known her for that long. Members of the Mardoxian Sect always had greater insight than any ruling council, but none of them sensed the evil in the Xiiginns. And if the Xiiginns ever learned of the Mardoxian potential in Humans, they would pounce on that star system with all their might. If we can help the Humans with their defenses, they stand a much better chance of survival," Gaarokk said.

"What if they don't want our help?" Kladomaor asked.

Gaarokk pressed his lips together. "That is their prerogative."

"I will keep Kaylan close to me and protect her myself," Kladomaor said.

"You may need to stand in line," Gaarokk said. "One thing I've noticed about these Humans is that they are willing to set aside their differences in order to survive. At the same time, their tolerance of deviant behavior will only go so far before they take it upon themselves to improve the situation."

"Some of them are quite clever. I may have been wrong in some of my assertions about the Star Shroud program, but I am right that the Humans are still an immature species," Kladomaor said, raising his hand to stave off Gaarokk's reply. "One with potential, but they still have much to learn."

"Agreed," Gaarokk said. "I meant to ask you why you agreed to the Human's plan for infiltrating the cruiser."

"Because I hadn't considered it, and I'm betting the Xiiginns haven't considered it either. The Xiiginns aren't equipped to repel boarders. They are too sure of their own power," Kladomaor said.

"We can still fall victim to that power," Gaarokk said.

Kladomaor nodded. "But we also have something they don't —a Human with the Mardoxian potential and another Human with a unique version of our artificial intelligence construct."

"Zack is quite clever. The artificial intelligence construct they're using is something unique when compared with what runs the listening stations. It merged with their own systems and works to protect their ship and its crew," Gaarokk said.

"And it can overcome the security protocols used by the Xiiginns," Kladomaor said.

Ezerah approached them. "There is something I think you should know."

Kladomaor nodded for her to continue.

"I was scheduled to leave on the Xiiginn cruiser as part of a research program. As part of standard practice, my access was already transferred to the ship during a scheduled data burst. There is no reason to think those orders have changed," Ezerah said.

"You believe you can help us access the ship using your credentials?" Kladomaor said.

"Yes, but I have one request," Ezerah said.

Kladomaor narrowed his gaze for a moment. "What is it?"

Ezerah turned to the tree line and screeched a call. The Nershal's call was answered in the form of a large protokar bursting from the forest and barreling toward them. The creature's clawed feet ripped into the ground, propelling it forward. Kladomaor knew those claws could tear into even their armor. Long, thick, yellow-and-purple hair whisked in the wind, and its barbed tail ended in a curved stinger. This protokar was loyal to Ezerah. Kladomaor knew the creature would die to protect her.

"I can't leave Dari behind," Ezerah said.

Gaarokk took several steps back as Dari closed in. The

protokar came to a halt at Ezerah's side. She scratched him along the back of his neck, which he seemed to like.

"The protokar could turn on us," Kladomaor said.

"Not likely," Ezerah said.

"We haven't encountered a species that can completely resist the Xiiginns," Kladomaor said.

Ezerah frowned. "He won't turn against me."

"That's what I thought when my own soldiers turned against me at the hands of the Xiiginns," Kladomaor said, and suppressed the bitter memories threatening to well up within him.

This gave Ezerah pause. She glanced at Dari, who watched her with twin sets of green eyes that almost glowed in the twilight of their camp.

"He can come. If he shows any sign of turning against us, I will have him put down," Kladomaor said.

Ezerah's lips thinned and her eyes narrowed, but she nodded.

"The ship is almost here. It's time to leave," Kladomaor said, and returned to the others with Gaarokk and Ezerah walking at his side. The protokar called Dari followed behind them.

Chapter Twenty

Zack sat aboard the Athena's shuttle. They were moments from lifting off, waiting for the signal from Kladomaor. Zack sagged against his seat and rested his eyes. They needed to get back to the Athena to resupply and prep for a short journey to Selebus's furthest moon, but Kladomaor had been fussy about moving their ship. He was concerned about it being detected or, more accurately, the fusion core being detected. Gaarokk had run some type of remote analysis from the Boxans' ship and decided that the power output from the Athena's fusion reactor was minuscule in comparison to other ships. The Athena would likely be undetected by anything the Xiiginns had.

Zack shivered as he recalled the image of the Xiiginns and their brief encounter with one at the research facility. He might have been feeding off the Boxans' fear of them, but Zack couldn't feel anything but apprehension at the thought of crossing paths with a Xiiginn in person. The likelihood of crossing paths was compounded by the fact that they were going to sneak aboard one of the Xiiginns' ships. Only a few of them were going, and

Zack was one of the lucky few who got to go. Zack snorted to himself. He wouldn't have had it any other way. He might not have been a soldier like Hicks and Katie or have some type of special ability that allowed him to see places he'd never been like Kaylan, but he had skills.

"Toolkit updated successfully with new parameters gleaned from the research facility," the Athena's AI said for Zack alone.

Zack sighed in relief. "Good. If it works, we might get lucky."

Katie looked up at him. "Who are you talking to?" she asked.

"Athena," Zack said. "It finished compiling the data from the research facility. I'm hoping it will help with access aboard the Xiiginn ship."

"What did you take?" Katie asked.

"The framework for their automated processes that I thought might be useful and a copy of Mar Arden's credentials," Zack said.

Katie shook her head.

Zack shrugged and smiled. "You're good with a gun and can fly a spacecraft. I'm good with computer systems and getting an artificial intelligence to help me bypass security protocols."

They got Kladomaor's signal, and Kaylan engaged the engines. The shuttle lifted off the ground and sped away. They broke through the atmosphere and headed back toward the Athena. As they got closer, Zack couldn't help but crane his neck to see the ship through the window. The gleaming silver hull of the Athena grew bigger as they approached. The half-moon, saucer-shaped front where the bridge resided, bearing the fiery wings of a phoenix with an astronaut standing in the middle, came into view. The large cylinders that hosted the different labs and living quarters came next. Zack couldn't explain why, but it filled him with a sense of pride that the

Athena was such a beautiful craft. The rest of the crew also silently admired their ship as the shuttle made its final approach.

Kaylan docked the shuttle with the Athena and they disembarked.

"We'll meet on the bridge in thirty minutes," Kaylan said.

Zack stowed his gear and swapped out the power supply to his suit so it would be fully charged in time for them to leave. Brenda insisted on subjecting them all to her medical scanners, but Zack decided he'd much rather have a shower first and slipped away in the opposite direction, stopping off at his room to deposit the Nershal jetpack. The thing had come in so handy that he was determined to bring it along on their current mission.

He grabbed a change of clothes and tiptoed across the hallway to the showers, where the sensors, knowing his preferences, automatically adjusted the water temperature. Zack stepped into the shower and sighed happily as the hot water cascaded down his back. Squeezing his eyes shut, he ducked his head under streams of water coming from the showerhead while blindly reaching for soap from the dispenser and washing himself. He hadn't realized how filthy he had been until he saw the last remnants of dirt cascading through the drain. Zack turned off the water and jets of warm air dried him in seconds. There were no towels because every bit of water had to be recycled and purified for later use, but the dryers worked wonders. He put on a fresh set of clothes and felt a hundred percent better than when he had walked in.

As Zack was leaving, Kaylan was coming in.

"I was just about to head to the med bay. I just wanted to shower first," Zack said.

Kaylan smiled. "Me too. You just beat me to it," she said.

Zack snorted. "I know Brenda means well, but she can be a tyrant sometimes."

Kaylan laughed, and Zack realized it had been a while since he had heard her do so.

"How are you doing?" Zack asked.

"I'm fine," Kaylan said.

"Yeah, me too, but given what we're about to do, I don't mind admitting that my prevailing sense of terror has become almost normal for me," Zack said.

Kaylan watched him for a moment. "I wanted to thank you for what you did on the planet. When Etanu . . ."

Zack felt his cheeks flush. "Oh, that was nothing. I'm sure Hicks—"

Kaylan stepped closer and placed her hand on his arm. Zack felt his skin grow warm at her touch.

"It wasn't 'nothing,' and then you had to risk your life in that stupid rite," Kaylan said.

Zack felt like his insides were twisting up. He swallowed hard. "You're welcome," he said.

Zack looked away, hearing a couple of voices from down the hallway, and when he turned back to Kaylan, he caught sight of her stepping into one of the shower stalls. He blew out the breath he'd been holding and headed for the med bay.

A short while later the crew of the Athena gathered on the bridge around the planning table.

"The Nav computer has the course for the rendezvous point. The Athena will remain near Selebus," Kaylan said. "A small team comprised of myself, Hicks, Katie, Zack, and Jonah will be going aboard Kladomaor's ship to infiltrate the Xiiginn cruiser."

"Commander," Vitomir said, "would you consider bringing one more?"

"No, I need the rest of you to remain with the Athena,"

Kaylan said, and could sense the frustration building from the others. "We can't all go. The rest of you will remain here and keep the ship prepped. In the event that we don't make it back, you are to make contact with Udonzari, who will help you return to Earth. Brenda will take command after we leave."

Vitomir nodded.

"I'm not sure why you're bringing me along," Redford said.

"Because," Kaylan said, "next to Zack, you're the foremost expert on alien technology. You helped with decoding the original message. You might notice something the rest of us miss."

Redford eyed her for a moment and then gave a single nod.

"I just wish we could take the Athena to the furthest moon," Brenda said. "Just in case you need us for something."

"It's better if you stay here," Kaylan said. "Their ships are faster than ours. We won't need help when we first get on board that cruiser. We'll need help as it gets close to this planet, which is where you'll be. Hicks believes that if Kladomaor sees an opportunity to either cripple or take out that ship, he will do so."

There were no other questions.

Kaylan looked around at all of them. "I just want to take a moment and thank you all for everything you've done in getting us this far. All of you have gone above and beyond what you signed on for, and I'm proud to be sharing this mission with each of you," Kaylan said.

Hicks and Katie stood at attention and saluted.

A dark shadow caught Zack's attention, and he glanced out the window. The gray hull of a ship easily more than twice the size of the Athena came into view.

"If that's what the Boxans call one of their smaller ships, I wonder what they have that's bigger," Zack said.

The Boxan stealth ship came to a halt next to the Athena, and more than one person commented on how big it was. Now that the ship was closer, Zack saw pale yellow markings that ran along the angular planes of the front.

"I guess a race of beings who average eight to ten feet in height require a much larger ship," Hicks said.

The hailing call chimed at the comms station, and Zack acknowledged it using his neural implants. Now that he had the implants, he couldn't imagine going back to a life without them. The benefits far outweighed the potential risks as far as he was concerned.

"They're ready for us," Zack said.

Kaylan nodded. "All right, that's our ride."

"Good luck, Commander," Brenda said.

They headed to the port airlock and put on their spacesuits. Zack engaged the helmet, and the suit's computers came online. Zack, Kaylan, and Redford once again donned a holster with the pulsar pistol. Since his experience with the pistol on the planet, Zack had a much greater appreciation for what it could do and how easy it was to use. Hicks and Katie had their assault rifles.

"Should we be armed with one of those rifles?" Redford asked, giving the pulsar pistol a disgusted look.

"If we ever get a chance to show you how they work and give you some practice time, then yes; otherwise, what you've got is probably best," Hicks said.

Katie went over to a locked container and entered a passcode. She retrieved several colored cylinders that were about three inches long and handed Hicks half of them, keeping the rest for herself.

"What are those for?" Zack asked.

"They're grenades," Katie said.

Zack shook his head. "I know I shouldn't be surprised, but why would you bring grenades into space?" he asked.

"We didn't know what we would find on Pluto. These were

one of the last-minute additions Ed Johnson was able to get put on board the Athena before we left Earth," Katie said.

"He and I didn't get along so well in the beginning," Zack said.

Kaylan snorted. "Well, you had just hacked one of Dux Corp's data storage facilities and exposed some of their best kept secrets."

Zack grinned. "If I ever see Ed again, I would thank him for thinking to include grenades on a list of must-have items on a mission of profound scientific discovery. Speaking of which, I wonder how NASA is reacting to the loss of contact with us?"

"They'll keep trying to make contact," Kaylan said, "but it will be a while before they can send a probe out to Pluto to investigate. They might try and repurpose a deep space telescope or two and see if they can glean any insight as to what happened to us. I just hope Michael somehow managed to survive. If he made it out of the wreckage, there were supplies enough to last him two months."

"If there is anyone who could do it, he could," Hicks said.

They filed into the airlock and sealed themselves in. The exterior airlock opened.

Zack gave a low whistle. "It's enormous," he said.

"They should be sending over something to help guide us across," Kaylan said.

"Couldn't we just use our suit jets and glide across on our own?" Zack asked.

"We could, but I want to save them for emergencies," Kaylan said.

A bright light shined across from them as the airlock on the Boxan ship opened. Zack squinted and saw a metallic line coming toward them. He checked his HUD, and the distance to the Boxan ship was a hundred and fifty meters.

Gaarokk greeted them over their suit comms. "You should be able to secure yourselves to the line, and we'll pull you across."

The stiff metallic line looked like corded steel. There were hooks that they could tether themselves to, and once they were ready, Kaylan gave the "all clear" to pull them across.

Zack felt himself jerk forward as the line was retracted, and they kept gaining speed as they zoomed across.

"Am I the only one concerned about not slowing down?" Zack asked.

"No," Redford grunted a reply.

The large open airlock loomed before them, and there was no sign of them slowing down at all.

This is it, Zack thought. *We're going to crash.*

They zipped past the open door, and the amber light in the room changed to green. Zack's stomach clenched as they came to a sudden halt. It wasn't just the line that stopped, but all of them were frozen in place. The airlock shut with a loud clang.

"They must have some type of gravity field that can zero in on each of us. Amazing," Redford said.

Zack felt himself being lowered to the floor and the gradual return of gravity that kept him rooted there.

"A little warning would have been nice," Zack said.

"That would ruin the effect," Gaarokk said over comms.

Zack would have sworn he'd heard the Boxan chuckle before he cut off the comms. The Boxans had been so serious that the attempt at humor caught them all off guard.

They detached the tethers, and the interior airlock doors opened.

Gaarokk waved at them. "Welcome, please step on through," he said.

They came out of the airlock and into a well-lit corridor beyond. Zack had the surreal feeling of being a child again. The interior was clearly designed for a much taller species than mere humans. The railing along the wall was at chest height for Zack and nearly to Kaylan's chin. Control panels at the door were six feet from the ground.

"You may remove your helmets. We maintain an atmosphere similar to Earth, but it might be a bit more humid than you're used to," Gaarokk said.

Zack removed his helmet. The moist air was soothing to breathe and carried the odor of garden soil after a rainfall. He removed his gloves and lightly touched the wall, expecting to find it slightly wet, but it was dry and cool to the touch. The yellow lighting along the ceiling reminded Zack of sunlight, and he briefly thought about whether he needed a vitamin D supplement today.

"While this ship isn't designed for prolonged space travel, we do take steps to ensure a similar atmosphere to our home world. The lighting we use on the ship emits light along the same spectrum as our star. And in different parts of the ship the wall screens will show images conducive to the personality of the occupants within range," Gaarokk said.

Redford frowned. "What happens if the occupants have dissimilar interests?"

"Then neutral images will be used," Gaarokk said.

Kaylan glanced at the computer readout on her PDA. "The lighting has ultraviolet rays," she said.

Gaarokk nodded. "We find it soothing and necessary for optimal health. Do you not have something similar on your ship?"

Kaylan shook her head. "Just in the hydroponic garden area. Later designs were going to take that into consideration."

Gaarokk began leading them down the corridor. "Our light

spectrum runs through cycles, and our internal sensors prevent overexposure."

Zack was glad to hear it. Although getting sunburned while on a spacecraft would be a first, it was something he preferred to skip.

Gaarokk led them to the bridge. Kladomaor sat on an elevated platform in the center of the bridge, giving him a bird's-eye view.

"We're ready to go," Gaarokk said.

"Acknowledged," Kladomaor said.

The bridge was sparse in terms of instrumentation available for actual input. Zack surmised that the Boxans relied heavily on their neural implants. There were no windows on the bridge, and Zack couldn't recall seeing any on the path they had taken to get to the bridge. There was no shortage of holoscreens at the various workstations on the bridge, along with a large central screen. The holoscreens were outlined in pale green, which took a moment to get used to.

"Are there any windows?" Zack asked.

"Windows are a structural weakness. We rely on our sensor net to observe the surrounding area," Kladomaor said. "Engineering, prepare for stealth drive engagement."

"The power requirements for stealth are extremely high," Gaarokk said.

Zack sent out sniffers to see if he could connect to the Boxan ship's computers, and Gaarokk immediately turned in his direction.

Zack shrugged guiltily. "I was just checking," he said, and killed his sniffer programs.

Hicks leaned in so only Zack could hear. "We don't want to wear out our welcome," he said.

Zack nodded.

"Stealth drive engaged," Kladomaor said. "Best speed to Arkeus."

A countdown timer appeared on the main screen.

"Do you know the position of the Xiiginn cruiser?" Kaylan asked.

The image on the holoscreen changed to show a close-up view of the gas giant that Selebus orbited. The moon they were heading to was pretty far from them.

"Is that moon breaking orbit from the gas giant?" Redford asked.

"Not for many cycles, but yes, it will eventually break free of its orbit," Gaarokk said.

A blip showed on the screen.

"That's the Xiiginn cruiser," Kladomaor said.

"Does it have some kind of designation?" Zack asked.

Gaarokk regarded him for a moment. "It does, but I doubt the translator you're using could make sense of it. It would just show up as a group of symbols."

Zack nodded. "Is that why I haven't been able to see what the designation of this ship is?" he asked.

"The references for our ships are a combination of alpha and numeric characters specific to the purpose for which the ship was designed," Gaarokk said.

Not very imaginative, Zack thought, but wouldn't dare voice his opinion out loud.

"How does the stealth technology work? What is it that masks our presence?" Kaylan asked.

Gaarokk glanced at Kladomaor, who nodded.

"There are two components that hide this ship. One is a stealth field that envelops the ship. Our presence is masked from the passive scanners the Xiiginns will be using. The second part blocks our power core from being detected," Gaarokk said.

"Does this ship have any weapons?" Hicks asked.

"Yes, but firing them would give away our position," Klado-maor said. "Also, while the stealth field is active, our shields are not. This ship cannot trade blows with a Xiiginn cruiser. We're simply outmatched in a stand-up fight. The strength of this ship is secrecy and striking our enemy where they believe they're safe."

"Are you sure they won't be expecting us?" Zack asked.

Kladomaor shook his head.

"How long would it take for them to repair communications at the research facility?" Zack asked.

"Not that long, but we've deployed suppressors that come online the moment one is discovered and taken out. It should give us the time we need to get on board that ship," Kladomaor said.

Zack nodded, finally understanding.

The doors to the bridge opened. Etanu and Ezerah entered, followed by four Nershal soldiers. They each wore black armor that could be seen under their long coats. A large, dark shadow loomed behind them, and Zack gasped, jumping back as a protokar sauntered in with the sleek grace of a predator. Zack had his pulsar pistol out instantly.

"Don't be a fool," Etanu said. "This one isn't wild."

Zack's heart thundered in his chest, but he lowered his weapon. He couldn't keep from looking at the protokar. Zack shuddered. He kept seeing the snarling faces that had chased him through the valley, but this beast was sitting passively, its giant tail resting on the floor.

Ezerah came over to Zack. "Etanu tells me you participated in the rite."

Zack nodded. "That's right," he said.

"I've raised Dari since he was born. He will not harm you unless I'm threatened by you," Ezerah said.

Just then, Dari turn its shaggy, yellow-and-purple-furred head toward Kaylan. It raised its head, sniffing the air, and cautiously approached.

Zack glanced at Ezerah, who frowned at the protokar. Kaylan stood perfectly still, but Hicks began to move in front of her.

"Don't," Kaylan said.

A low rumble sounded from deep in Dari's chest, and the protokar cocked its head to the side as it peered at Kaylan.

Ezerah moved to stand in front of the protokar, but it stretched its neck around her, focusing on Kaylan. Ezerah spoke a word Zack didn't understand, but the protokar ignored her.

"Let it approach," Kladomaor said.

Kaylan stepped forward and let the creature come closer. The protokar came before Kaylan and sat on its haunches. Kaylan reached out, and the protokar shook its head as if there were something buzzing around it.

"Shhh, it's okay," Kaylan said.

Zack wanted to tell her it couldn't understand her but didn't think it would help.

The protokar closed both sets of eyes and leaned its head forward into Kaylan's hand. Kaylan's eyes widened, and an unexpected smile came to her face. She glanced at the others. "It won't hurt me."

"How do you know?" Zack asked. He kept dividing his gaze between Kladomaor and the protokar, figuring the Boxan would have greater insight into what was happening.

"I don't know. I just do," Kaylan said.

Dari opened its eyes and glanced at Ezerah, leaning over into her as if he'd just seen her for the first time. The protokar then turned back to Kaylan and did the same thing.

Ezerah's eyes were wide with shock. "I don't believe it. Protokars bond with only one other, and the bond holds for the duration of its life except—" She broke off and looked at Kladomaor.

"Except when in the presence of a Mardoxian priestess," Kladomaor finished.

Kaylan turned toward Kladomaor. "A what?" she asked.

"Protokars can sense the Mardoxian potential in you. We don't know how. I've only seen this one other time, and the greeting was the same. It was described as meeting a long-lost friend you never knew you had," Kladomaor said.

The protokar turned around and padded off to the side. Every so often it would stop and glance at Ezerah and Kaylan.

"The Xiiginns used them to hunt our species, looking for ones with the potential so they could study them," Kladomaor said.

Ezerah looked down for a moment.

A chime rang, drawing their attention to the main holoscreen.

"We've made it," Kladomaor said.

The image changed to show the gray pockmarked surface of a small moon. Although the sensors showed the Xiiginn cruiser closing in, they still couldn't see it.

"No change in cruiser trajectory or speed," Gaarokk said.

"Good. Helm, take us in," Kladomaor said.

The bridge became silent as the Xiiginn cruiser drew steadily closer. The cruiser's sleek design was a triangular shape that reminded Zack of an arrowhead. Gun turrets were strewn across the bow of the ship. The Boxan crew became even more somber as they each took in the view of the ship. Zack had no idea how long the two species had been waging this battle, but the strain of it was clearly evident on each and every Boxan on the bridge. As strong as the Boxans appeared to Humans, they were severely vulnerable to the Xiiginns. Zack didn't know what effect the

Xiiginn would have on him, but he felt tensions grow as fear settled in around them.

As the Xiiginn cruiser passed, the Boxan stealth ship zipped around the moon and flew along the underbelly, matching speeds with the behemoth of a ship.

"Ready the clamps," Kladomaor said. "Attach."

Zack heard a loud clang and wondered if anyone on the cruiser had heard the same thing.

"We're attached," Gaarokk said. "No alarms have been raised."

"Excellent," Kladomaor said. "Move out."

The Boxans rose from their consoles and engaged their power armor. Zack walked next to Gaarokk.

"Doesn't anyone need to stay with the ship?" Zack asked.

"No. If it had to, the ship could remote pilot to our position; however, some will remain behind to provide backup if we need it," Gaarokk said.

Zack nodded. Hicks and Kaylan were walking in front of them with Kladomaor.

"This puts us by the engines," Hicks said. "Couldn't we sabotage the ship and give us more time?"

"Negative," Kladomaor said. "It would alert the Xiiginns to our presence. Stealth is our safest bet."

Kladomaor led them through the ship to the upper level where they would cross over to the Xiiginn ship. Zack became aware of Etanu walking behind him and glanced back at the Nershal.

"Stay focused at all times and we may get through this alive," Etanu said.

Zack faced forward. He didn't know what to make of Etanu. There were times when the Nershal seemed to hate him, and other times the Nershal regarded him with grudging respect.

Zack engaged his neural implants and the interface appeared on the HUD of his helmet. He focused his attention to put the words on screen.

::Athena.::

::I'm here.::

::Anything come up on passive scans?:: Zack asked.

::I thought it prudent to wait until we're on board. This way our scans won't be detected,:: Athena said.

Zack could have gotten the scan status himself through his neural interface. It amazed him how much he'd grown to like conversing with the AI. Sometimes the AI was keenly observant and offered valuable insight. Other times it was completely obtuse to the situation and kept its insights to itself.

Kladomaor came to a halt at the end of the corridor in front of large gray doors. The doors were outlined with a thin yellow light. There were ten Boxans with them in full battle armor. The crowded corridor was silent.

"Beyond the doors is an engineering access hatch. We'll be going through in a moment," Kladomaor said.

"Won't they detect the hatch opening?" Kaylan asked.

"They will," Kladomaor said. "Once on board, Ezerah will use the maintenance console to update the status. The crew is a mixture of Xiiginns and Nershals, so it shouldn't raise any suspicion."

Kaylan nodded.

"I need each Human to pair off with a Boxan. Kaylan, you're with me," Kladomaor said.

Zack glanced at the others in alarm. This was the first any of them had heard this.

Kladomaor noted their hesitation.

Gaarokk stepped forward. "The cloaking of our armor can be extended to close proximity of the wearer. This proximity is enough to envelop each of you if you pair off with one of us. It's the only way to mask your presence on the ship."

"No way. We should stick together," Hicks said.

"You agreed that on this mission you will obey my commands," Kladomaor said.

"He's right," Kaylan said. "Pair off."

Hicks clamped his mouth shut and nodded toward Katie.

"Zack, you're with me," Gaarokk said.

Zack nodded, a bit relieved. Gaarokk was the most reasonable of the Boxans he'd encountered so far. "What do you need me to do?" Zack asked.

"Just stay close to me. I'll link up with your suit's computer so you'll know when the cloak is engaged," Gaarokk said.

They lined up. Ezerah and the other Nershal soldiers dispersed between them. Etanu stuck close to Gaarokk and Zack.

The Boxans unholstered their weapons and held them ready. Zack and the others followed their example, but the Nershals did not.

Zack focused on the door and felt a slight squeeze in his chest. He took in a slow breath and held it for a moment. Kaylan stood in front of him next to Kladomaor. The two commanders disappeared as an active connection registered on Zack's HUD. He looked down at one of his hands, and it vanished in front of him. His HUD changed, and he saw the green silhouette of the Boxans with their cloaks engaged. Zack faced forward and saw Kaylan's silhouette next to Kladomaor.

The doors opened, revealing the cruiser's maintenance hatch. Gaarokk prodded him gently forward, and Zack exhaled.

Here we go again, Zack thought.

Chapter Twenty-One

The maintenance hatch shut behind them, and Zack started scanning the ship's systems as soon as they were on board. Ezerah accessed the console and was able to use her credentials to submit the routine maintenance code for the hatch. Anyone monitoring the system wouldn't be any the wiser that they were there.

They were in an engineering subsection near the power core of the ship. Dari pushed ahead to walk near Ezerah.

"Likely Ma'jasalax would be held in the detention center," Kladomaor said as they went. "We should be able to get to it quicker if we cross over near the power core."

"I don't see her listed as a prisoner," Gaarokk said.

Zack had requested the AI monitor communications from the Boxan's power armor. Since there was an open connection, the AI was able to decode the protocols used to access the ship's systems so Zack could run his own search.

"They wouldn't list her," Kladomaor said. "Search the logs for Enforcer check-ins. They should be systematic and on schedule."

Multiple windows showed on Zack's HUD as the AI searched through the ship's computer. "I've got it," Zack said. "Sending the data over now."

Gaarokk gave him a sideways glance. "Should have realized this would happen with an open connection."

Kladomaor cursed. "She's not in the detention center but in one of the med bay levels."

"That makes sense," Gaarokk said. "They've never captured one of the Mardoxian Sect before who didn't follow protocol. They're observing her."

"Or testing her resistance to the Xiiginn influence," Kladomaor said. "She might already be under their influence, and we're being lured into a trap. Either way, we're not leaving until we know for sure."

They came to a door that automatically opened at their approach. Beyond was a well-lit, stark white hallway. The cloaked Boxans immediately stayed to the side, as close to the wall as possible. Ezerah raised her chin and walked briskly in front of them as if she owned the place. They crossed an intersection where there were several Nershals conversing. One looked over as they passed. None of them were armed. Zack hardly dared to breathe and double-checked that he was safely within the confines of Gaarokk's cloaked field. Ezerah paid the Nershals hardly any notice, and after a moment they resumed their conversation.

Doors opened at the far end of the hallway, and a large group of Nershals could be seen heading toward them. Zack craned his neck to get a better look, but they were still too far away.

"We need to get out of this hallway," Kladomaor said quietly.

Without skipping a beat, Ezerah turned down the next intersection and quickened her pace. Zack risked a glance behind

them, but the large group of Nershals hadn't come to the intersection yet.

They came to the end of the hallway.

"We need to go left," Kaylan said. "There is a group of
Nershals inside a room not far away and . . . something else,"
Kaylan said and frowned. "I'm not sure what it is."

Ezerah hesitated. According to the map on their HUD,
access to the shortest way across the power core was to the right.

"Do as she says," Kladomaor said.

Zack kept monitoring the maintenance hatch they had used
to come aboard the ship, and a recent event appeared in the log.
"They're sending someone to investigate the hatch we came
through," Zack said.

Kladomaor sent a message back to their ship to detach and
move to the secondary site.

Zack's stomach clenched. He had the sickening feeling that
the Xiiginns knew they were here. He tried to reason his way
through his doubts but couldn't shake the feeling.

::*Athena, can you run a search on the security status of the
cruiser?*:: Zack asked.

::*Status is normal. No heightened security protocols have been
engaged,*:: Athena said.

They turned down another corridor and headed to the door
at the far end. Ezerah opened it and they went through. A blast
of air sounded beneath them as they stepped onto a walkway that
circled a massive chamber. Dark gray panels adorned the walls.
In the center of the chamber was a black sphere surrounded by a
semi-translucent field. The sphere hovered above the ground far
below them.

Gaarokk gently prodded him along, and he tore his eyes
away from the sphere to check his suit readings. There was no
sign of radiation. In whatever way that thing powered the ship, it

didn't emit anything they could detect. It took them almost fifteen minutes to circle around to the other side of the chamber. With each passing moment, the risk of discovery grew. It was taking longer for them to get to Ma'jasalax than they had originally expected.

Zack kept glancing down at the network of walkways beneath them. His balance started to shift when someone grabbed onto him.

"Focus," Etanu said.

Zack gasped, and his eyes snapped in front of him. "Thanks," he said.

Kaylan turned around, and Zack gave her quick wave that he was okay.

They came to a door, and Ezerah entered her credentials as she'd done before, but the door didn't open. She tried again with the same result.

"Try this," Zack said, and told her the sequence for Mar Arden's identification.

The door opened and they quickly passed through.

"We need to move," Gaarokk said.

"I know," Kladomaor replied.

They quickened their pace and came to the end of the corridor. A group of Nershals in black uniforms turned around at their sudden appearance in the corridor. Ezerah turned to lead them in the opposite direction.

"You're not supposed to be here," one of the Nershals said.

Oh crap, Zack thought. He gripped the pulsar pistol, which had become slippery in his sweaty palms.

"Apologies," Etanu said. "We've gotten a bit turned around. Perhaps you might be of assistance."

The Nershal narrowed his gaze suspiciously. "Where do you need to go?"

"We're heading to the research lab on this deck," Ezerah said.

"That area is restricted. I'm going to need to call this in," the Nershal said, and raised his left hand to his head. The others with him reached for their weapons.

"Don't do that," Etanu said to the Nershal who had challenged them, stepping closer. "This is the second time something like this has happened. If this gets reported, I'll never be accepted into the Academy."

The Nershal lowered his hand and smirked. "Which house are you from?"

"The one loyal to all Nershal," Etanu said. He grabbed the soldier by his uniform and slammed his fist into the soldier's smirking face.

Gaarokk grabbed Zack and held him in place. The others sprang into action. A few seconds later the unconscious soldiers were bound and gagged, then stuffed into an empty room.

"Good work," Kladomaor said.

"They weren't going to let us go," Etanu said.

"You heard him," Kladomaor said, addressing the rest of them. "Weapons ready. The area up ahead is restricted, so it's likely guarded. There will be no talking our way through."

"Should we split up?" a Boxan soldier asked. "I can take a few of us and cause trouble in another part of the ship, then meet up with you later."

Kladomaor considered this. "Negative, we stick together."

They started to move on, and Kaylan stumbled. Kladomaor stooped to help her up.

"I'm sorry," Kaylan said. "It's getting harder to focus the closer we get to her."

Kladomaor nodded. "I should have anticipated this. The closer we get to Ma'jasalax, the stronger the connection."

"I'll be fine. Let's keep moving," Kaylan said.

Ezerah led them down the corridor. Etanu once again took up position near Zack's side. Zack scanned the ship's network, but there had still been no alarms raised. Ezerah came to a halt. A short distance from them the corridor branched off.

"The med bay is just around the corner," Ezerah said.

They heard the door open and they waited. A tall, pale figure rounded the corner. The Xiiginn was looking down at some type of tablet computer in her hands. Her nostrils crinkled as she sniffed the air, and her platinum-colored hair shifted as she looked up at them. Her tail flicked to the side.

Zack froze.

The Xiiginn opened her mouth as a large blast came from Kladomaor's gun, reducing the Xiiginn to ashes.

They charged forward. Gaarokk grabbed Zack by the shoulders and pushed him ahead. The Boxans dropped the cloaked field as they burst through the door to the med bay.

Zack focused on the ground, trying to keep his legs under him. Bright flashes lit up the area. The Boxans moved through the room, destroying anything that moved. Zack saw the body of a dead Nershal sprawled alongside a desk and felt himself go numb. He'd known what would happen when they came here, but to see it firsthand sent his mind reeling.

"Check each room," Kladomaor said.

Katie came over to him. "Are you okay?"

Zack finally looked up. "I think so. I didn't even fire my weapon."

"Never mind that. What matters is that you're not hurt," Katie said.

Kladomaor called them over.

Zack followed Katie. He glanced behind him and saw that Etanu was still there. There were a few Xiiginns mixed in with the

Nershals who were in the med bay. None of them looked sick or injured. The Xiiginns in the room were all female. There was a tranquility in their deathly expressions that made Zack shiver. Their skin was so pale that it had a purplish hue. None of them were armed as far as Zack could tell, but Kladomaor wasn't taking any chances.

"They weren't even armed," Zack said.

"Don't let their appearance fool you," Gaarokk said. "They may look peaceful now, but they are fierce killers. We're lucky we took them by surprise."

They stood outside a closed door. Ezerah was trying to get it to open.

"Nothing is working," Ezerah said.

Zack blinked away the sight of the dead bodies he'd just seen and used his implants, searching for a security override for the door.

Kladomaor motioned to the door, and one of the Boxan soldiers came up and placed a small round device over the console. Kladomaor had them step back. There was a flash and the console fizzled, with wisps of smoke rising around it. The door opened to a darkened room beyond.

Kaylan stepped through first. The lights in the room flickered on and then immediately turned off, but the sensors on her helmet swept the darkened room, enabling her to see. She heard Kladomaor's footsteps pounding the floor behind her as she rushed inside. There were instruments on top of metallic shelves that hung along the walls. She headed toward a large window that had another door alongside it.

"Wait," Kladomaor said.

Kaylan stopped at the window and peered through. There was a shifting in the shadows beyond the dimly lit room.

"She's in there," Kaylan said.

"We can't burst into that room. There could be fail-safes engaged," Kladomaor said.

Kaylan glanced helplessly at the door. She felt Ma'jasalax's presence in the other room.

"I'm checking," Zack said. After a moment he frowned. "The door isn't locked."

Kladomaor reached out, and the door opened. Low-level lighting shone from the panels along the floor.

Kaylan entered and saw that Ma'jasalax was strapped to a table in the middle of the room. Her face was covered with a white mask that was connected to hoses that ran to the floor. A holodisplay flickered on and showed a readout of Ma'jasalax's vitals.

Kladomaor grumbled as he went over to the holo-interface and started navigating through the options.

Kaylan slowly approached the Boxan she had come into contact with through the Mardoxian Chamber on Pluto. She remembered how afraid she had been when she'd first seen Ma'jasalax. But now, seeing her lying on the table made her look so vulnerable. Her eyes were shut. Kaylan reached out and placed her hand on top of Ma'jasalax's hand. The Boxan's brown, roughened skin was hard to the touch. Kaylan's hand appeared like a child's in comparison to Ma'jasalax's large hand.

"Gaarokk, can you make anything of this?" Kladomaor asked.

The Boxan leaned down to examine the mask on Ma'jasalax's face. They might have thought she was sleeping if not for all the hardware connected to her body. Gaarokk circled around the table and joined Kladomaor at the holo-interface.

Zack came to Kaylan's side. "Have you tried talking to her?" he asked.

Kaylan glanced at him and then turned back to Ma'jasalax. "I did as you asked. We found you. Now you have to wake up."

No response—just the steady rise and fall of the Boxan's chest.

"Whatever you're going to do, you need to do it fast," Etanu shouted from the other room. The Nershals had stayed outside to secure the way.

"I'm seeing comms chatter being logged for weapons fire in this area," Zack said.

"We're running out of time. We have to disconnect her," Kladomaor said.

"If we don't have the right sequence, she could die," Gaarokk said, and kept navigating through the interface. "I've got it." The hoses connected to Ma'jasalax disconnected of their own accord and retracted back into the floor. Kladomaor carefully removed the mask from her face, but she remained unresponsive. Kladomaor gave her a slight shake to try to wake her up, but it didn't work.

Gaarokk came to her side, removed a small device from his pack, and attached it to her arm. The device started to glow, sending a wave of light over her body. Ma'jasalax opened her eyes. Her bright green irises captured the light, and Kladomaor helped her sit up. She looked at them all, and then her gaze settled on Kaylan. Ma'jasalax's gaze softened, and Kaylan felt the same connection blossom between them that she had felt in the chamber a few weeks before.

"The Xiiginns are on their way," Kladomaor said.

Gaarokk helped Ma'jasalax to stand up, and she almost collapsed when she tried to stand on her own.

A loud blast sounded from the outer room, followed immediately by another. Reacting without thought, Zack ducked his head. Hicks and Katie were at the doorway. The snap hiss of weapons fire could be heard beyond.

Zack noticed one of them was missing. "Where is Redford?" he asked.

Hicks glanced into the outer room where the Boxan and Nershal soldiers were firing their weapons through the open doorway to their only way out. One of the Boxan soldiers came back to the room they were in and deposited Redford on the floor. He wasn't hurt.

"We need another way out of here," the soldier said.

Kladomaor walked up to the doorway and checked the room beyond.

Zack came to Kaylan's side. "Can you find another way out of here?" he asked.

Kaylan's brows drew up. "I'm not sure," she said and glanced at Ma'jasalax, but she was barely conscious. Gaarokk was doing the best he could to hold her up.

Zack watched as Kaylan closed her eyes. Sounds of more blasts came from the outer room, and Zack heard Kladomaor bellow out orders.

"Fall back," Kladomaor said, and returned to them. "I can take out one of these walls so we can escape. I just need to know which one," he asked.

Zack watched as Kaylan stepped toward the back of the room. He'd been trying to find detailed schematics for the rooms they were in but couldn't find anything other than standard maps of the area.

"There is some kind of service tunnel behind this corner," Kaylan said, and backed away.

Kladomaor raised his weapon and changed a setting. The weapon gathered a charge and belched out a huge blast that melted through the corner, leaving a gaping hole. Kladomaor grabbed Ma'jasalax's other arm and helped haul her away.

Zack glanced back at Redford, who was shaking his head and muttering to himself.

"Jonah, come on," Zack said.

Redford looked over at him and nodded.

They moved down the service tunnel as quickly as they could, and Zack could hear the muffled sounds of alarms blaring. The Boxan soldiers at the end of the line fired their weapons, holding up whomever was pursuing them as best they could. A few minutes later they squeezed through the maintenance hatch to the ship's power core. Beyond the hatch was a narrow walkway that led straight out over the core and then branched off in two directions.

At this point, Ma'jasalax was able to stand on her own with assistance from Gaarokk, who refused to leave her side.

"Deploy charges. Timed detonation primary. Remote detonation secondary," Kladomaor said. A storage compartment opened on his suit near his hip, and three blue spheres were deposited into his hand. He tossed them into the air, and they flew off, guided by forces Zack could neither see nor understand.

Etanu weaved his way through them until he was behind Zack. "Are you still in the ship's system?" he asked.

"I'm still in," Zack said. "What do you need me to do?"

"Upload the data from the research facility and broadcast it to the entire ship," Etanu said.

"But your people . . ." Zack said.

Etanu's gaze hardened for a moment. "Their blood will not be on your hands. The Xiiginns are responsible. Will you do this thing that I have asked you to do?" Etanu asked.

Zack nodded.

::*Athena, compile the data recorded from the research facility.*

*Have the video playback on an automated loop with this message . .
.::*

Zack finished the short message, but his suit computer was compiling the message at a frustratingly slow rate. The progress bar inched its way across, and Zack minimized it on his HUD. *How did I ever function without neural implants?* He wondered.

"It will take a few minutes to compile," Zack said.

Etanu nodded.

They continued on the walkway, and Zack tried to ignore the dizzying heights that assaulted his senses the farther out they went. They reached the middle of the vast power core chamber and spread out on either side to cover the others. A strangled cry sounded behind them, and Zack turned around to see one of the Boxan soldiers plummet over the side. He had been knocked off by another Boxan soldier, who held one of the glowing spheres that was set to explode. The Boxan's movements were slow and jerky, as if he couldn't control his limbs.

"Kladomaor," the Boxan soldier cried. "I can't stop. Kill me!"

Energy bolts fired at them from below.

On the walkway behind them was a Xiiginn. A male. His face twisted in a sneer.

"Go ahead, Kladomaor, kill him. I will have you soon enough," the Xiiginn said.

Katie squatted next to Zack, aimed her assault rifle, and fired. Her shot hit the Xiiginn in the face but ricocheted off of some type of shield.

Kladomaor growled as he fired his weapon, taking out the Boxan under the Xiiginn's power. The sphere fell from his grasp and bounced along the walkway, heading in their direction.

Zack's breath caught in his throat. He pushed Katie to the side and turned to see where Kaylan was. He leaped over and threw himself in her direction. The sphere exploded behind him, and Zack felt the heat of the blast burn through part of his suit. He rolled onto his back, and Kaylan was shouting his name. It took him a moment to get his bearings.

"Get up," Kaylan said, and dragged him to his feet. Ma'jasalax was behind her.

Zack steadied himself on the railing and reached down to pick up the pulsar pistol.

"Go," Kladomaor said. "We'll meet you at the ship."

Zack looked over. The walkway ended at Kladomaor's feet. He was shouting across to the others. Zack craned his neck to see who was on the other side of the expanse. All of them were there. It was just himself, Kaylan, Ma'jasalax, and Kladomaor stuck on this side. The space between the two sections of the walkway was too great to jump across.

Etanu and one of the Nershal soldiers unfurled their wings and flew over to them.

Katie locked her gaze onto Zack across the expanse that separated them. Hicks came up behind her, and it took him a few tries to get her attention.

Zack opened up a comms channel to them. "Go on, we'll meet up with you," Zack said.

"Keep your head down—" Katie said, and was cut off by energy bolts fired at them from below.

The bolts smashed against the bottom of the walkway, which was starting to buckle under their weight.

"Run!" Zack shouted, and watched as Ezerah was the first to realize the danger they were in. She called out to the others and ran the other way.

Etanu and the other Nershal soldier reached them. *His name is Lok*, Zack thought. Kladomaor helped Ma'jasalax onto her feet and bellowed for them to keep up. Zack stayed by Kaylan's side. She had her pulsar pistol out and so did Zack. As they ran away from the edge of the walkway, Zack felt it shudder beneath his feet. It was going down at any second. Ahead of them the walkway connected to another section that would bring them to the edge of the chamber. They just had to reach it in time.

Etanu and Lok hovered just above them and provided covering fire. Kladomaor picked up Ma'jasalax and carried her. Zack and Kaylan ran side by side. A Nershal soldier appeared by the edge of the walkway, and Zack fired the pulsar pistol, taking him by surprise. Zack felt his stomach rise into his chest as the walkway dropped several feet.

Kaylan cried out. A Nershal soldier had grabbed her and was trying to pull her over the side. She struggled against the Nershal and its flapping wings. Zack couldn't get a clear shot. He raced forward without any thought at all other than getting to Kaylan fast enough. He slammed the stock of his pistol into the Nershal's face. The Nershal released its grip and shook its head as if it couldn't see what it was doing. Zack seized the opportunity, grabbing Kaylan's arm and half dragging her away.

Kladomaor called out to them to hurry. As they closed in to where Kladomaor waited, Zack watched in horror as a jagged tear separated the walkway into sections, causing it to tilt wickedly to the side.

Kladomaor backed away, carrying Ma'jasalax to safety.

Zack stumbled and fell to the ground. Kaylan, barely keeping her feet under her, staggered back to him. The walkway lurched beneath them.

"Grab onto something!" Zack said, grasping the railing with one hand and Kaylan with the other hand while she did the same.

The groaning supports snapped, and the walkway twisted as it swung down, dangling. Zack squeezed his eyes shut and held on as tightly as he could.

Chapter Twenty-Two

Hicks kept his weapon ready. Years of combat training provided the foundation that allowed him to stay focused. They had left Kaylan and the others. He'd had no choice. There was no way to get over to them. Katie had gone grimly quiet and took to coldly killing anything they came across. They'd made it to the edge of the power core chamber and were heading to the door.

Hicks kept a careful watch on the Boxan soldiers still with them. One of them had betrayed them—perhaps the Xiiginn influence. He didn't understand how one's control could be overridden so easily. He'd hardly caught a glimpse of the Xiiginn before Kladomaor had taken it out. Could all Xiiginns control other species? Maybe only some of them could.

"We're almost there. Quickly now," Ezerah said while waving them on as she made sure no one else had been lost.

Redford stumbled in front of him, and Hicks helped steady him on his feet.

"Your helmet," Hicks said, noticing the jagged crack on Redford's faceplate.

Redford reached up and felt along the edges. "I, uh . . . don't remember," he said.

"Never mind. Just keep going. I'm right behind you," Hicks said.

Katie provided cover fire from behind them.

They were now close to the rendezvous point with the ship. A loud crash sounded from some other part of the chamber, startling Hicks.

"We have to move," Ezerah said. "Kladomaor will make sure the others get out."

Hicks pressed his lips together, fighting the urge to run back to find the others, and saw the same reflected in Katie's eyes. The walkway shuddered beneath their feet, which caused their pursuers to stop firing on them. The ship was coming apart. The Boxan soldiers ushered them onward, and they left the power core behind to race for their ship.

ZACK STRUGGLED to hang on and slid down the railing several feet.

"I'm slipping," Kaylan said.

The damn walkway was swaying back and forth. Zack wasn't sure how long they could hold on.

"We need to let go," Kaylan said.

"What! Are you crazy?" Zack said.

"Look," Kaylan said. "If we time it right, we can land on the walkway below us."

Zack glanced down, and his attention was divided between

plunging to his death or the slight chance of hitting the walkway on the next level down.

"There's no way we can make it," Zack said. "We need to climb up."

With each passing moment he slid farther down, with Kaylan doing the same.

"Trust me," Kaylan said. "We go together."

This is gonna hurt, Zack thought, and nodded.

The walkway swayed away from the one beneath them, and Zack fought off the feeling of vertigo.

"Now!" Kaylan said.

They let go, and Zack felt as if his heart were going to burst through his chest. He focused on the grip of Kaylan's hand in his and screamed. The angle of the dangling walkway decreased their velocity and functioned as a slide. Kaylan landed on the walkway below, and Zack slammed into the railing, knocking the breath from him. Kaylan scrambled to her feet and pulled him from the railing to the walkway. Zack kept coughing, trying to catch his breath. Each breath he took sent a lance of pain through his side.

"Get up," Kaylan said, pulling him up.

There was a loud snap overhead, and the dangling walkway started to crash down on them. They ran toward the edge of the chamber. Severe pain in his leg nearly brought Zack to his knees. He grabbed onto the railing to propel himself onward. The section they were on split in two directions, with both leading to a door.

Kaylan's eyes widened in fear. "They're coming. Come on, we've got to move," she said, pulling him in one direction.

Zack's leg twisted under him and they went down. "My leg," he gasped, and pulled himself back to his feet. "I can't breathe. I just need a second," Zack said.

The door behind them opened and out poured Xiiginns,

wearing dark armor that covered their bodies but left their heads exposed.

Zack grabbed his pulsar pistol and took aim while he and Kaylan backed away. A piece of wreckage whooshed by them, coming dangerously close. The Xiiginns noticed them and started heading over. According to the map on his HUD, there was an elevator through the doors behind them. He sent a signal to summon the elevator so it would be there waiting for them.

A green energy bolt singed the railing where Zack's hand had been.

"Stay back," Zack said. Both he and Kaylan had their pulsar pistols raised.

There were ten Xiiginn soldiers closing in on them. The leader cocked his pale head to the side as if he didn't quite understand them.

"What sort of species are you?" the Xiiginn asked.

Zack and Kaylan continued to back away.

The Xiiginn's green eyes narrowed menacingly. "Take another step and we'll open fire."

More wreckage from above crashed down around them.

"Your control is tenuous at best," Zack said. "The Nershals won't sit back and allow what you've done to go on."

The Xiiginn sneered. "You refer to the broadcast that invaded our systems moments ago. Who do you think authorized the research in the first place?"

"You lie," Zack said.

"One rogue faction doesn't condemn an entire species of wrongdoing," the Xiiginn said. "Surely you have experienced deviants on your home world."

"Liar!" a voice bellowed from above.

Zack looked up and saw Etanu and Lok swoop down and land in front of them.

The Xiiginn leader held up his hand to keep his soldiers from firing.

"Nershals would never sanction what you've done," Etanu said.

"You've been infected with Boxan lies. We've been nothing but honest in our dealings with you," the Xiiginn said. "I am Sion Shif, First Commander of this ship. You know the Boxans lied to us all. They cannot be trusted."

"Perhaps," Kaylan said. "But neither can you."

Sion Shif smiled. "Yours is an interesting species. I look forward to learning all about it."

Kaylan felt as if her head had been submerged into a thick fog. She shook her head and glanced at Zack. He seemed to be waiting.

Resist. Ma'jasalax's voice whispered in the depths of Kaylan's mind, and the fog was driven back.

Focus on something important to you, Ma'jasalax said.

Sion Shif stepped forward, and his soldiers followed. Kaylan's eyes darted to Zack. His bleeding side was getting worse and he still favored one leg, but he stared defiantly at the Xiiginn. He was strong in ways she had never suspected, and she cursed herself for not seeing it sooner.

Etanu and Lok leaped to the side and hovered in the air, firing their weapons at the Xiiginns. A few soldiers went down, but not before taking out Lok, whose limp form plummeted down.

Kaylan heard the snap hiss of Zack's pulsar pistol firing. She glanced upward and saw more wreckage barreling toward them. Kaylan grabbed Zack and pulled him back, out of the way.

Pieces of the walkway crashed down in front of them, cutting off the Xiiginns. They backed away, and she could see Zack looking for Etanu, but they couldn't find him. The Nershal must have gotten caught in the wreckage.

"Come on," Zack said. "There's an elevator."

Together they headed for the open elevator doors. She heard Zack's labored breathing as he clutched his side. They stopped a few feet from the elevator, and Zack collapsed to the floor, almost dragging her down with him. She dropped her pistol and had moved to pick it up when she noticed more of Zack's blood soaking through his uniform.

"Come on. Please," Kaylan said. "You've got to get up."

Zack cried out as she tried to get him to stand back up.

"Go," Zack said, clutching his side.

"I won't leave you," Kaylan said, and pulled Zack to his feet.

They made it to the elevator, and there was an explosion behind them. The wreckage on the walkway was blasted away by the Xiiginn soldiers.

Zack was leaning against the elevator doorway and he suddenly pulled her toward him. "I'm sorry," he said. He pressed his lips onto hers and shoved her into the elevator.

The glass doors began to shut.

"No! Zack!"

The doors shut with her safely inside and Zack outside. He had grabbed her fallen pulsar pistol. Kaylan slammed her fist onto the door and tried to open it, but the controls wouldn't respond.

"Open the door!" Kaylan said. The elevator started to rise. "Open the goddamn door!" She repeatedly banged her fists on the window. "Why?"

Zack watched her, pressed his lips to his hand, and placed his hand on the window. With her eyes brimming, she choked back a sob and waited until he was out of sight to scream.

WITH THE ELEVATOR out of sight, Zack turned back to face the Xiiginns, the pulsar pistols weighing heavily in each of his hands. He felt so tired and could barely stand.

The Xiiginns pushed their way through the rest of the fallen wreckage with Sion Shif in the lead.

Etanu climbed over the railing, onto the walkway near Zack. One of his wings was damaged and wouldn't fold in right. The Nershal glanced at the approaching Xiiginns before coming to stand near Zack.

"Thanks for coming," Zack said.

"An honor to stand at your side, Human," Etanu said.

Zack raised his pistols and started firing at the Xiiginns. The Xiiginns returned fire, and a green energy bolt struck him in the chest and knocked him off his feet.

Zack heard the rapid approach of muffled footsteps. He tried to open his eyes but couldn't. The pain in his side vanished. He felt as if he were floating in a pool of water.

"Keep them alive," Zack heard Sion Shif say before everything faded to black.

Chapter Twenty-Three

Kaylan screamed herself raw and her heart felt like it was going to burst. All Zack had needed to do was get on the elevator with her. Then everything would have been okay. She kicked the elevator door again, her bruised fists shaking. He had kissed her before he pushed her onto the elevator. He wouldn't have done that if he thought he was going to live. Kaylan wiped her eyes. "You're not going to die," Kaylan said to the empty elevator. "Not if I have anything to say about it." Kaylan clenched her teeth. She would get Kladomaor and the others and return for Zack, even if she had to tear this whole goddam ship apart to find him.

There was a loud pop of some far-off explosion. The force of it shook the elevator, which came to a stop, and the doors opened. Kaylan pressed her back to the side to hide from whomever might be outside.

"Kaylan?" Kladomaor called.

Kaylan sighed in relief and sprang out of the elevator.

"Zack is down there. We have to go back and get him," Kaylan said.

Kladomaor still had his arm around Ma'jasalax, who could barely stand by herself.

"We can't. We have to go," Kladomaor said.

Kaylan's brow furrowed. "No. Didn't you hear me? Zack is still down there. So is Etanu. They need our help."

A siren started blaring. A message sounded, advising all hands to abandon ship.

"The ship is coming apart," Kladomaor said. "Zack sacrificed himself so you could get free."

"I don't care. I'm not leaving without him," Kaylan said.

Kaylan went back to the elevator, but the controls were locked out.

"We can't help him now," Kladomaor said. "I won't force you to come, but know that if you stay here and die, he will have sacrificed himself for nothing."

Kaylan's lip trembled as she glared at the locked-out control panel. In her mind she was still seeing him press his lips to his fingers and place them on the translucent elevator door, his pained expression oddly peaceful. She tried to focus her mind to locate Zack, but nothing worked. She couldn't find him. *Is he dead?* Kaylan wondered for a second, then banished the thought just as quickly.

Kaylan left the elevator and blindly followed Kladomaor, and pieces of her heart felt like they were being torn away with each step she took. She heard Kladomaor coordinate with the ship to meet them at a new location closer to where they were.

Kladomaor glanced down at her. "The others got off safely and are on the ship," he said.

Kaylan nodded but didn't trust herself to speak. The corridors were deserted. She felt the impact of explosions shimmy through the floor. Then another explosion blew out the wall near them. Ma'jasalax collapsed, pulling Kladomaor off balance, and Kaylan stumbled over to the wall.

"Boxans!" a Xiiginn sneered as he stepped over the wreckage.

Kladomaor struggled to free his weapon, and Kaylan sucked in a breath. The Xiiginn aimed, and his weapon began to glow red at the tip.

Kaylan scrambled over to help Kladomaor.

Suddenly the Xiiginn cried out, and Kaylan saw a large black stinger protruding from the Xiiginn's chest. Blackened blood pooled at its feet as a protokar stepped into view from beyond the wreckage.

"Dari," Kaylan breathed.

The protokar's jade eyes were fiercely fixed on the Xiiginn as it hoisted the body into the air and flung it behind them. Dari circled back and trotted over to Kaylan, giving her a soft push with its muzzle.

Kladomaor lifted Ma'jasalax up. "We must hurry."

They quickly made their way to the airlock and returned to the Boxan ship. Kladomaor handed Ma'jasalax over to be taken to the sick bay, and they headed toward the bridge.

"Gaarokk," Kladomaor said, "get us out of here."

Kaylan saw the others and could hardly make herself look at Katie.

"Where is Zack?" Katie asked.

The question felt like a blow. Kaylan tried to form the words, but her tongue became thick in her mouth. She shook her head and glanced at the main holoscreen.

The hull of the Xiiginn cruiser raced past the screen as their ship moved away. There was a bright flash at the rear of the Xiiginn ship, and the breath caught in Kaylan's throat.

Zack!

Warning alarms blared on the bridge as they cleared the Xiiginn cruiser. There was another flare from the center of the cruiser, and then the ship blew apart. Large sections tumbled through space. Kaylan cried out and doubled over. Katie wrapped her arms around Kaylan's shoulders.

"I'm sorry," Kaylan whispered, her lips trembling. "I shouldn't have left. I shouldn't have left you," she said, her eyes fixed on the holoscreen.

Katie coaxed her off the bridge so they could have some privacy. She heard Hicks ask where the med bay was, and someone led them there. Hicks and Redford stayed close but also kept their distance.

"Calm down," Katie said. "Just tell us what happened."

Kaylan took several deep breaths. She kept seeing the Xiiginn ship coming apart. Katie handed her some water, which Kaylan sipped, and she slowly recounted what had happened.

"I wouldn't have left him," Kaylan said. It sounded like she had said it a hundred times, and no matter how many times she said it, it didn't change the fact that she had left him on that ship.

"I know you wouldn't have," Katie said.

Kladomaor entered the med bay, and Hicks and Redford went to speak with him.

Kaylan made herself look Katie in the eyes. "I love him," she said.

Katie met her gaze. "I know."

AFTER SPEAKING WITH THE HUMANS, Kladomaor sought out Ma'jasalax, who was resting nearby. If the Mardoxian priestess had any issue with his abrupt entry, she didn't give any indication. Ma'jasalax looked through the doorway to where Kaylan was speaking with her crewmates.

"The connection between them is strong," Kladomaor said.

"Not as primitive as you thought then?" Ma'jasalax asked.

"They are more than what I thought they would be, but they still have much to learn," Kladomaor said.

Ma'jasalax leveled her eyes at him. "Perhaps we can learn something from *them*."

Kladomaor drew his chin up and then sighed. "Are we wrong? Should we not have used the Star Shroud to keep the other species ignorant of each other? Is our suffering because of our own actions? Our own pride?"

"What do you think?" Ma'jasalax asked.

"I want to know what *you* think. Those of the Mardoxian Sect have greater insight than I have," Kladomaor said.

"I know your experiences say otherwise," Ma'jasalax said.

"I don't know," Kladomaor said. "Until the Xiiginns, we had peace in our section of the galaxy, but now I think an outcome involving a species like the Xiiginns was inevitable. One thing that has been proven is that all the species we worked to cultivate into harmony resent having been kept ignorant of the universe, even those who recognize that we did it for their own protection, and ours. The Nershals will fight the Xiiginns and each other for a time, but that doesn't mean they will want to have anything to do with us."

"That is their right," Ma'jasalax said.

"Was it your right to pull the Humans into this? They are here because of the message you sent," Kladomaor said.

"I made a decision to reach out to them, just as you made a decision to return to the Nershals' star system to show them the truth about the Xiiginns," Ma'jasalax said. "Would it have been better to let the Humans develop on their own, only to emerge from the Star Shroud to be enslaved by the Xiiginns? By then they wouldn't have stood a chance at surviving a conflict with them. Now at least they have a chance, and the rest of our species cowering on our last colony must take action if we're to survive."

"What do you know of war?" Kladomaor asked.

"I know that we've been on the defensive for many years, and you alone have chosen to take the offensive against the Xiiginns. Perhaps others will be inspired to such actions," Ma'jasalax said.

"I thought the Mardoxian Sect was to promote harmony in the universe."

"It is, but not at the expense of our civilization," Ma'jasalax said. "We are a prideful race, believing that our wisdom and intelligence made us infallible to the repercussions of our decisions. This mindset has prevented us from adapting. Stagnation is the death of any species, including our own."

Kladomaor frowned in thought. "You speak of influencing our entire species into action. That seed could make us come undone."

"Are we any different than the Nershals? Some of them will still choose to ally with the Xiiginns despite what you've accomplished here. The same applies to us. Some will strive to return to the days of old where we asserted our mastery. Others, like yourself, will realize that we can never go back to that," Ma'jasalax said.

Kladomaor felt as if he was being manipulated, but at the same time he agreed with Ma'jasalax. If the Boxans were to survive, they had to change. Would the Humans be the catalyst for that change? Or would they be yet another species to fall victim to the Xiiginn?

KAYLAN ROSE TO HER FEET. She and Katie hadn't said anything else. What else was there to say? Both had succumbed to a numbing silence.

She crossed the Boxan medical bay to where Kladomaor was speaking with Ma'jasalax. The two Boxans stopped speaking as she approached.

"We have to go back to the wreckage to search for Zack," Kaylan said. As she spoke she became aware that the others in the med bay became silent.

"I've lost members of my own crew—" Kladomaor started to say.

"He's not lost. He's not dead. They have him," Kaylan said.

Kladomaor glanced at Ma'jasalax for a moment. "Are you able to see him?"

Kaylan's brows drew forward, and she shook her head. Try as she might, she couldn't make herself concentrate enough to see anything. "I know he's alive."

"How?" Kladomaor asked. "He locked you on the elevator to save you because he thought he was going to die."

"He's not dead," Kaylan said. She felt her chest tighten and knew she was being irrational but didn't care. "If you won't help me, we'll take our own ship and search the wreckage," Kaylan said, and turned to leave.

"Wait," Ma'jasalax said.

Kaylan stopped.

Ma'jasalax looked at the others. "Please give us a few moments."

Kladomaor left, and Kaylan nodded to Hicks and the others to follow the Boxan commander.

"Have a seat," Ma'jasalax said.

A stool rose from the floor and Kaylan sat on it.

"Kladomaor told me that you and your crew were the reason

they were able to find me in the first place. Please accept my thanks, and I'm sorry for all that you've suffered since coming here," Ma'jasalax said.

Kaylan nodded and felt as if her tears were going to overwhelm her eyes. She wiped them away and clamped down on her feelings. She needed to be strong.

"This member of your crew is important to you?" Ma'jasalax asked.

"Yes," Kaylan said, her voice sounding thick with emotion.

"I know the feeling," Ma'jasalax said, and glanced the way Kladomaor had gone. "The ones closest to us are the most difficult to see."

Kaylan closed her eyes and pinched her lips together. "I can't see Zack. I know he's alive, but I'm not able to find him," Kaylan said.

"You remember what happened in the chamber?" Ma'jasalax asked.

"We were able to communicate."

Ma'jasalax nodded. "The Mardoxian Chamber can amplify our abilities."

Kaylan's eyes widened. "You mean we can use the chamber to find Zack?"

"Perhaps, but first let's see if he is, in fact, alive," Ma'jasalax said.

"How?" Kaylan asked.

"Take my hand," Ma'jasalax said.

Kaylan placed both her hands in Ma'jasalax's large hands. The Boxan had brown, roughened skin, but Kaylan could also feel warmth radiating from her.

"Now close your eyes," Ma'jasalax said.

Kaylan did as she asked. She felt more focused than before, as if holding Ma'jasalax's hand gave her the foundation she needed.

Kaylan focused on Zack, from his deep, penetrating eyes to the last press of his lips on hers. She saw him kiss the tips of his fingers and place them on the door. The side of his spacesuit was stained crimson with his blood. Kaylan's chest tightened and a soft moan escaped her lips. Memories of their time on the Athena played through her mind—both the times when they'd laughed and when they'd argued. She eagerly sought both, strengthening her image of Zack. Then the memories faded in her mind until there was nothing but darkness. She heard her own beating heart in her ears and something else. She strained, reaching deeper inside than she had ever done before. She knew that if Zack were alive, she should be able to focus on that. She held her breath, and in that moment she heard a slight gasp and a sigh.

Zack.

Chapter Twenty-Four

E arth Star System
Mission Control, Houston, Texas

Gary Hunter glanced at the computer readout, checking the logs and waiting for anything new to come from Pluto. This had been his daily routine at Mission Control since all communication with the Athena had ceased. There had been plenty of speculation, and an effort to send a probe to Pluto was currently in the planning phases. Nothing they had in space now could match the Athena's speed. Even the guys monitoring SAT comms, who used to complain daily about their telemetry data being incorrect, only grimly nodded in his direction. Quite a few of them had gotten a good laugh when they learned that Zack Quick had poked a bit of fun at their satellites by having them suddenly report that they were on the other side of the known galaxy. He wished one of the SAT comms guys would come over with a new occurrence like that one. At least then they would know that the Athena and her crew were alive. The lack of communication and the fact that they were unable to establish a connection to the Athena's comms systems grated on everyone's nerves at Mission Control and beyond. Edward Johnson with Dux Corp had rarely left Mission Control when they first announced the Athena's disappearance. The last communication sent from the ship had been a partial data dump that cut off in the middle. They were still working through the part they had received.

"Good morning, Gary," Ed Johnson said.

Gary glanced at his watch. "It's three a.m."

Ed shrugged. "I couldn't sleep. Here, I brought you some coffee."

Gary took the proffered cup. "Thanks," he said, and took a sip. Cream and sugar, just as he liked it.

"Anything new?" Ed asked.

Gary shook his head. "Not yet. Still waiting for today's report."

The main screen at Mission Control flashed, indicating an incoming transmission. The various groups pulling the graveyard shift perked up.

"What is it?" Ed asked.

Gary frowned, his fingers tapping through the interface with practiced efficiency. "I'm not sure . . . Hold on, it's a video feed."

"From the Athena?" Ed asked.

Gary examined the data headers as the feed was still coming in and compiling. "No, but it's coming from Pluto."

A few minutes passed and the data dump completed. An image appeared on the main holoscreen at mission control.

Hello, this is Michael Hunsicker, Commander of the Athena Mission. I'm sending you this message from the alien outpost on Pluto. First and foremost, we have confirmation that we are not alone. The structure on Pluto was built by a race of beings who call themselves Boxans. Included in this message is a set of instructions to build a communications device that will allow us to speak in real time. The status of the Athena is unknown. The ship went through a wormhole to another star system. I'm not alone here. There was a Boxan named Chazen who was in stasis for a very long time. He woke when we powered the station up. I will send another update tomorrow, but until you build the communications device, we will have no way to communicate with each other.

Gary's mouth hung open in shock, and after a moment he glanced at Ed, who had a broad smile on his face.

"Time to wake up the world," Ed said. "We've got work to do."

THANK YOU FOR READING STAR DIVIDE.

The Ascension series continues with the next book, but before you grab the sequel, I'd like to offer you a free science fiction story I wrote. If you join my mailing list, I'll send you a free copy of **Crash Landing**, a story that features Kladomaor and the earliest events in the Xiiginn uprising that plunged the Boxans into an interstellar war. You can read Crash Landing for free by signing up by clicking the link below.

Click Here to download your FREE copy of Crash Landing

The Ascension series continues with the 3rd book. Also click the link for a FREE short story - **The Star Alliance**

About the Author

I've written multiple science fiction and fantasy series. Books have been my way to escape everyday life since I was a teenager to my current ripe old(?) age. What started out as a love of stories has turned into a full-blown passion for writing them.

Overall, I'm just a fan of really good stories regardless of genre. I love the heroic tales, redemption stories, the last stand, or just a good old fashion adventure. Those are the types of stories I like to write. Stories with rich and interesting characters and then I put them into dangerous and sometimes morally gray situations.

My ultimate intent for writing stories is to provide fun escapism for readers. I write stories that I would like to read, and I hope you enjoy them as well.

If you have questions or comments about any of my works I would love to hear from you, even if it's only to drop by to say hello at KenLozito.com

Thanks again for reading *Star Divide*.

Don't be shy about emails, I love getting them, and try to respond to everyone.

Also by Ken Lozito

ASCENSION SERIES

STAR SHROUD

STAR DIVIDE

STAR ALLIANCE

INFINITY'S EDGE

RISING FORCE

ASCENSION

FIRST COLONY SERIES

GENESIS

NEMESIS

LEGACY

SANCTUARY

DISCOVERY

EMERGENCE

VIGILANCE

FRACTURE

HARBINGER

INSURGENT

INVASION

IMPULSE

INFINITY

EXPEDITION EARTH

FALLEN EARTH

SPACE RAIDERS SERIES

SPACE RAIDERS

SPACE RAIDERS - FORGOTTEN EMPIRE

SPACE RAIDERS - DARK MENACE

FEDERATION CHRONICLES

ACHERON INHERITANCE

ACHERON SALVATION

ACHERON REDEMPTION

ACHERON RISING (PREQUEL NOVELLA)

SAFANARION ORDER SERIES

ROAD TO SHANDARA

ECHOES OF A GLORIED PAST

AMIDST THE RISING SHADOWS

HEIR OF SHANDARA

IF YOU WOULD LIKE TO BE NOTIFIED WHEN MY NEXT BOOK IS
RELEASED VISIT KENLOZITO.COM